LOST HEIR

BLOOD WEAVER TRILOGY
BOOK 2

KARINA ESPINOSA

Copyright © 2024 by Karina Espinosa

All rights reserved.

No part of this book may be reproduced in any form or by any electronic or mechanical means, including information storage and retrieval systems, without written permission from the author, except for the use of brief quotations in a book review.

Cover design by © Christian Bentulan
Edited by Stacy Sanford
Map by Cartographybird Maps

Copyright 2024 by Karina Espinosa

ISBN-13: 9798327404052
ASIN: B0CSRB3YL9

For my readers.
Who are still patiently waiting for the final book in the Sevyn Rose Series. I'll get there soon! Promise!

TO THE UNCHARTED NORTH

THE LUMINAR SEA

KELDARA
SEAT OF THE
KELDARAN KINGDOM

CENTRA

ALTHERA
RIVER

LOMEWOOD

ELLYNDOR

THE
TIDAL
STRANDS

TERRITORY OF THE
CRIMSON CLAN

THE GRASSLANDS

THE GREAT LANDS OF
ASTERIA
MAPPED
IN THE PRESENT AGE

TO THE FAR SOUTH

VALORIA

SEAT OF THE
VALORIAN KINGDOM

LAINS

SILENT
MOUNTAINS

SEAT OF THE
ELDWAIN KINGDOM

ELDWAIN

SERELUNE
RIVER

OBSIDIAN OCEAN

SAPPHIRE DEPTHS

PROLOGUE
RONAN

The first time I saw Eldwain, I thought I'd stumbled into a dream; one of those vivid dreams where every color was brighter, and every scent was sweeter. I was only ten, a boy from the Crimson Clan of the Grasslands, where the earth was our bed and the sky our roof, where the wind told our stories and the earth cradled our sleep. But here... here was a fantasy turned vivid reality, a land where magic didn't just linger, it thrived. I had never seen anything like Eldwain, a land whispered about in our clan as the place where the half-fae, half-humans lived, descendants of the legendary fae of Ellyndor.

My father, the clan chief, led our procession with a steady grace, but I couldn't help but gape at the spectacle around us. We were on horseback, every single one of us, from my father, to me, to the warriors who accompanied us for protection.

Eldwain was beautiful, but it wasn't just the land that enchanted; it was its people as well. Their hair was silver, and they moved with an effortless grace as we entered town, their light eyes sparkling in bright shades compared to our crimson eyes. Their laughter wove through the air, a melody that promised stories of endless wonder. In them, I saw the marriage of fae and human, a beauty too profound to fully grasp.

As we approached the heart of Eldwain, the palace emerged like a vision from the mist, a masterpiece sculpted by both nature and an artisan's skilled hand. It was not a structure of stone and mortar, but a living testament to the harmony that existed between the fae and human realms. The palace walls, if they could be called walls, were woven from living trees. Their trunks twisted and merged to form elaborate patterns, branches arching overhead to create a canopy that shimmered with a mosaic of leaves, filtering sunlight into dappled hues of emerald and gold.

The entrance was flanked by two massive sculptures, not carved but grown from the earth itself, shaped over centuries into guardians that seemed to watch over the palace with serene vigilance. Their features were both fierce and beautiful, embodying the strength and grace of the creatures of Eldwain.

"Name?" one of the guards called out to us as we were stopped at the entrance.

"Chief Aryan of the Crimson Clan of the Grasslands," my father's voice boomed from within the procession. His presence dominated amongst the group of fierce warriors. His long, dark hair fell below his hips with loose braids woven throughout his hair. He possessed crimson eyes darker than any other I'd seen, and his skin was covered in cerise markings that told stories of the clan and of victorious battles. My father was a sight to behold as he sat tall atop his black stallion.

The Eldwain guard nodded respectfully and motioned for the other guards to allow our company to enter. "Welcome, Chief Aryan. Please leave your horses here. Only you and your immediate family members are to enter. Please leave all weapons behind."

My father turned his attention to me and nodded, telling me to follow him. I slid off my horse and handed the reins to young Silas, who rode beside me.

"Good luck," he whispered as I passed, following my father into the Eldwain palace.

Stepping inside, the boundary between the outdoors and indoors blurred. A stream, clear as crystal, wound its way through the palace floor, its gentle babble resonating against the walls, mingling with the soft glow of bioluminescent moss that clung to the interior. The ceilings soared high above, supported by pillars that resembled the trunks of giant trees, their branches intertwining to form natural archways.

The heart of the palace was the Great Hall, a vast space that seemed to hold the essence of Eldwain within its bounds. The floor was a tapestry of living grass, soft underfoot and scattered with flowers that opened to the gentlest touch. The room was lit not by torches, but by clusters of glowing orbs that floated lazily in the air, casting a soft, ethereal light that made shadows dance.

At the center of the Great Hall, a throne of intertwined branches sat upon a dais of smooth stone, cushioned with moss and blooms. It was not a seat of intimidation, but one of unity, embodying the bond between the land and its rulers.

Above, the ceiling was a living canvas, where the branches of the trees that formed the palace met and mingled, creating a natural dome. Here and there, gaps in the foliage allowed shafts of sunlight to pierce through, creating beams of light that spotlighted the hall in a celestial display.

The Eldwain King's marriage celebration unveiled wonders I hadn't dared to imagine. Lights danced without flame, music rose from the very ground, and the feast... it sparkled as if the dishes themselves were alive with enchantment. Performers summoned illusions that spun tales of love and valor, weaving the essence of Eldwain into every gesture.

As we stepped into the vast expanse of the Great Hall, my father, Aryan, halted and laid a weighty, reassuring hand upon my shoulder. With a solemn yet encouraging glance, he spoke. "I must pay my respects to the king. Seek out the princes and princesses, Ronan. It's time you began forging alliances."

Nodding, I dipped in a bow, my eyes trailing after him as he strode purposefully towards the throne, where the king and his new wife presided over the festivities.

Alone now, I surveyed the hall, its splendor dwarfing my presence. Not a single peer in sight, just a sea of strangers whose glances cut sharper than blades. Their eyes, filled with disdain, brushed over me, an unspoken reminder of the divide between us. Though we shared borders with Eldwain, my people seldom ventured beyond the Grasslands. To these courtly folk, we were mere tales of savagery, our ways as foreign as our lands.

Eager for escape, I found solace in the palace gardens. Slipping through an archway, the cool embrace of the open air greeted me, and there, amidst the lush whispers of nature, I discovered a gathering of children. Their laughter, a melody foreign to my ears, sparked a flutter of excitement beneath my ribs, tinged with the anxiety of the unknown.

They were like creatures from a different realm, adorned

in silks that captured the essence of the sky at dawn, so at odds with my attire. My battle leathers, worn with pride back home, suddenly felt coarse, a stark reminder of the worlds that lay between us. A glance down at my garb, then back to their finery, and a wave of self-consciousness washed over me.

Gathering every shred of bravery I possessed, I advanced towards them, my gaze drawn to a girl whose dark tresses flowed like the night sky. Her eyes, a startling blue, outshone the very heavens, and her smile, radiant and warm, beckoned me closer without a word. It was as if the sun had chosen to shine through her, dispelling shadows of doubt and kindling a smile on my lips to mirror hers.

Venturing into their circle, my heart hammered against my chest, a mix of hope and apprehension swirling within me. "Hello," I attempted, my voice stronger than I felt, accompanied by a tentative wave. "I'm Ronan from the Crimson Clan."

A boy, his hair the color of moonlight but without the pointed ears that marked the fae, telling me he was from Eldwain, turned sharply towards me. His eyes narrowed and a sneer curled his lips. "We don't associate with barbarians," he declared dismissively, turning his back to signal the end of the interaction.

The others, a blend of night and silver-haired youths, mirrored his move, drifting away with a wave of cold shoulders and whispered judgments.

All of them left except for one.

The young girl who had captured my attention stood before me, her bright smile almost blinding as she waved at me. "Hello, Ronan! Ignore Caelan," she added with an eye roll. "My name is Lyanna," she said as she extended a hand to me.

Hesitation gripped me for a heartbeat before our hands met, and a jolt like the first breath of a storm raced up my arm. "I'm Ronan." I stumbled over my words, caught in the net of her vibrant presence.

She laughed, a sound as clear and melodious as a crystalline brook in spring. "You said that already," she teased, her fingers gently releasing mine only to venture closer, curiosity lighting her features. She reached out, her fingers grazing the ends of my hair that fell in waves to the middle of my back. "Wow, you have such pretty hair. And your eyes..."

Her words trailed off and I braced for scorn, my cheeks warming under her gaze. But instead, she whispered, "It's beautiful," her admiration clear and sincere. "Could I... could I braid your hair?"

The question took me aback. In the Grasslands, our hair was a tapestry of our identity, touched only by the women of our clan, a sacred tradition. Yet, as her request hung between us, something in her genuine interest, her disregard for the barriers that had just been so painfully enforced, nudged me towards acceptance.

I found myself nodding, granting her permission. Her smile broadened and she circled to my back, her fingers beginning to comb through my hair. "It's so soft. I wish my hair was this soft."

As she spoke, her fingers danced through my hair, weaving it into a braid with care that felt like a whisper of wind through the Grasslands. In that moment, with Lyanna's kindness wrapping around me, the walls that seemed so impenetrable began to crumble, replaced by a bridge built on a simple, shared moment between two souls from worlds apart.

"Uh... where are you from, Lyanna? You don't seem like

you're from Eldwain," I ventured, my curiosity piqued as her fingers continued their gentle exploration of my hair.

She paused, her laughter ringing softly in the air. "Oh, no, I'm from Valoria," she confessed, a hint of pride in her voice.

Valoria? The word sent a jolt through me, and my eyes widened in disbelief. "Are you... are you the princess?" The question stumbled out, cloaked in a mix of awe and nervousness.

Her hands stilled for a moment before she resumed her task, her voice laced with amusement. "Yes! Have you heard of me?"

Heard of her? The realization crashed over me like a wave. Lyanna, the Princess of Valoria, wasn't just any royal. She was the first female blood mage since the moon goddess, a legend reborn. Her birth had been a beacon of hope and power, whispered about even in the far reaches of the Grasslands. And more than that, she was the one my father had spoken of, the one destined to be my future, woven into my fate since childhood. Yet, standing here with her hands buried in my hair, she was no longer a mere promise or a distant dream; she was real, and breathtakingly so.

"I... yes, I've heard of you," I admitted, my voice barely above a whisper, the weight of the moment pressing down on me. "You're... famous. Not just for being a princess, but a blood mage. The first in centuries."

Her touch paused, and for a heartbeat, I wondered if I had said too much. But then she leaned closer, her voice a mix of curiosity and surprise. "And you? Who are you in the grand tapestry of our lands?"

I swallowed, the gravity of who we were—of what we

might become to each other—suddenly very real. "I'm Ronan, son of Aryan, chief of the Crimson Clan."

As Lyanna completed her artful braid, she stepped around to face me, her smile bright and carefree, revealing the gap where her two front teeth once were. "It's nice to meet you, Ronan," she said, her eyes sparkling with a playful light.

Just then, a young boy's voice pierced the tranquil garden. "Lyanna!" he called. "Our parents are looking for us!"

With a graceful twirl of her dress, she called back, "Be there soon!" Her voice carried a melody of reluctance and duty.

The boy, likely her brother, darted away, leaving us in a momentary bubble of silence. Lyanna turned to me, her expression softening. "I have to go. Thank you for letting me braid your beautiful hair," she said, her voice tinged with a hint of sadness for the abrupt end to our encounter.

As she pivoted to leave, a sudden urge gripped me, compelling me to reach out and gently grasp her wrist. "I—" Words failed me, a rare occurrence. My heart yearned for more time, for another moment in her radiant presence. "Do you want to meet later tonight? Maybe we can look at the stars. They might not be as pretty as they are in the Grasslands, but I bet they're stunning from here."

Her eyes lit up, a mirror to the stars we wished to watch together. "Sure! Want to meet back here at the stroke of midnight?" she proposed, her voice a mix of excitement and conspiracy.

I nodded, unable to contain my eagerness. With a shared promise hanging between us, she slipped away, chasing after her brother.

That night, I waited under a cloak of darkness where the

garden transformed into a realm of whispered secrets and shadowed beauty. Midnight came and went, the stars tracing their paths across the sky in silent witness to my lonely vigil. Yet, as the hours slipped by, the realization dawned with the chill of the early morning air: Lyanna was not coming.

The night ended in solitude, her absence echoing louder than the promises made. But our brief connection, the shared laughter and plans we made under the canopy of Eldwain's sky, lingered like a ghost of what could have been, leaving me with a mix of disappointment and a faint, unyielding hope.

1

It was a sleepless night. My cot, nestled within the confines of my tent in the Valorian camp, offered no comfort as scenes from the previous night's battle against the Crimson Clan replayed in my mind. My spirit was troubled and unease settled deep within me. Ronan had deceived me, yet despite his betrayal, concern for his well-being gnawed at me as a persistent ache. Even though I was the one who put him in his current situation as a hostage for Valoria, the weight of that decision lay heavily on my heart.

As dawn painted the sky in strokes of light, I escaped the confines of my tent only to be met by the messenger I had dispatched under the cloak of night. His approach was marked by a deference, his bow a silent acknowledgment of my returned status. "Your Highness," he greeted, extending a letter retrieved from the secrecy of his vest. "Apologies, Your Highness. I could not find the fae Orion, nor Miss Selene."

The letter, a failed attempt at communication from the night before, felt heavy in my hands. "She wasn't at the Rose

Petal Lounge?" My voice betrayed my concern, a wary tremble beneath the surface.

His head shake confirmed my fears. "No, Your Highness. She was not there."

A storm of worry churned within me, thoughts spiraling into dark possibilities. Did Orion go back on his word, or was this all a trick from the start? The uncertainty was frightening. Without confirmation of Selene's safety, I couldn't even think about leaving for Valoria; her liberation from Madam Rose's grasp was paramount.

"Lyanna?" Caelan's voice sliced through my turmoil, his presence a sudden beacon as he made his way toward us across the camp.

"Thank you for your help," I told the messenger, my gratitude for his efforts a brief interlude in the storm of my thoughts. He departed with a bow, leaving me alone with Caelan.

Caelan, with his untamed silver hair and a smile that spoke of undisturbed slumber, stood in stark contrast to my unrest. The imagined dark circles under my eyes felt like badges of my sleepless vigil.

"Are you unwell?" His concern pierced the morning air, his smile fading as he drew closer.

I mustered a smile, a feeble shield against my worries. "I'm fine, just a bit worried."

His frown deepened and his hazel eyes scanned my face as if searching for clues. "What's wrong? Whatever it is, we can solve it, I promise—"

"It's Selene," I interrupted, the urgency in my voice cutting through any pretense of calm. "I can't get ahold of her, and I'm worried. I can't leave for Valoria without knowing her whereabouts."

Caelan cleared his throat. "About that ... She's here."

My brows shot up. "Pardon?"

He ran a hand through his hair. "Marcellus bought her last night. It was why he was missing from the battle."

"Wait. He *bought* her, or he *freed* her?"

Caelan bit his lower lip and paused before answering. "He bought her," he clarified.

I felt the blood rush up to my head as if I was upside down. Fury was evident in my heated glare. "Where is he?" I demanded as I attempted to push past Caelan.

"Wait!" He stopped me, his hands going to my upper arms. "If you go to him while you're still upset, it could turn ugly. Remember his reaction last night? He still needs time to process your return."

I shrugged off his hands. "I don't care! He's not a child anymore, Caelan! You need to stop coddling him as if he still was. This is why he's so damn spoiled!" I pushed past him, toward where I assumed his tent was located. Going from tent to tent without asking permission, I checked all within the vicinity, barging in on soldiers undressing and doing things I probably should not have witnessed. Finally, I found Marcellus's tent.

Barging in, I saw him standing on one side and Selene seated on the edge of his cot, looking nervous. "Selene!" I yelled.

She breathed a sigh of relief at the sight of me, but when she started to stand and approach me, Marcel cut into her path.

"What are *you* doing here?" Marcellus asked, his voice dripping with disdain.

I scoffed. "What am *I* doing? What are *you* doing?" I shouted. "Did you really buy her instead of freeing her?"

He lifted his chin and peered down at me. "As if I have to answer to you. You're nothing but a Crimson whore who—"

Just then, Caelan darted past me and slapped Marcellus across the face.

I flinched, surprised by the swiftness of his movements. He glared Marcel down. "How *dare* you speak to your older sister in that manner!" Caelan yelled.

"She is no sister of mine," Marcel gritted between his teeth, holding the side of his face. "I didn't peg you as the type to want Ronan's sloppy seconds."

Caelan went to slap him again, but I caught his wrist and stopped him. "Enough. His words don't bother me, and they shouldn't bother you. They're nothing but the ramblings of an insecure little boy."

"How dare you!"

Marcel attempted to step up to me, but Caelan stood in his way. His glare was icy and deadly. "Don't even think about it," Caelan warned. "I have patience, but you're testing it right now."

"Your Highness, *please*," Selene pleaded as she tentatively approached. "She's my best friend and she's worried. Please understand!"

I wanted to tell Selene to stop begging him, but I felt as if it would only make matters worse, so I kept quiet.

Marcellus turned his chilling blue eyes towards Selene. She stared back unflinchingly and slowly, Marcel softened his gaze and nodded.

I went around them to Selene and pulled her into an embrace. "What happened?" I whispered into her ear.

She sniffled and clung to me. "Orion came to fetch me, but Madame Rose had already sold me. Orion didn't stand a chance."

"Do you know where he is?" When she shook her head, I pulled back. "Okay. As long as you're okay," I murmured.

"Of course she's fine. I would never hurt her!" Marcel yelled indignantly.

I scoffed and rolled my eyes. "You claim you wouldn't hurt her, but what do you think you're doing by bringing her to Valoria? You're bringing her to a den of vipers!" I nudged Selene behind me protectively.

"I've already sent word home," my brother sniffed. "She'll be my concubine—"

"The hell she will!" I shouted and charged toward him, but Caelan and Selene caught me before I could throw the first punch. "How can you be so damn selfish, Marcellus? She had a hard life at the pleasure house, and now you want to make her not your wife, but a concubine? You're so egotistical!" My voice trembled toward the end, and I felt as if I was at the brink of tears. "Did you ever ask her what *she* wants?"

Marcellus's face hardened at the accusation and his eyes flicked to Selene where she stood quietly behind me. He pondered my question for a few moments and then cleared his throat. "What do you want, Selene?"

I peered over my shoulder at her and nodded. "Speak freely, Selene. Don't be afraid. Tell us what *you* want, not what others want for you."

She bit her lip before speaking. "I—I want to be free, Your Highness."

I sagged in relief and turned my attention back to my brother. "You heard her. Now tell me, Marcel, what are you going to do?"

His brows furrowed as he stared intently at Selene. "I'll give you your freedom ... as long as you return to Valoria with me."

"You can't—" I attempted to argue, but Selene clutched my wrist, stopping me.

"I agree," she said quickly. "Wherever Leila goes, I'll go."

I whirled around to face her. "Selene, this is your chance at freedom. Return to the Luminar Sea and be reunited with your people, with your home—"

"You *are* my home, Leila. Please. Let me stay by your side." Her green eyes pleaded with me as she reached for my hands and squeezed. "Please," she repeated.

"We can keep her safe, Lyanna," Caelan interrupted. "I'll see to it."

My gaze locked on Selene's. I wanted her to change her mind, but then I remembered I'd just told her to decide her path based on no one's choice but her own.

"Fine. But you can forget about making her your concubine," I said to Marcel.

He kept quiet, though he sent me a nasty glare.

"Come on, Selene, you can ride with me—"

"Can I talk to the prince for a moment ... alone?" Selene asked, looking at me intently. "I won't be long."

I was hesitant to leave her, but she was her own person and she deserved to make her own decisions. I couldn't control her, no matter how badly I wanted to keep her safe. "Fine. Just ... be careful," I warned, giving her one last embrace before exiting the tent with Caelan following closely behind.

We crossed the vast camp and headed back toward my tent, the sun beaming down on us with buttery rays that attempted to chase away the early morning chill. Along the way, Caelan stopped me by gently touching my elbow. "Are you okay?"

I ran a hand through my hair. "I guess," I muttered. "Selene is her own person. She's been controlled by Madam Rose for so long, I couldn't bear it if she was turned over to yet another master. She deserves her freedom."

He nodded. "I'll prepare a carriage for you both. And I promise, Lyanna, I'll make sure nothing happens to her. You have my word."

I gave him a tight smile. "Thank you, Caelan."

He smiled down at me, his hazel eyes drifting to the crescent moon birthmark on my forehead. After releasing the magic that kept it hidden last night, I noticed he couldn't stop staring at it.

I self-consciously touched my forehead. "Does it look funny?"

He chuckled. "No. Not at all. It looks beautiful, Lyanna. *You* are beautiful."

I didn't know what to say so I kept quiet. I knew how he felt about me. He'd admitted as much when he knew me as Leila. But I couldn't string him along. Eventually, I would have to tell him how I felt. Eventually.

Just not right now.

2

The camp buzzed with the muted chaos of departure; the air filled with the anticipation of our journey back to Valoria. I gingerly navigated the maze of tents and supplies that were being packed and loaded, my heart a tumult of unspoken goodbyes and unresolved threads. I made my way toward the carriage where I would ride with Selene. I felt odd leaving without notifying anyone from my former life as Leila, the healer. The few friends I had would have no idea what happened to me. I did manage to send a messenger to find Henry and tell him he could stay in my clinic indefinitely. I didn't know if he'd remained with the Crimson Clan or not, now that Ronan was our hostage. But just in case he was staying behind, I didn't want to leave without saying goodbye.

As I approached the caravan, Caelan's familiar voice pierced the chaos. "Lyanna!" he called out, though the name felt like a garment ill-fitted after years of wearing Leila. I'd been Leila for ten years. Ten very long years.

"Selene is waiting for you," he said as he approached.

"I just had to get a few things." I pointed to my satchel and lifted the strap over my shoulder before following Caelan toward the procession of horses and carriages that would carry us back to Valoria. It was then, amidst the flurry of preparations, that I caught sight of him.

Ronan.

The Crimson Clan chief's son was crouched in a wooden cage atop a wagon being pulled by two horses. He looked completely disheveled, but otherwise appeared to be unharmed. At least from where I stood.

"Is ... is he okay?" The question escaped me, a whisper of concern to Caelan, even as my gaze remained locked on Ronan, searching for any sign of distress.

Caelan's response, laced with disdain, struck a wary chord. "Don't worry about him, Lyanna. He's a savage. He's probably used to being caged," Caelan sneered, his words igniting a spark of anger within me.

I whirled on him, my voice carrying the weight of many years spent in the shadows. "If this was ten years ago, I wouldn't have thought twice about it. But now I know what you're capable of, Caelan. So let me ask again: *Is he okay?*"

The color drained from his face, perhaps ignited by memories of my captivity under his torturous care. "Lyanna," he began, his voice a mix of regret and plea. "I'm sorry. Truly, I'm sorry," he declared. "The last thing I would ever want to do is hurt you. You know that, right?"

I narrowed my gaze to let him know his artful deflection had not gone unnoticed. "Don't change the subject, Caelan. Is he hurt?"

His frustration was palpable. "Why do you care so much? You were barely friends ... unless ..."

"Unless what?" I challenged, defiantly meeting his stare.

Caelan's approach turned menacing; his question laced with accusation. "Unless you were *more* than friends ... Did he touch you?" he growled. His hazel gaze bore into me, a storm of jealousy and concern mingling in his eyes.

Shocked by the intensity of his suspicion, I recoiled. "What? Of course not!" I countered, my response a lie draped over the truth of my almost-intimacy with Ronan, a moment interrupted by Silas and now locked away in the silence between us. How could I confess that to Caelan, when I was still untangling the web of feelings and loyalties that bound me?

In that brief interlude, amidst the tension and whispered confrontations, Ronan's weary head rose as if drawn by the current of our discord. Our gazes collided across the distance, a silent exchange fraught with complexities and unvoiced confessions. It was a fleeting connection, yet in that moment, a torrent of unarticulated thoughts and feelings surged between us, a silent conversation that spoke volumes.

But the moment was shattered when Caelan's hand abruptly shadowed my vision, his palm cold against my skin. "Don't look. He's not worth it," he murmured through clenched teeth, a protective yet possessive gesture that felt as much an assertion of control as it was an attempt to shield me. With a firmness that brooked no argument, he steered me away, guiding me towards the carriage and away from Ronan, away from the silent exchange that momentarily bridged the gap between captive and onlooker.

I wanted to scream and rage. Caelan's prejudice was painfully obvious. I smacked his hand out of my face and stormed toward the carriage without looking back. I'd had enough of men in this lifetime.

As the caravan lurched into motion, setting its course towards Valoria, I was nestled beside Selene in the confines of our carriage. The rhythm of our journey was dictated by the uneven terrain beneath us, a gentle jostling that served as a constant reminder of the land's untamed spirit. Outside the window, the world unfurled like a tapestry of living hues and textures, each mile revealing a new facet of the landscape that stretched between our current location and the distant allure of Valoria.

The terrain of the Central Plains was a mosaic of tall grasses that swayed rhythmically with the wind, their tips brushing against the sky in a silent dance. Here and there, clusters of wildflowers added bursts of color to the placid sea of green, their presence a vivid reminder of nature's resilience and diversity. The horizon was a distant line, a blend of earth and sky where the early morning light cast long shadows that played hide and seek with the land.

Our horses, led by a mage whose subtle gestures cut a serene path through the wild expanse, moved with a steady pace.

As we traveled, the plains stretched out in every direction, a testament to the vastness of the land. Occasionally, a lone tree or a small copse would rise against the expanse, their presence marking the passage of miles and the slow change in scenery as we moved arduously northward. The air was fresh, carrying the scent of grass and earth, a constant companion through the open windows of our carriage.

"Leila?" Selene's voice, soft as the rustle of grass outside our trundling carriage, drew my attention away from the window. She leaned her head on my shoulder, a silent request for comfort as the plains rolled by. "How long will it take us to reach Valoria?"

"Two to three days," I replied, gazing out at the Central Plains unfurling before us. "We have to cut through the Central Plains to cross the border."

She straightened and turned her gaze towards me, a shadow of concern in her eyes. "I know I've been silent on matters, but I'm curious about what happened. I thought ... I thought you were on good terms with Ronan?"

A wearisome sigh escaped me, the memory bitter on my tongue. "I thought so, too," I whispered, the words thick with betrayal. "I ... I almost gave myself to him. And to think it was all part of some elaborate plan."

Selene's eyes widened and she gasped. "He was tricking you?"

Nodding, I let the truth sink in. "I learned of a prophecy. One that states the Crimson Clan needs to sacrifice me in order to resurrect the Demon Fox."

"But he seemed so ... so *genuine*!" Selene sputtered. "How could he?" she exclaimed, anger and disbelief warring within her.

I couldn't help but chuckle despite the gravity of our conversation, soothing her with a gentle pat on her arm. "Calm down there, firecracker. Luckily, I found out before anything could happen."

"Did you tell Prince Caelan about it?" she probed, her curiosity unyielding.

I shook my head. "No."

"Why not?"

I blew out a breath as I fiddled with the frayed edges of my blouse. "Honestly, I don't know why. But I don't want him to know about it. Just in case ..."

"In case it puts Ronan in even more danger?" Selene whispered.

I nodded. "How did you know?"

Selene's soft smile was knowing. "Because regardless of what has transpired, I know you care for Ronan deeply. It's the first time in the five years I've known you that I've seen you care about someone other than me."

"I care about my patients and others," I scoffed, slightly offended.

Selene chuckled. "Yes, but it's not the same. You wouldn't risk your life for others. Not like you've done for me and Ronan."

She wasn't lying, but it wasn't easy hearing the truth. In the short expanse of time I'd known Ronan, he'd gotten under my skin and wormed his way into my heart. Now it seemed I couldn't rid myself of him.

"Enough about me. What's going on with you and Marcellus?" I deflected, eager to shift the focus.

Her cheeks flushed and she looked away. "Nothing," she whispered, too quickly.

I threw my head back and laughed, her denial too flimsy to be believed. "You can't call me out and expect me not to do the same. Be honest with me, Selene. What happened that day at the Rose Petal when he spent an hour in a private room with you?"

She bit her bottom lip and nervously twiddled her thumbs. I elbowed her, snapping her out of her daze. "Nothing. Honest! I played the lute, danced, and … and I sang."

My eyes widened. "You *sang* for him?" I choked out in shock. "Selene, why would you do that? A siren's call is not only rare … it's incredibly dangerous."

She shrugged. "I don't know. He was just so genuinely

nice, and I wanted to do something special for him. I promise it was tame, so ..."

"I know he liked you before then, but he could become obsessed with you because of this. Is this why—"

"No!" she exclaimed as she whirled on me. "That's not why he bought me, I swear. It was just one little song; nothing too impactful."

"Selene ..." I urged.

"He's really not that bad, Leila. Honest. I can tell he wouldn't let anything bad happen to me."

"You hardly know him—" I started, then caught myself. I hardly knew Ronan, either. I sighed. "What did you want to talk to him about in private? Will you tell me?"

She shook her head and dropped her gaze. "I'd rather not."

I slowly closed my eyes and took deep breaths to calm down. "I hope you know what you're doing, Selene," I whispered as I opened my eyes again. "Valoria is nothing like the Central Plains. And my brother ... is no prince charming."

"I know," she said softly. "Will you trust me?"

I stared into her emerald eyes, trying to see into her soul for a snippet of an answer, but she was like a stone wall. Not a crack in sight. "I trust you," I finally said. "Just ... be careful, Selene."

She smiled brightly. "I will."

∽

As twilight wrapped its cloak around Asteria, our caravan came to a halt and settled into the embrace of the Central Plains for the night. The landscape stretched endlessly in all directions, a sea of grass beneath the burgeoning stars, its vastness both a comfort and a reminder of our isolation. I was unsure how close we were to the border.

Gathered around a crackling fire that pierced the growing darkness, its warmth a small bulwark against the evening's chill, Caelan, Selene, Marcellus, and I formed a makeshift circle. The flickering flames cast dancing shadows over our faces, reflecting in Caelan's eyes as he tended to the fire with practiced movements. Beyond our little circle, the silhouettes of soldiers moved with efficient grace, their actions blending into the rhythm of the wilderness as tents rose from the ground and the scent of cooked meat filled the air.

"How far are we from Valoria?" My question broke the comfortable silence, a query borne of the same restlessness that stirred the fire.

Caelan paused, his gaze measuring the distance in his mind before answering. "We're roughly two hundred kilometers away from the border, and maybe another hundred kilometers from the border to the palace." His voice, steady and sure, did little to quell the nervous anticipation that buzzed beneath my skin.

Selene and I shared a log for seating, our proximity a small comfort in the vast, open plains. Across from us, Marcellus and Caelan mirrored our arrangement, yet an unspoken tension hovered between me and my brother, his attention occasionally straying towards Selene but never lingering long enough to bridge the gap of silence.

Selene's voice, soft and reflective, cut through the crackle of the fire. "I haven't left the Central Plains since I was twelve," she said as she rubbed her upper arms to warm herself from the night chill.

She was twelve when her father sold her to the pleasure

house, and she hadn't seen him since. The thought ignited a silent fury within me.

"If you want to return to the sea, we can still make it happen, Selene," I said, unsure whether she was excited or frightened about leaving the Central Plains.

She hesitated, her whisper barely audible over the fire's crackle. "I know," she said, a tremor of unresolved emotion in her voice. "But I don't want to. Not yet, anyway."

Acknowledging her response with a nod, I respected her silence and allowed the topic to fade into the night. Our conversation dwindled as we settled into the rhythm of the camp, the fire's warmth a small beacon of solace in the whispering plains. The wilderness of the Central Plains enveloped us, a reminder of the long journey that still lay ahead.

"Lyanna?" Caelan called out, breaking the silence. "I've been meaning to ask ... what happened after you left Valoria? Why didn't you return home?"

At that question, Marcellus looked up at me, curiosity lingering in his gaze.

I blew out a breath. "Sir Edric and I crossed the border into Keldara, thinking their back yard would be the last place they would look if they wanted to find us." My mind wandered to memories of the past. "We travelled throughout Asteria, never staying long in one location. It was hard to get news from Valoria, but when we heard that Keldara's invasion had failed, I asked Sir Edric if we'd be going home, but he said it was still too dangerous. He warned I couldn't return or my life would be in danger. I believed him. To this day, I don't know what the danger was that he spoke of," I lied, knowing full well what it was after speaking with him through one of the Crimson Clan's witch doctors. "The coin that Sir Edric brought lasted less than a year. He couldn't leave me alone in case someone found me, so finding employment was difficult. He'd do odd jobs here and there, but nothing stable. We spent many nights hungry, with no food or shelter. But Sir Edric did his best. I do not fault him for a single thing."

"What happened to Sir Edric?" Marcellus asked quietly.

I wrapped my arms around myself as I prepared to tell them. "We were in Ellyndor. I was sixteen years old, I believe, and I remember Sir Edric coming home furious beyond belief. He wouldn't tell me what happened before he stormed out of our home. It wasn't until midnight struck and he still wasn't home that I got worried. It was unlike him to be gone for such long periods of time, so I went searching for him. That's when I found him, dead in an alleyway. I tried to revive him, to feed him some of my blood, but it was too late," I whispered. "If I'd just been faster, or gone to look for him sooner ..."

"You were in Ellyndor?" Caelan asked in shocked surprise. "Why couldn't I find you there?"

I smiled bitterly. "We were in a small town on the outskirts of the capital."

"How did you end up in the Central Plains?" Caelan gritted between his teeth as he internally raged with fury.

"I'd already been training as a healer, and I wanted to go somewhere that I could rest my head longer than a few months, possibly permanently. I was tired of running. When I found Sir Edric, his last message to me, which was written in his blood on the stone wall beside him, was *Central Plains*. So I took that as a sign."

Marcellus scoffed. "And you just left him there without trying to figure out who killed your guardian?"

I tamped down my irritation. "No. I stayed for a while and investigated until I couldn't stay any longer. I kept in contact with the authorities, but the case came to a dead end. When he died, the magic concealing the crescent moon birthmark on his forehead disappeared and they started to question who he was. That was when I knew I couldn't stay much longer. Not unless I wanted to risk being caught."

Caelan's hands tightened into fists atop his knees. His jaw ticked, and I feared that at any moment he would explode. "How could you have been forced to endure so much hardship?" he gritted. "You're the princess of Valoria! This is—"

"I stopped being the Princess of Valoria ten years ago," I cut him off. "Being royalty didn't matter. It was all about survival."

"I swear, I will investigate what happened to him. I won't let this disappear into the ether," Caelan promised.

"Why didn't you come home after Sir Edric passed? You could have returned then!" Marcellus shouted.

I smiled bitterly. "Sir Edric died with a secret. A secret that was potentially dangerous to me. I couldn't risk returning until I found out what it was."

"And you didn't trust us to help you? To protect you?" My brother shot to his feet. Selene jumped up and followed as Marcellus stormed away angrily.

Marcellus's exclamation tore through the fragile peace of our campsite. My brother's frustration was palpable in the crackling air as he receded into the darkness, his departure marked by his thunderous footfalls against the soft earth.

Exhaling deeply, I watched the space where Marcellus had been, feeling the weight of his expectations and the gulf of my decisions. The night seemed to hold its breath, the only sounds the gentle crackle of the fire and my brother's footfalls fading into the plains.

Caelan closed the distance between us and sat where Selene had been, his presence a calm amidst the storm of emotions. His body language was open yet protective.

"Ignore him." Caelan's voice, softer now, carried a comforting tone, an attempt to soothe the sting of Marcellus's words and diminish the complexity of our situation. The fire between us seemed to grow brighter with his care, its warmth a barrier against the night's chill and the coldness of unresolved conflicts.

Under the canopy of a starlit sky, my voice barely rose above a whisper, carrying the weight of unspoken fears. "Do you resent me as well?" The words hung between us, delicate and fraught with vulnerability.

Caelan's movements stilled and he turned, his gaze meeting mine in the firelight. Shadows danced across his face, softening his features. "No, I don't," he replied, his voice firm yet tinged with quiet remorse. "I don't have the right to resent you, not after all I've put you through." His admission was a balm to old wounds, a recognition of past wrongs from which we both wished to heal.

The past was a ghost that lingered, its presence unwelcome yet undeniable. I sought to shake off its chains and step into a future unburdened by the shadows of what had been.

A sudden gust of wind swept across the plains, cutting through the warmth of the fire and wrapping its cold fingers around us. I shivered and instinctively hugged myself tighter in a futile attempt to ward off the chill.

Noticing my discomfort, Caelan acted with a tenderness that spoke volumes of the recent shift between us. He reached out, his hands enveloping mine, a shield against the biting wind. His breath, warm and steady, flowed over my fingers, a small gesture of care. He held both my hands in his, his actions gentle as he rubbed them together.

His touch, though filled with a gentleness meant to comfort, sparked unease within me. I wanted to pull away, but I was afraid he'd be offended. I knew he meant well, but I also knew his intentions. I couldn't keep quiet much longer. He had to know how I truly felt.

"Caelan," I began, my voice a mere whisper as I gently extricated my hands from his. "I think we should talk."

His curiosity piqued, evidenced by a lifted brow. "Hmm?"

"I—" The words lodged in my throat, a barrier to the confession I needed to make. "I don't want to make things uncomfortable between us, but you should know that I ... I only see you as a friend. My best friend. And nothing more."

He froze and slowly turned to face me. "Why?" was all he said, catching me off guard.

"Why?" I repeated dumbly. "Well ... it's just how I feel, how I've always felt. There's really no explanation I can give you." I stood my ground, although my heart raced.

Caelan's reaction was immediate and intense, his physical presence overbearing as he stood. "When we were young, we promised to—"

"I was barely ten!" I protested, the absurdity of holding onto such words evident in the heat of my rebuttal as I stood to face him. "And you were what, twelve? We were *children*, Caelan. You can't hold that against me."

He gripped my shoulders and squeezed hard enough to make me wince. "I love you, Lyanna. I always have. Nothing can change that. You've been gone for ten years, just ... just give us time. We'll find our way back to each other," he declared, his words a mix of plea and conviction.

But love was not a chain by which to be shackled. I

shrugged out of his hold, rubbing my shoulders where his fingers bit into the skin. "I don't need time, Caelan. I love you ... I really do. But only as a friend."

His denial was soft-spoken. "You don't mean that."

I frowned. "Yes I do."

"No," he muttered to himself as he began to pace. "You don't know what you want. You'll realize with time that I'm the only one for you. That no one will ever love you as much as I do."

He was rambling, and I was starting to get a headache. He obviously wasn't listening to anything I said.

"You can't make me love you in that way, Caelan. It won't happen."

He stepped toward me, encroaching into my personal space and glaring down at me. "Is it because of *him*?"

"Who?"

"Because of the savage we've taken hostage!" he yelled, spittle flying out of his mouth. "Don't make me say his name," he growled.

His accusation, linking my feelings—or the lack thereof—to Ronan, was a strike too far, a blow to the fragile bridge of understanding upon which we treaded. Caelan's anger, raw and unfocused, pushed me further away.

I winced and took a tentative step back. "You're angry and you're not thinking clearly. I think maybe we should get some sleep."

I turned to leave when he snatched my upper arm roughly. "We're not done!"

I ripped my arm out of his grasp. "Don't you *dare* grab me like that again!"

"If it were *him*, you wouldn't have a problem with it," he scoffed.

"I would," I countered. "I am not property that can be handled as you please!" I snapped.

"Lyanna, please," he begged. "I didn't mean to—"

"I think you did," I said. "You're not the boy I once knew, and the truth of that terrifies me. I think it's best if we put some space between us. I'm leaving. Please don't follow unless you really want to see what I'm capable of." I spun on my heels and left him alone.

As I stormed away, leaving him in the grasp of his turmoil, the distance I put between us was not just physical, but a necessary division. He needed to learn that he couldn't get everything he wanted—including me.

3

The next day I avoided Caelan at all costs, managing to scramble into the carriage with Selene before he could see me. He hadn't approached me since last night, for which I was extremely thankful. Something about Caelan made me uneasy, but I couldn't seem to pinpoint just what was bothering me, which only frustrated me further.

The caravan resumed its journey with the first light, the rhythmic trot of the horses and the gentle sway of the carriage a constant as we navigated the path towards Valoria. By noon I was getting antsy and peered out my window to catch a glimpse of the world outside. I quickly realized we were no longer in the Central Plains. Without being told, I knew we'd crossed the border to Valoria.

Rolling hills covered in a quilt of green and gold stretched towards the horizon, dotted with clusters of trees that swayed in a gentle breeze. Fields of wildflowers bloomed in riotous colors, painting the landscape with strokes of lavender, yellow, and crimson. The air was fresher, imbued with the scent of earth and blossoms, a marked departure from the dusty openness of the plains.

Amid the enchanting scenery, a figure caught my eye—a mage soldier marching with a casual grace that set him apart from his companions. His presence piqued my curiosity. For a reason I couldn't explain, he looked familiar compared to the others who marched nearby. I glanced at Selene sleeping soundlessly beside me and then back at the soldier.

Leaning slightly out the window, I beckoned to the mage. "Excuse me!" I called out, then waved him over. "What's your name?"

He paused and turned towards the sound of my voice. In that moment, he was transformed. His dirty blond curls that sat as a chaotic crown atop his head were brushed aside to reveal a crescent moon birthmark—a mark of distinction for those of Valorian descent. His smile, bright and disarming, crinkled the corners of his eyes, reducing them to mere slits of vibrant green that sparkled with an unreadable emotion.

"Viktor, Your Highness." His voice bridged the gap between us as he stepped closer, the distance shrinking with each deliberate pace.

My gaze drifted beyond the carriage, seeking the horizon's secrets. "Do you know how far we are from the capital?" The question lingered in the air, mingled with the scent of fresh earth and the distant murmur of our caravan.

Viktor's gaze followed mine, squinting to get a better look. "Roughly another hundred kilometers," he estimated, his eyes reflecting a sliver of the journey ahead. "We crossed the border about an hour ago."

That meant we would arrive by noon tomorrow at the latest. With such a large caravan, we couldn't travel faster.

I bit my lip. I was hesitant to ask, but decided to take the risk. "How have things been in my absence?" I ventured.

"We've made many advances, building our army and even training some female mages. But ..." A pause laden with something unsaid hung between us.

"But what?" I prodded, sensing the undercurrent of his hesitation.

He leaned in subtly, his voice a hushed tone meant for my ears alone. "Keldara's silence has been deafening. Our preparations have mirrored the quiet, but we believe Keldara has been secretly preparing as well. It's been far too quiet across the border. We expect they're working on something big," he confided, the concern in his eyes mirroring the tension in his voice.

Surprise flared within me, and realization dawned sharp and clear. Valoria, for all its advancements, remained blind to Keldara's quiet storm. Keldara had found a material called Aetherite that muted a mage's power. I felt it firsthand when Mykal captured me. Didn't my father and the others know about it? Not wanting to alarm him, I kept quiet, knowing that when I arrived at the palace, I would have to tell my father immediately.

As Viktor moved parallel to the carriage, his silhouette a constant companion to our journey, I was enveloped by a sense of familiarity. There was something unmistakably known in the curve of his jaw, the set of his shoulders—echoes of a past interaction, perhaps, or a shared moment lost to memory.

Leaning forward, my curiosity thoroughly piqued, I posed the question that had been gnawing at my thoughts. "Do we know each other?" My arms found a perch on the windowsill, bridging the distance between us. "You look very familiar.".

His response, a chuckle muffled by the distance, drew my gaze to his movements. Viktor glanced down with a momentary contemplation of his boots before meeting my inquiry with an air of amusement. "Something like that," he offered cryptically.

The ambiguity of his answer furrowed my brow in confusion. "What do you mean by that?" I pressed, seeking clarity.

He lifted his gaze and we locked eyes. The smirk that played upon his lips carried a depth of knowledge, a shared secret yet to be revealed. "I'm Sir Edric's son," he disclosed, the words landing with the weight of a thunder bolt.

Surprise seized me and a silent gasp escaped as Viktor's words settled into reality. My seat became a necessary anchor, preventing the physical manifestation of my shock from sending me tumbling to the carriage floor. "You-You're Sir Edric's son?" The words tumbled from me in a stutter of disbelief.

He affirmed with a simple nod, embodying the legacy of his father with quiet pride. "The one and only."

Memories of a young Viktor filtered through my mind. He was fifteen or sixteen when his father smuggled me out of Valoria. Sir Edric often spoke about him. Viktor, the beacon of Sir Edric's life, now stood before me, a bridge to a past marred by sacrifice and separation.

"Viktor …" My voice softened, laden with the weight of unspoken apologies, a heart burdened by the price Sir Edric paid for my safety. "I'm so sorry." The guilt, a shadow companion of mine, grew darker with the acknowledgment of his loss. Sir Edric had risked it all for me. As if I was his own daughter. Worse still, I didn't even have an answer for why he was murdered. I couldn't help but feel responsible.

"Your Highness?" His gentle voice made me look up at

him. "You don't owe me an apology. You did nothing wrong. I hold no resentments." His reassurance was a balm, yet my heart wrestled with the burden of what remained unsaid.

"I know, but—"

"But nothing, Your Highness. Please." He glanced down at his booted feet again. "I'm assuming he is no longer with us ... Would you mind telling me what happened?"

"Of course." I situated myself and recounted the story I shared with Caelan and Marcellus the first night of our journey back to Valoria.

Viktor listened intently, without becoming upset or emotional. He simply nodded with each word I spoke.

"Sir Edric was like a father to me," I admitted. "He protected me from everything and everyone. He trained me well so I could eventually protect myself. When things got hard, he never once abandoned me. He always made sure we had a roof over our heads, and even if he went without food, he made sure I was never hungry. Sometimes we could only afford a single meal a day which we shared, but he hardly ate to make sure I had my fill. I can't express how sorry I am that I couldn't protect him. I owe you a debt, Viktor."

A sad smile spread across his face as he looked up at me again. "Thank you, Your Highness. I've spent many years wondering, and I'm glad to finally have closure ... I hope to protect you just as my father once did."

The offer, noble and heartfelt, sparked an immediate refusal. "I could never ask that of you!" I insisted, the weight of his proposal too great. "How ... how is your mother?"

At my question, Viktor's eyes turned glassy and he looked away again. "She passed two years ago."

A tear slid down my face. I could only hope that she and

Sir Edric were reunited in the Underworld after being apart for so long.

"I'm—I'm sorry," I whispered, lowering my head and then quickly looking up. "Whatever you may need, you can count on me. I owe you that much."

"Thank you, Your Highness, but truly, I am fine. I just hope to be of service one day."

∽

THE EVENING'S encampment sprawled beneath a twilight sky, situated a mere twenty to thirty kilometers from the Valorian capital. Restless, I navigated the periphery of our makeshift settlement, the need to evade Caelan propelling my steps. I wanted to bring Selene with me, but she'd been spending more and more time with Marcellus. I worried she was becoming too attached, but I didn't have the heart to stop her. At least not yet. I knew eventually I would have to step in, especially if my mother caught wind of their relationship.

As I strolled through camp, the sight of Ronan ensnared within his wooden prison halted my steps. His gaze, a piercing crimson, found mine across the distance, tethering me to the spot. Compelled by a mix of unresolved emotions and lingering questions, I approached with measured steps until I crouched before him a respectful distance away.

"Are ... are you okay?" The words felt inadequate, but they bridged the silence between us.

He stared at me intently, his face covered in grime, his long hair disheveled, and met my question with a weary acknowledgment. "I'm fine, Leila," he exhorted, a mixture of concern and resignation in his voice. "Go before anyone catches you here. Before Caelan finds you here."

Millions of questions swarmed my mind. I didn't care who might find me here. There was just one question to which I needed the answer. "Ronan?" His name escaped me like a plea. "I need to know why ... Why did you betray me?" It was a silly question. The inquiry was born of a heart still entangled in past affections, but I couldn't leave without knowing the truth.

He regarded me, his expression a complex tapestry of emotions, the weight of unsaid words palpable between us. "Does it matter? What's done is done," he deflected, his voice a low murmur in the encroaching night.

"It *does* matter, Ronan! I trusted you! So please, just give me an answer, any answer."

Ronan's response was a mirror to the complexity of our situation. "The truth doesn't matter, Leila. Not everything is black and white."

I pressed on, undeterred by the ambiguity of his warnings. "I'm not afraid of the in-between. I just need the truth, whatever it is." I crept closer to the wooden bars of his cage.

He hesitated, a silent struggle evident in his demeanor. "You might not like what you hear," he cautioned, his voice laced with somber foreboding.

My frustration boiling over, I clenched my fists around the bars of his cage as I sought to bridge the physical and emotional distance that separated us. "I don't care!" I declared, my voice rising in a mix of anger and desperation. "Are you prepared to be taken hostage to Valoria? Is this what you want?"

Ronan's retort was laced with grim amusement, a stark reminder of the political chessboard on which we were mere pawns. "Do you think I'll remain their captive?" he challenged, his words painting a picture of inevitabilities yet to unfold. "Valoria's king would not dare, not without risking war with the Crimson Clan. I'm just indulging Caelan for the moment."

"You truly believe my father will release you?" I pressed, skepticism lacing my voice. Truthfully, I didn't know much about Valorian politics, and I didn't know what my father was like anymore.

Ronan's confidence didn't waver; his smirk was a beacon of certainty. "I know he will," he assured me. "Your father is a smart man, Leila. He wouldn't dare bring another war to Valoria's doorstep."

My skepticism morphed into weary frustration. "Even so, I wouldn't be as confident. Caelan is ..." I hesitated, the name alone conjuring a storm of complications.

"Tricky?" he finished for me, a hint of wariness creeping into his voice. "I know. I know better than anyone what Caelan is capable of. And so should you. So ... be careful."

His concern, genuine and unexpected, drew a furrow between my brows. "Are you actually worried? About me?" I couldn't mask the surprise in my voice.

"Always, Leila. Always," he returned, his voice devoid of humor.

I scoffed. "Why do you keep calling me Leila? It's Lyanna," I corrected, a thread of irritation weaving through my words.

"Is it?" he challenged softly, an underlying acknowledgment in his gaze. "I'm sure you're not used to being called such. Leila suits you better. The great healer of the Central Plains who fears no man or beast. Not Princess Lyanna of Valoria who, in Caelan's eyes, is defenseless and weak. No, you're no such thing."

His assertion that he understood me better than I realized stirred a complex whirl of emotions. "You think you know me so well," I whispered, disbelief shadowing my tone. "But you don't."

He moved closer, his hand reaching out between the bars to gently caress my cheek. The warmth of his touch sparked an involuntary lean towards him. "But I do," he whispered back, his thumb grazing my lips in a tender motion that belied the complexity of our connection. "I know you very well, just as you know me."

"Do I?" The question was barely a breath, a soft surrender to the moment as I leaned into his touch. "All you've done is lie to me."

His hand stilled and I slowly opened my eyes. "I didn't mean to, Leila. Everything I did was for your wellbeing. In that, you can be sure. I would never hurt you."

The softness in his crimson gaze contradicted the harshness often attributed to his people. "But you *have,* Ronan. You lied to me—"

"No I didn't," he interjected with quiet intensity. "Mykal thinks he knows everything, but he doesn't. He doesn't know what I had planned."

I frowned, my curiosity piqued. "Which was?" I sought the truth hidden beneath layers of deception.

In response, Ronan closed the distance between us, his hands gently framing my face and pulling me closer until our breaths mingled, his lips grazing mine in a whisper of a kiss that stole my breath away.

"Nothing you need to concern yourself with," he whispered, but the gravity of his dismissal could not quell the storm of questions within me. "Just forget about the prophecy. There's no use in—"

I pulled away abruptly. "This involves my *life*, Ronan. I can't forget it that easily."

"Do you love me, Leila?" Ronan's voice softened, vulnerability cloaking his usually guarded demeanor. "Truly, do you love me?"

"I—" The words snagged in my throat. I was speechless, trapped in a moment that demanded a truth I wasn't ready to confront. Frozen in place, I stared at the man who had captured my heart. A man who was supposed to be my enemy.

"Because I lov—"

"Your Highness?"

The interruption was abrupt, a voice slicing through the thick air, breaking the spell Ronan and I were under. I spun around to find Viktor, his expression a mix of concern and confusion as his eyes darted between Ronan and me.

Scrambling to my feet, I sought to mask my turmoil. "Hi, uh, are you looking for me?" My voice wavered, betraying my flustered state.

Viktor offered a strained smile, his glance fleeting towards Ronan before settling on me. "Caelan is," he informed, a cautious glance over his shoulder hinting at the urgency of his message. "It's best if you leave here, Your Highness ... before he finds you."

"Listen to him, Leila." Ronan's voice, a blend of resignation and hope, urged me to heed Viktor's advice. "Go. I'll see you soon."

I peered back at Ronan, hesitant to leave him alone, but nodded with weary resignation before letting Viktor escort me back to my tent. His assurance, however comforting, couldn't ease the reluctance that weighed my steps as I followed Viktor away from Ronan's cage.

Our return to the heart of the camp was marked by silence, a mutual contemplation of the events that had just unfolded. I finally broke the quiet, curiosity guiding my words.

"Can I ask you a question, Viktor?"

"Of course, Your Highness," he said as we walked side by side.

"Why does the Valorian army listen to Caelan? He's from Eldwain."

Viktor nodded, his steps unfaltering. "Yes, but he spent much of his youth in Valoria and earned the King's trust. Especially since Prince Marcellus hasn't shown any interest in politics, Caelan's influence has only grown."

"And you, Viktor? Do you trust Caelan?" I asked cryptically.

He halted, the suddenness of his stop mirroring the gravity of my inquiry. "Do you want the truth, Your Highness?" At my affirmation, he exhaled a weary sigh. "I believe Caelan is up to something, I just don't know what. It worries me."

I hadn't known Viktor long, but he was Sir Edric's son. If there was anyone I could trust, it was him. At least until proven otherwise.

"Will you do me a favor?" I ventured, lowering my voice as I scanned our surroundings for eavesdroppers.

"Anything, Your Highness," he assured, his stance resolute.

"Investigate Eldwain's political climate. Rumors suggest the King is ill, and a successor remains unnamed. Can you—"

Viktor's agreement was swift, his promise a lifeline in the tumultuous sea of court intrigues. "I'll look into it, Your Highness. You have my word."

4

The trek into the capital was filled with shouts and cheers as we passed through the streets of Celeste where the people of Valoria eagerly awaited our return—or rather *my* return.

I peeked at the town I once called home through a slit in the curtain. The people appeared joyous, throwing grains of rice as if they were witnessing a wedding processional. The excitement for my return was evident in their faces.

Celeste, the heart and capital of Valoria, unfolded before me like a tapestry woven with threads of joy and anticipation. Its streets, lined with cobblestone paths that shone brightly under the mid-day sun, thrummed with life. Buildings, their architecture a harmonious blend of elegance and strength, rose on either side. Here, in the capital, the reverence for the moon goddess was palpable, her influence interwoven into the very essence of the city. Crescent moons were etched into doorways and hung from balconies where they danced in the breeze, a constant homage to the divine protector of Valoria.

The people of Celeste, their foreheads marked with the

sacred crescent moon birthmark, gathered in droves along the caravan's path. Their cheers and jubilant cries filled the air, a cacophony of welcome and celebration. The warmth in their eyes combined with genuine smiles spoke volumes of their elation at my return. I, who had wandered far from the land that birthed me, was home again, embraced by a community I thought had long forgotten me.

Once we entered the palace grounds, my surroundings changed drastically.

The palace came into view, a majestic structure that stood as a testament to Valorian artistry and devotion, marking the culmination of our journey. Rising from the heart of the capital, its spires reached towards the heavens, a silent prayer to the moon goddess. As we made our way to the palace, the atmosphere shifted from the communal warmth of the town to the solemn grandeur befitting the heart of a kingdom. The palace grounds, a sprawling expanse of meticulously tended gardens and imposing structures, stood as a beacon of Valoria's might and majesty.

Slowly, the caravan came to a halt. Once we were safely behind the palace gates, Viktor opened my carriage door.

I turned to Selene, who was seated beside me and whispered, "Stay here. I'll send someone for you. If Marcellus comes to get you, don't go with him. It's best if you're not seen together just yet."

"Leila ..." she started, her face creased with worry.

I took her hand and gripped it tightly. "I promise to keep you safe, Selene. But for me to do that, I need you to listen to me. Do you understand?"

She nodded stiffly.

"I won't be long." I released her hand and slowly exited the carriage, gratefully accepting Viktor's hand as he helped me out of the carriage. Before he could pull away, I whispered, "Get someone you trust to escort Selene out of here and into my quarters. Don't let any of the ladies from my mother's court see her."

"Understood, Your Highness," he replied, his voice equally low, a shared understanding of the task at hand.

Together, we approached the Grand Hall, the palace's heart, where history and the present converged. The courtyard, a vast expanse of cobblestone interlaced with verdant patches of grass, was alive with blooming flowers and the gentle murmur of fountains, their waters catching the sunlight and scattering it like jewels. Statues of past rulers and heroes of Valoria stood sentinel, their stone gazes fixed eternally forward as if guiding us along our path.

The walk to the Grand Hall was a journey through time, the air perfumed with the scent of lavender and rosemary from the surrounding gardens. The towering doors of the hall loomed before us, their wood carved with scenes of lunar worship and Valorian victories, evidence of the country's enduring reverence for the moon goddess and its storied past.

"Are you sure you don't want to change first?" Caelan called out as he stood a few paces ahead, waiting for us.

I looked down at my trousers and blouse and knew he wanted me to change into attire more appropriate for a princess. But the truth was that I was no longer the pampered girl covered in silks and gowns. This was who I was now, and I wanted my parents to see who I had become.

"No. I'm fine the way I am." I lifted my chin and attempted to walk past him, but he gripped my arm, stopping me.

"Lyanna," he whispered into my ear. "You—"

I narrowed my gaze on his grip. "Release me," I gritted between my teeth. "Unless you want me to cause a scene."

As if I'd thrown acid at him, he jerked back and released me at once. "I didn't mean—"

"I know. But I would prefer if you kept your hands to yourself," I retorted.

He exhaled loudly before nodding. "Very well."

After motioning us to walk forward, I followed Caelan towards the Grand Hall. We crossed the threshold in silence, the weight of the occasion settling around us like a leaden cloak. The Grand Hall, with its high vaulted ceilings and walls adorned with tapestries depicting the phases of the moon, welcomed us into its hushed embrace. Light filtered through stained glass windows, casting the room in a kaleidoscope of colors. Each measured step echoed on the marble floor, announcing our arrival.

It was in this moment, balancing between the beauty of the courtyard and the majesty of the Grand Hall, that I felt the full weight of my return to Valoria—a blend of duty, anticipation, and the silent promise of challenges to come.

The doors were opened by mages who stood guard as our arrival was announced. Their robes fluttered gently in the breeze, a silent witness to their vigilance.

"Her Highness, Princess Lyanna with Prince Caelan of Eldwain," announced a guard, his voice echoing off the stone walls as we stepped into the grandeur that awaited.

At the far end, seated upon thrones that seemed to capture the very essence of the night sky, were my parents.

My father, once the embodiment of Valorian strength, bore the marks of a decade's passage. His hair, formerly a dark cascade, now whispered tales of wisdom and trials in strands of silver and gray. The lines at the corners of his eyes spoke volumes, each a story of laughter, worry, and the burden of rule. Yet his eyes, those clear pools of blue, ignited with a light I hadn't seen in years as he rose to greet us.

My mother, the epitome of regal poise, had managed to cloak the years in an aura of timeless beauty. Her hair, styled in a perfect chignon, betrayed no hint of silver, though I wondered at the magic that might have kept the years at bay. Her face, taut with the efforts to preserve her youth, softened into a smile that, despite its warmth, couldn't quite reach the cool detachment of her gaze.

Together, they presented the dual faces of Valoria—strength tempered with grace, power cloaked in beauty. As we advanced, the distance closing with each step, the weight of the moment settled upon me, a mantle of expectation and reunion that was ten years in the making.

My father's voice, rich with emotion, broke the ceremonial silence that had cloaked our procession. Meeting us halfway he exclaimed, "Lyanna!" His steps quickened until he enveloped me in an embrace that bridged the chasm of years. "Oh, how I've missed you, my darling girl."

The warmth of his hug thawed the lingering chill of uncertainty within me and tears, unbidden, traced paths of relief down my cheeks. "I missed you, too." My voice barely rose above a whisper, laden with a decade's worth of unsaid words.

As he stepped back, his gaze swept over me, a mixture of awe and something unreadable. "You've ... changed," he observed, his tone tinged with a hint of surprise and perhaps uncertainty.

A light laugh escaped me, an attempt to bridge the gap his words had inadvertently forged. "I'm no longer eleven," I reminded him, trying to infuse lightness into the moment. "I'm bound to change."

The sound of my mother's heels announced her approach; the unmistakable cadence of authority in her step heralded her arrival into our reunion. "I can only imagine the years of poverty you've endured," she said as she came into view around my father. "But do not dwell on the past. You're home now."

Stepping forward to acknowledge her, I dipped into a curtsy, a gesture of respect and distance. "Mother," I greeted, my voice soft, courteous.

Her response was immediate, her touch light on my elbow as she guided me upright. "Welcome home, Lyanna. No formalities needed," she reassured me, her voice carrying a warmth that belied the coolness of her gaze.

My father, ever the host, interjected with a question that seemed to herald a return to normalcy. "Are you hungry?" he asked, his enthusiasm bubbling over. "You must be hungry. We'll hold a feast! And in ten days' time, we will hold a banquet in your honor."

The proposal was overwhelming, a grand gesture that felt disproportionate to my desires. "That's really not necessary—" I began, only to be cut off by his fervent insistence.

"Of course it is!" he declared, his determination clear. "All of Asteria needs to know you're home."

I knew what he meant. He wanted to invite everyone from Asteria so he could parade me around and celebrate the fact that the only female blood mage had returned. And to prove that I was not, nor had I ever been in the clutches of the Crimson Clan. This homecoming was not just a reunion but a reentry into a world of political machinations where my very existence was a statement of power and a tool to be wielded.

I couldn't argue. I was in no position to do so. I might be a princess, but even I was limited in power, especially after being gone so long.

I smiled tightly and bowed. "Of course," I agreed, my tone betraying none of my reservations.

My father's joy was palpable, his hand finding Caelan's shoulder in a gesture of gratitude. "Wonderful!" he beamed, his eyes alight with relief and celebration. "Thank you for bringing my daughter home safe and sound."

Caelan's response was tinged with discomfort, his laughter not quite reaching his eyes as he glanced away. "It was my honor, Your Majesty," he murmured, the formality of his words a stark contrast to his unease.

"Nonsense. Please be Lyanna's escort to the banquet. It'll be a wonderful day for us all to celebrate!"

The announcement that I would accompany Caelan to the banquet ensnared me in a web of emotions I had yet to untangle. I stilled as I peered over at Caelan. He wore a tense smile, but remained quiet about all the things he had done. For some reason, even though I told him the past was in the past, his reaction upset me. Which had to mean that I hadn't truly forgiven him, and if I did, I hadn't forgotten. He was the last person I wanted as my escort.

"Father—" My attempt to voice my concerns was abruptly cut short by my mother.

"Where is Marcellus?" she asked. "Did he not arrive with you as well?"

"He did."

Caelan's brief acknowledgment was overshadowed by the Grand Hall's doors swinging open as the guard's voice boomed, "His Highness, Prince Marcellus!"

Marcellus walked in … with Selene behind him.

The room seemed to hold its breath as Selene stepped into the light, her beauty stark against the grandeur of the hall, her apprehension clear in the wide set of her emerald eyes. My eyes widened at the sight of her, and I attempted to regain my composure. I dared to look behind me, back at my mother. Her gaze was sharp and calculating as it shifted to Selene, her interest piqued by the unfamiliar face.

"Marcel..." My mother's voice was smooth, her curiosity veiled behind a veneer of courtesy. "Who is this you've brought with you?"

"This is—"

"My best friend," I interjected, a desperate bid to shield Selene from her scrutiny. "She was my assistant back in the Central Plains. I did not want to leave her behind."

"Is that so? She's beautiful. Quite a rare oddity. Do I dare say, one of the Merfolk?" my mother asked.

I cleared my throat. "Yes. Yes, she is."

Admitting to Selene's Merfolk lineage was a gamble, one I hoped would satiate my mother's curiosity without inviting further examination.

Marcellus and Selene approached us, and he took ahold of my mother's hand, offering a peck on the back of her hand with a slight bow. Selene stood by awkwardly, unsure what to do.

"Tell me, Marcel, is this the concubine you said you'd be taking in your letter?" my mother asked as she looked Selene up and down with mild interest.

"No!" I yelled quickly, then cleared my throat. "No, she's not. That was another girl, but Marcel changed his mind about her. Selene is here just as my friend." I sent a glare in Marcellus's direction, daring him to disagree. He looked away.

"Come, dear," my mother beckoned Selene. "Let me look at you."

Selene tentatively stepped forward and my mother inspected her more closely. Wearing a modest dress that she hadn't changed since we left the Central Plains, we all looked a bit rough for wear.

"It—It's a pleasure to meet you, Your Majesty," Selene stuttered.

My mother's focus shifted back to me, her disdain thinly veiled. "At least you had someone attending to your needs while you were away."

The assumption that Selene served merely as a maid irked me, but I held my tongue and chose my words carefully. "Mother, she wasn't attending to my needs. I was a healer in the Central Plains. Selene assisted me in my work," I clarified.

My mother gasped, looking aghast at what I'd just said. "You dealt with the ill?" she echoed, her voice a blend of disbelief and dismay.

"I did," I affirmed, meeting her incredulous gaze with a steady one of my own.

My father cleared his throat as he cut between me and my mother. "That is very admirable, Lyanna. We're proud of you."

"She's a very well-known healer in the Central Plains," Caelan added. "Many travelled far and wide to receive her care."

"Did you ... did you use your blood?" my father asked with furrowed brows.

I gave a small nod. "Sometimes, but not often. Only when the situation was too dire for more traditional methods," I admitted.

"She saved me," Caelan hurried to say. "When I was poisoned by fae fruit."

"Well, I guess you owe our Lyanna a life debt," my father chuckled.

"I owe her more than that," Caelan murmured, but didn't speak further.

Seeking to steer the conversation away from dangerous

waters, I introduced a new topic. "Father, there is someone else we brought with us."

"Lyanna—" Caelan warned, but I ignored him.

"Oh?" My father raised a questioning brow.

"Ronan, the Crimson Clan Chief's son is with us ... as a hostage," I said.

As the truth spilled from my lips, a ripple of tension swept through the Grand Hall like a cold gust. My father's reaction was a silent storm brewing. His stance was rigid as he processed the information, running a hand through his hair before spinning around to walk back to his throne.

"Caelan!" My father's voice sliced through the thick atmosphere with a gravity that demanded everyone's full attention. "Explain."

Caelan cleared his throat and stepped forward, the weight of the moment pressing upon him. "Your Majesty, during our encounter with the Crimson Clan in the Central Plains, Ronan was taken prisoner. It was a strategic move, one that—"

Marcellus, ever the provocateur, couldn't resist stirring the pot further. "He was in a relationship with Lyanna," he interjected, his voice laced with mischief as he cast a glance my way that was both accusatory and gleeful. "Quite the scandal, indeed."

I glared at my brother as he openly took delight in our mother's shocked expression. Her body swayed as if the ground beneath her had shifted. Only Marcellus's quick reflexes prevented her from faltering completely, his arms steadying her as she regained her balance.

"Lyanna!" she gasped, her eyes searching mine for the truth. "Is there any truth to what your brother claims?"

"Lies, I'm sure of it." Caelan's growl resonated with protectiveness, his stance beside me both a shield and a proclamation. "Ronan deceived Lyanna. She has no fault in this matter," he countered, his gaze fierce.

Marcellus's snort was dismissive, a silent challenge to Caelan's defense. "If you say so," he murmured under his breath, skepticism coloring his tone.

"I *know* so!" Caelan's voice rose, his declaration ringing through the hall. "Regardless of the circumstances, Lyanna would never betray her people, much less lay with a beast like him!"

The heat of embarrassment and the sting of guilt flushed my cheeks, Marcellus's words and Caelan's vehement defense wove a complex tapestry of warring emotions. Caught between the scandal Marcellus delighted in unveiling and the fervent protection Caelan offered, I found myself unable to meet the eyes of those who were gathered, my heart torn asunder by the revelations and the rapid pace at which they were unfolding.

"Enough!" my father yelled, banging his fist on the throne's armrest. "You'll not speak ill of your sister. Caelan is right. She would never betray her people. But …"

"But what, dear?" my mother pleaded as she fanned herself. "We cannot let these rumors stand. They will spread like wildfire and her reputation—"

"We cannot keep him prisoner," my father interrupted. "It would ignite a war with the Crimson Clan. While they would be easy enough to defeat, I will not expose Valoria's people to danger."

"But—" my mother attempted.

"But nothing. Marcellus!" he called out. "Release him at once. Send him to the Northern palace to rest and dispatch a messenger with a letter to Chief Aryan, informing him that his son is safe with us. We will also invite him to the banquet to be held in ten days' time."

"Of course, Father," Marcellus gritted between his teeth and quickly stormed out of the Grand Hall, sending one last lingering look at Selene before leaving. Thank the gods my mother didn't see him. She was still in disbelief at my father's command.

"There's always some truth to rumors," my mother said as she turned her icy glare to me. "Explain yourself, Lyanna."

With my hands clasped behind my back, I hesitated, unsure whether to be truthful or lie through my teeth. "I—" I croaked, but the words stuck in my throat.

"Enough." My father sighed as he ran a hand through his hair. "Lyanna, you don't know everything, much less the truth—"

"That's where you're wrong, Father. I know *everything*," I growled, staring at my parents with a look that could kill a hundred men.

My father jerked back as if I'd slapped him, his eyes widening and his breath hitching. My mother clutched her chest with her handkerchief in hand and I knew she was just as shocked. Her bottom lip trembled.

With one last, searing look, I grabbed Selene's wrist, spun on my heels, and left the Grand Hall. This was one topic I didn't want to discuss with them.

At least not yet.

5

Even after stepping out of the Grand Hall, the weight of the conversation still hung heavily in the air around us. Viktor, his posture tense with apprehension, was the first to greet us, his loyalty as evident as his concern.

"Your Highness," he greeted, bowing deeply, a sign of respect mingled with urgency. "Apologies, but—"

I waved off his concerns before he could finish. "Don't worry, Viktor. I'm well aware of Marcellus's ways. He leaves little room for dissent," I reassured him, hoping to ease the obvious tension in his shoulders.

He offered a solemn nod, acknowledging the truth in my words, the complexity of court dynamics playing silently between us.

Selene wore a mask of contrition. "Leila ... I'm sorry, I should have listened to you—"

"It's too late for that now," I snapped, still holding her wrist. I realized I might have been a bit harsh and slowly released her. "Sorry, I didn't mean to ... I'm just a bit stressed."

Selene shook her head. "It's okay. I understand. I—"

"Not here," I whispered.

Seeking a semblance of privacy, I glanced around the opulent expansiveness of the palace courtyard. "Is my room still situated in the Eastern palace?" I inquired, the need for solitude pressing.

"Yes, Your Highness. Allow me to escort you both." Viktor's tone shifted to one of dutiful assurance as he led the way.

Our path to the Eastern palace was a journey through the heart of Valorian splendor. The palace grounds unfurled like a meticulously designed tapestry, each step revealing more of its intricate beauty. Marble pathways bordered by lush, fragrant gardens guided our way, the air filled with the scent of blooming night jasmine and lavender, a soothing balm to the day's tensions.

Archways carved with effigies of the moon goddess marked our passage, their silvery sheen casting a soft glow under the afternoon sun, a reminder of the divine protectorate who oversaw Valoria. The rhythmic splash of fountains and the gentle rustle of leaves in the breeze accompanied our silent procession, the natural harmony a stark contrast to the discord we'd endured in the Grand Hall.

The Eastern palace, with its soaring towers and gleaming domes rose majestically against a backdrop of azure sky. Its façade, adorned with crescent moon motifs and celestial imagery, demonstrated Valoria's enduring devotion to the moon goddess. The entrance was flanked by statues of guardian spirits, their faces serene yet vigilant, welcoming us into the sanctuary of the palace's most private quarters.

As we traversed the final stretch, the Eastern palace's

grandeur enveloped us, its corridors whispering stories of the past, each step taking us deeper into the place I once called home. The walk, a transition from the public spectacle of the Grand Hall to the intimate seclusion of my chambers, was a journey back to myself, away from the princess and back to the person I had become during my years away.

We approached the ornate doors leading to my chambers and Viktor reached forward, pushing them open with a reverence that suggested we were entering a sanctuary rather than mere living quarters. The first thing that struck me was the soft light filtering through the tall, arched windows, casting the room in a warm, golden hue. The air was scented with the subtle fragrance of jasmine and rose, a comforting embrace that welcomed me back to a place I hadn't realized I'd missed so profoundly.

"My room ..." I whispered, Selene's startled gasp echoing my delight. Stepping inside, my gaze swept over the familiar yet changed surroundings. The walls were adorned with fine tapestries depicting the moon in various phases. An opulent rug woven with threads of silver and blue covered the floor, soft underfoot, leading the way to a large canopy bed draped in gossamer fabrics that fluttered gently in the breeze from the open windows.

"Your Highness, we prepared the chamber for your return," Viktor said, breaking the silence. "We hoped it would make you feel welcome."

Clasping Selene's hand again, I turned to him, a smile finding its way to my lips despite the day's earlier turmoil. "It's more beautiful than I remembered. Thank you, Viktor."

He bowed slightly, a gesture of deference. "It was our honor, Your Highness. If there's anything else you require, please don't hesitate to ask."

My attention was drawn to a small, intricately carved table by the window, upon which lay a collection of scrolls and books. Beside them was a crystal decanter filled with a luminescent liquid that seemed to glow with its own inner light, and a single glass. "Is this ...?"

"Aetherwater," Viktor explained, following my gaze. "Infused with moonstone to aid in relaxation and healing. I thought you might appreciate it after your journey."

I nodded, touched by the thoughtfulness. "That's very considerate. Thank you."

"If there's nothing else, I'll exc—"

"Are the court ladies still the same?" I inquired before he left.

He stilled, opening his mouth then closing it again.

"What is it, Viktor?"

He cleared his throat. "Her Majesty changed them."

I snorted and gave a dry laugh. Of course my mother did. No doubt my new court ladies were all dutiful spies for her. I knew returning to Valoria would be tricky, but if I didn't have a safe place to rest, I would surely lose my mind.

"I can always change them, Your Highness," he whispered softly, as if unsure about his suggestion.

I smiled. "It's like you were reading my mind," I said. "Do you know of any trustworthy court ladies who aren't loyal to my mother?"

He nodded. "They aren't court ladies, but they work in various sections of the palace, from the kitchen to laundry duty. But they're loyal, I can guarantee it."

"Perfect. If anyone asks, tell them it was me. I'll write up a letter just in case."

"Yes, Your Highness."

After Viktor excused himself and left me and Selene to settle in, I wandered over to the window, drawn by the view it offered. The gardens below were a riot of color, evidence of the palace's dedication to beauty and harmony. From this vantage point, the worries of court politics and personal entanglements seemed a distant memory, if only for a moment.

Turning back to the room, I took in the small writing desk with its quill and ink neatly arranged, the comfortable chairs positioned by a low-burning hearth, and the wardrobe doors slightly ajar, revealing hints of the gowns nestled within. Each detail was a stark reminder of the life I was stepping back into, a blend of duty and personal sanctuary.

Selene's voice, soft and laced with concern, pierced the serene silence of my chambers, drawing me back from my reverie. "Are you okay, Leila?" she asked, her eyes searching mine for signs of unrest. "Won't your mother be upset if—"

Cutting her off, I nodded slightly, the weight of realization settling on my shoulders. "She will be, but she'll get over it," I admitted. The thought of navigating palace intrigues without becoming ensnared in my mother's web of surveillance was a cumbersome burden. "If I allow her court ladies to remain, I won't have a moment of peace. My every move will be reported to her. They have to go."

As understanding dawned in Selene's eyes, her earlier excitement at our arrival was now tempered by the complexity of our situation. "I didn't realize how ... *complicated* things would be," she confessed, a hint of worry threading through her words. "No wonder you were in no rush to return home."

A rueful laugh escaped me, the irony of the situation not lost. "You're right about that. I think this is the part I dreaded the most. Palace life is akin to being a bird trapped in a gilded cage. It's ... suffocating," I mused, the analogy bitter on my tongue. "After a decade of freedom, the confines of these walls feel more like shackles. I'm not sure I'll assimilate well."

Selene's response was a gesture of solidarity. Her hand found mine, her grip firm and reassuring. "I'll be with you every step of the way," she promised, her determination a beacon in the uncertain path that lay ahead. "You're not alone."

Her words, simple yet profound, offered a sliver of comfort amidst the turmoil. "Thank you," I whispered, allowing myself a moment to lean into the strength of our friendship. "In this nest of vipers, you're probably the only one I can count on. But ..."

Her brows knitted together in concern. "But what?"

Exhaling an onerous sigh as the weight of our situation seemed to press down on all sides, I met her gaze, the conflict within me evident. "But being that anchor, you also become my most vulnerable point, a lever others might use against me. Are you certain you wouldn't rather return to the Luminar Sea? To your people?" The question hung between us, saturated with the implication of her safety and the potential cost of our bond.

Her response was immediate, her resolve unwavering. "Would you have me leave, then, to safeguard yourself?" Her tone, gentle yet firm, challenged the notion of separation as a solution.

"No, of course not!" I hurried to clarify, the mere thought of her departure a bleak prospect. "I just ... I fear what they might do, and how they might exploit our friendship to meet their ends."

Selene took a step closer, her presence a comforting certainty. "Leila, or Lyanna," she corrected softly, "whichever name the world knows you by, I choose to stand with you.

Not as a maid, not as a mere assistant, but as a friend. The Merfolk can wait. This ... all of this," she gestured around us, "is where I need to be. Where *I* can protect *you*."

Her declaration, bold and without hesitation, fortified my resolve. In the intricate dance of palace intrigues, Selene's loyalty was my unwavering point of light, a reminder that not all battles were fought with swords or spells, but with steadfast hearts and unbreakable bonds.

I took a step back, creating a small space between us, driven by a need for clarity. "By the way," I ventured, a thread of confusion lacing my words. "What happened earlier? Why did you arrive in the Grand Hall with Marcellus? I understand why Viktor couldn't override my brother's demands, but why—"

Selene's response was a quiet retreat; her gaze shifted towards the window, the open vista a silent witness to her turmoil. "He ... he thought if his parents saw us together, it might ..." she trailed off, her uncertainty palpable.

I pressed for more, needing to understand. "Might what, Selene?"

With a ponderous sigh, she glanced back, her vulnerability framed against the backdrop of the room. "Might offer us a better chance at being together," she admitted, her voice barely above a whisper.

"Selene," my voice was laced with concern, "why would you entertain such thoughts? Engaging with Marcellus in this way ... it's dangerous. My mother—"

She interrupted with a nod, a silent acknowledgment of the precarious path she treaded. "I know, I do. After seeing her reaction ... Well, it's clear she disapproves. She already doesn't like me."

I reached out, offering reassurance by squeezing her hand. "It's not about dislike, Selene. My mother operates within a realm of caution. She doesn't know you, and that's where her distrust stems from. Don't take it personally, but also remember what kind of person she is and guard yourself against her."

Selene's eyes met mine, a mix of gratitude and resolve within them. "I will. I promise."

6

The relief of shedding the journey's grime in a bath left me feeling rejuvenated, yet the solitude of my chambers was stifling with the knowledge that the court ladies were watching my every move. With Selene comfortably settled in her own room and Viktor tasked with the delicate matter of staffing, the Eastern palace's corridors echoed with a silence that spoke volumes of my isolation. Each step felt calculated, a stark reminder of the scrutiny that waited around every corner.

Seeking a small reprieve, I ventured to the kitchens and returned laden with simple comforts—a bowl of grapes and a modest jug of wine. It wasn't the luxurious A Thousand Roses wine from the Rose Petal Lounge, but it promised a semblance of solace for my solitude.

The sight that greeted me upon my return to my chambers, however, was anything but solitary. Caelan, perched on the edge of my bed as if he belonged there, stirred a mix of irritation and surprise within me. "What are you doing here?" I asked, my voice low, a blend of curiosity and caution coloring my words.

His gaze swept over me, a smile playing on his lips as he noted the changes in my appearance. "You look ... different. In a good way. You look like Princess Lyanna again," he observed, his eyes lingering on the subtle transformation wrought by a dress and my freshly braided hair.

A snort escaped me at his approval, laced with a hint of derision. "I'm guessing you prefer me this way," I retorted, moving past him to place the wine and grapes on my desk, enacting a barrier between us.

"I do," he confessed, unabashed. "This is who you are. Who you should have been all along."

His words, meant as a compliment, felt like chains tightening around me. I braced against the desk, the wood creaking under the force of my grip.

Caelan glanced at the wine with open disapproval. "You really shouldn't drink so much. Why don't I get one of the court ladies to bring you some tea instead?" he offered.

His suggestion was the spark that lit the powder keg of my frustration. Spinning around, I blocked his path, the word "No!" a sharp rebuke. "I don't want tea. If I did, that's what I would have brought."

"Lyanna—"

"Caelan, stop!" The plea burst from me, a mix of anger and desperation. "Please, just stop. If I wanted someone to dictate my choices, my mother is more than capable of doing so."

He paused, his advance halting as he processed my outburst. "I'm not trying to control you, Lyanna. I'm trying to help," he said, his voice softer, an attempt to bridge the gap that had opened between us.

Yet, in that moment, the gap felt like a chasm. His presence in my chamber was an unwelcome reminder of the liberties he'd already taken and the autonomy he threatened. His proximity, once a source of comfort, now felt like an intrusion, a challenge to the independence I'd fought so desperately to reclaim.

I found myself cornered, both physically by Caelan's imposing presence and emotionally by the weight of his accusations and expectations. Exhaling a frustrated breath, I leaned back against the desk, the cool wood a minor relief against the tension that crackled between us. "I know you believe you're helping, but this—this constant *oversight* is suffocating, Caelan. I can't live like this."

His reaction was immediate, a mix of hurt and anger sharpening his words. "So, it's suffocating when *I* do it, but if it was Ronan, you'd be fine?" His voice was a low growl, his jealousy barely contained.

I met his challenge head-on, my patience fraying. "If it was Ronan, he wouldn't be telling me what to do," I shot back, standing my ground.

Caelan scoffed bitterly and closed the distance between us, his movements deliberate. "You think you know him so well, but you don't, Lyanna. He's a—"

"You don't know *anything* about him!" I exploded. My voice rose and I pushed him away, needing to reclaim my space.

He paused and surprise flashed across his handsome features before he regained his composure, his gaze sharpening. "And you do?" he challenged, skepticism lacing his tone. "Wasn't Ronan the one who deceived you with his lies? Or did I get that part wrong?"

I furrowed my brows. "How did you—"

Caelan's frustration boiled over, and his pacing became a physical manifestation of his inner turmoil. "Nothing is a secret around here, Lyanna! When will you get that through your thick skull?" His warning was clear, tinged with a protective fervor that bordered on possession. "And just as a warning, don't even think about going to the Northern palace to see him. Don't give the rumors credence."

I couldn't hide my irritation, my voice laced with defiance. "I'm well aware of what I should and shouldn't do."

"Good." He started toward me again.

Before I had time to react, Caelan took ahold of my wrist, pinned it behind my back, and pulled me flush against his chest. I attempted to push him away with my free hand, but his grip was firm.

"Caelan!" I gasped, surprised he would manhandle me this way.

"Lyanna, why won't you look at me? Why do you only have eyes for a barbarian like Ronan?" he murmured, his gaze lingering on my lips.

My patience frayed past the breaking point. "Let *go*, Caelan," I insisted, my voice a mix of warning and anger.

"Why?" he whispered, his lips inching closer to mine. "Do you think I don't know that he's already touched you in ways he shouldn't?"

"You don't know anything!" I retorted sharply, struggling against his grip. "Release me."

"And if I don't?" he muttered. His eyes, dark and searching, fixed on mine, seeking an answer that was obvious to everyone but him.

"I am a blood mage, Caelan, and a damn good one, too." The threat spilled from me, cold and clear. "If you don't release me this instant, then I won't apologize for what happens next."

His gaze pierced me. If looks could kill, I'd be dead on the spot. Before he could speak, the doors to my chambers burst open with a resounding boom.

Someone cleared their throat. "Your Highness?" Viktor

called out from behind Caelan. I peered over his shoulder to look at my guard. "Is everything all right?"

My gaze shifted from Viktor to Caelan and I grinned. "Everything is perfectly fine. Caelan was just leaving."

Caelan's grip on my wrist tightened, no doubt leaving a bruise before he released me with a sneer, taking a step back and putting distance between us. "This conversation is not over," he whispered before spinning on his heels and pushing past Viktor, nearly knocking him over as he stormed out of my chambers.

Once he was gone, Viktor quickly closed the doors and rushed toward me. "Your Highness, are you okay?" His gaze dropped to my wrist, which already bloomed with Caelan's fingerprints.

"I'm fine. Thank you for coming in," I assured him, massaging the tender skin.

"I would have been here sooner, but I was down by the river, meeting with the laundry maids." He winced. "I should have been here."

I waved off his concern. "Don't worry, Viktor. It would have happened at some point. Were you successful, at least?"

He nodded. "I've swapped out the current court ladies with new ones, and I sent their promotions to the senior lady-in-waiting with your seal. There shouldn't be any issues."

"Thank you, Viktor," I sighed. "I feel as if I can breathe properly for the first time since I arrived."

"Of course, Your Highness," he said. "But ..."

I frowned. "But what?"

"Would you like me to send a message to our guest in the Northern palace?" he inquired.

While I appreciated his offer to send a message to

Ronan, I knew better than to have anything in writing. In the wrong hands, any missive could be used against me. No matter how innocent the contents may be.

I shook my head. "No. It's fine. I'll see him at the banquet in ten days."

"Very well, Your Highness. Before I go, let me introduce you to the lady-in-waiting who will accompany you and handle all your needs. She is a mage warrior—"

Viktor's introduction of a mage warrior masquerading as a court lady caught me off guard. "A mage warrior?" I echoed. "Wouldn't becoming my lady-in-waiting be a demotion?"

He affirmed with a solemn nod, his gaze earnest. "Well ... yes, it would be. But from my recent observations, Your Highness, I would feel more comfortable leaving someone more capable by your side in case I'm not around," he said delicately. "Female warriors are rare, and Tessa is exceptional. She readily agreed to be your main lady-in-waiting."

"Oh," I managed, the reality of my situation settling in. I knew what he was getting at. With all the danger that surrounded me, I needed more than a mere court lady by my side. I needed a bodyguard.

"Tessa!" Viktor called, his voice echoing slightly in the spacious chamber. "Come in."

The doors parted and a young woman strode in, dressed in the lady-in-waiting's customary uniform of sky blue and pink. Her blonde hair was pulled back in a tight chignon, with silver hair pins as decorations. Tessa approached and stood beside Viktor before offering a deep bow.

"Your Highness," Tessa began, her voice steady and sure, "I am honored to meet you. My duty is to ensure your safety, a responsibility I accept with all seriousness."

Her declaration, sincere and forthright, momentarily

eased the tension coiled within me. "Thank you, Tessa." The gravity of her role—a protector in the guise of a court lady—sank in. "I must admit, I'm surprised you'd accept what many might see as a lesser position."

Tessa's response was immediate. She lifted her head and met my gaze directly. "To serve and protect you, Princess, is no demotion in my eyes. It's a privilege I embrace wholeheartedly."

Her words, infused with a sense of honor and duty, offered a sliver of comfort. "Then I am grateful for your service." I offered her a genuine smile, a small gesture of appreciation for the warrior who had willingly stepped out of the shadows to be my shield.

∽

As darkness enshrouded the Eastern palace, marking the end of my first day back in Valoria, the surreal nature of my return settled over me. Accompanied by Tessa, my new protector and chief lady-in-waiting, I explored the familiar yet altered corridors of my childhood home, introducing myself to the new faces assigned to attend me. Freed for the moment from my mother's scrutinizing gaze, I found a semblance of peace.

"Your bed has been made, Your Highness," Tessa announced, deftly turning down the covers of my large bed, her movements efficient yet gentle. "Would you like me to brush your hair before bed?"

I picked up the hairbrush and positioned myself in front of the vanity mirror, a simple act of normalcy. "No, it's fine, Tessa. I haven't had these sorts of luxuries in ten years. It will take a while for me to adapt. But in all honesty, I hope I don't," I admitted softly, running the brush through my hair.

Tessa paused, her reflection joining mine in the mirror as she knelt beside me, her presence comforting yet unobtrusive. "Why, Your Highness?"

As I met her gaze in the mirror, a silent understanding passed between us. "I don't want to forget."

"Forget what?"

"Forget what's normal," I confessed, the brush pausing mid-stroke. "Here, living in the palace where you're waited on hand and foot, it's not normal. Everyday citizens don't live this way. For the last ten years *I* didn't live this way. I'd rather do things on my own the way I've gotten used to."

Tessa let out a soft sigh, her understanding clear. "I understand, Your Highness," she cautioned, her voice low. "I just hope you're aware that Her Majesty would not agree. Within the confines of these chamber walls, your wishes are paramount. However, beyond them, adherence to royal customs is advisable to avoid Her Majesty's ire."

In the hushed ambiance of my chamber lit only by the soft glow of bedside candles, I placed the brush aside and turned to acknowledge Tessa's presence. Her silhouette was framed by the warm light, her expression a blend of duty and concern. "You're right. Thank you for the reminder," I conceded, feeling the weight of her advice settle over me.

"Ready to change into your nightgown?" she inquired, moving gracefully towards the wardrobe, her hands poised to select the fabric of my repose.

"Yes," I agreed, my fingers working at the clasps of my dress. With a fluid motion born of necessity, the dress pooled at my feet, a whisper of silk against the cool stone floor. Gathering it, I draped it over the vanity chair.

Viktor's voice, muffled by the chamber doors, intruded upon the tranquility. "Your Highness?" he called, his tone respectful yet urgent.

"I'm undressing!" I called back. Tessa, understanding the delicate timing, assisted me into the soft embrace of my nightgown, its fabric a gentle caress against my skin. "Come in!"

The doors opened and Viktor poked his head inside. "You have a visitor, Your Highness."

I frowned. "This late at night? Is it Selene?"

He shook his head. "It's the guest from the Northern palace," he whispered.

My eyes widened and I turned to Tessa. "Please give us a moment."

Her hesitation was palpable, her loyalty clashing with her duty. "Are you sure, Your Highness?" she questioned.

"Yes. I'll call for you if I need you. Thank you," I said. She left with a backward glance that spoke volumes of her concern.

After a few seconds, the doors opened wider and a cloaked figure stepped inside, shutting the doors behind him. He paused for a moment before turning around to face me. Pulling back his hood, Ronan stood before me, a mischievous smirk splayed across his face.

"What are you doing here?" I hissed so Viktor and Tessa wouldn't hear me.

He shrugged. "I thought I'd pay you a visit." He slowly walked around my chambers, looking around as he sized me up and down, taking in my pink silk nightgown. "Cute nighty," he said as he walked around me.

I wrapped my arms around myself. "This is inappropriate, Ronan," I stated, a vain attempt to marshal some semblance of propriety.

He snorted. "As if I haven't seen all of you already."

My face flushed and I avoided eye contact. "Ronan," I warned.

His laughter, rich and unapologetic, filled the room. "Okay, I'll stop," he whispered as he hovered behind me, his chest to my back. "I've just missed you." His lips grazed the shell of my ear, making me shiver.

The reminder of the risk his presence posed was barely audible, a whisper against the gravity of his closeness. "You shouldn't be here," I breathed, the danger of discovery looming over us. "Leave before—"

"No one's going to know," he said as his hands caressed my bare arms. "I jumped the wall instead of coming in through the front gates."

I spun around to face him, not realizing how close he was, and stumbled backward. Before I could fall, Ronan wrapped an arm around my back and tugged me toward him. My heart galloped like a thousand horses as I was brought flush against his warm body. I didn't want to pull away, but I had to. I needed a clear mind when speaking to him.

"Are you going to tell me why you lied to me?" I pushed him away, putting some much-needed distance between us.

He sighed. "If I tell you, will it change anything between us?" he asked as he started circling me again. "You'll still feel as if I've deceived you."

I raised my chin. "You don't know that. Maybe I won't."

Under the flickering candlelight, Ronan crossed the dimly lit room toward my bed. With a deliberate motion, he shrugged off his heavy boots, one after the other, the sound echoing softly against the stone walls. He then reclined with casual grace on my bed, resting his hands behind his head on the pillow, creating a relaxed, yet decidedly confident pose. The low light danced across his sharp features, casting half his face in shadow and emphasizing the intensity of his crimson gaze. "Fine. But if I tell you, you must fulfill one wish of mine," he proposed, his voice carrying a weight of seriousness masked by a playful undertone.

"Which is?" I asked, my curiosity piqued yet guarded.

He tsked, a mischievous glint in his eyes as he wagged a finger at me in a scolding manner. "Not yet, Leila. When I'm ready to make the wish, I'll tell you."

I scoffed, feeling the tension rise within me as I crossed my arms over my chest, my posture stiffening in defiance. "I don't make open-ended deals."

His challenge hung between us; a gauntlet thrown. "Then I guess you don't want to know," he sighed, his voice laced with feigned disappointment. He lay there, an enigmatic figure bathed in the interplay of light and shadow near the bedside candles.

Feeling as if there was no way out, I approached the bed and stood my ground. "Fine," I sighed, my voice filled with resignation. "But I won't do anything illegal, or something that goes against my morals, or ... sexual."

He snorted in response, his laughter short and disbelieving. "What do you take me for, Leila? Have I ever ravaged you against your will?"

"I'm just making things clear!" I nearly shouted, my voice echoing slightly in the room, betraying my rising frustration. "So you got a deal. Now tell me. Why did you lie?"

Ronan regarded me with piercing intensity, his gaze searching mine for a moment that felt like an eternity before he exhaled loudly, a gesture of concession. He moved his hands to rest atop his abdomen. "Fine. What do you know, or should I say, what did *Mykal* tell you about the prophecy?"

"That I need to be sacrificed to the fox demon in order for the Crimson Clan to resurrect him. That ... that one of the rituals includes giving my maidenhood to you," I murmured, my voice barely above a whisper, laden with a mix of fear and confusion.

"Did you ever wonder why it has to be *me* who takes it? Why couldn't it be anyone else from the clan?" he probed, lifting a brow in a gesture that challenged me to question deeper and look beyond the surface.

I frowned when I realized I'd never questioned the motives behind the ritual. "No, I didn't. I just assumed—"

"You assumed I wanted to take advantage of you," he finished for me, his tone somber yet tinged with an underlying frustration. "I get it. But that's far from the truth, Leila. The truth of the matter is that the one who takes the maidenhood of the Blood Weaver is entitled to one wish from the fox demon."

"What?" My confusion was palpable, the revelation sparking a myriad of emotions within me.

He sat up and turned to face me directly on the edge of the bed, his movements deliberate, as if preparing himself for the weight of his next words. "The fox demon has resurrection powers. I had hoped—"

"You hoped after sacrificing me and resurrecting the fox demon, you could wish for him to bring me back," I finished for him, the pieces of the puzzle finally clicking into place in my mind.

"Yes." His admission was simple, yet it carried the burden of his intentions and the complexity of his plan.

"Then why does it have to be you? So what if that's your intention—"

"Because the one who makes the wish …"

"Yes?"

He sighed. "Because the Blood Weaver and the one from the Crimson Clan must have feelings for one another … like that shared by the fox demon and moon goddess."

I scoffed and began to pace back and forth, my mind racing. "Do you think that makes it all okay?"

He sighed deeply, the sound laden with resignation. "I knew you would still be against it, which was why I never brought it up. Why I told you I'd bring you to the Grasslands and never divulge your identity. Leila—"

"Why does the Crimson Clan have to resurrect the fox demon? What good will it do for your people?" I asked, my gaze piercing his to search for the truth in the depths of his crimson eyes.

"It's complicated, Leila," he answered curtly, his voice strained with a mixture of frustration and desperation. "Things in the Grasslands aren't as simple as they seem. My people ... are suffering."

I furrowed my brows, my curiosity and concern deepening. "What?"

Ronan rubbed his sweaty palms on his thighs nervously as he blew out a breath and struggled to find the words. "It's a deal the Crimson Clan made with Keldara during my great-grandfather's reign. In exchange for war horses and weapons, we provide Keldara with tributes," he whispered, his voice dropping to a hushed tone as he lowered his head in shame.

"Tributes?" I repeated, my heart sinking at the implication.

"Women and children, Leila." His admission was a whisper, yet it reverberated through the room like a thunderclap.

I gasped and covered my mouth with my hand in shock. "Why?"

"Keldara is a military-run country. Their birthrate is fairly low, almost nonexistent. They need ..." He trailed off, unable to finish his sentence, but the implication was clear. Keldara had a strong military; alone, the Crimson Clan would never be able to defeat Keldara. But with the fox demon? They might stand a chance.

"If they're doing this to your clan, why did your people align themselves with Keldara ten years ago?" I asked, stepping closer as I sought answers to the questions swirling in my mind.

"My father was desperate. He wanted to capture you as soon as possible and resurrect the fox demon to save our people. Unfortunately it backfired, and we've been searching for you ever since." His voice was a mix of regret and determination, revealing the depth of his struggles and the lengths he would go to protect his people.

Ronan gently captured my hands in his, drawing me nearer with a tenderness that belied the gravity of our conversation. His eyes, a stormy mix of determination and despair, locked onto mine as he whispered, "I never meant to deceive you." His voice, barely louder than a breath, carried the weight of his dilemma. "But I'm stuck between a rock and a hard place."

The crease of worry between my brows deepened as I considered his confession. "Does ... does Mykal know the whole truth?" The question emerged from me, tinged with a mix of hope and skepticism.

He gave a noncommittal shrug and his gaze drifted away momentarily. "Honestly, I don't know. The King of Keldara is aware, but who among his advisors is privy to the same knowledge remains unclear. But Mykal must suspect something, given how readily he shared the prophecy with you."

A wave of frustration crashed over me, causing my jaw to clench tightly. The realization that I was a pawn in Mykal's game ignited a fierce anger within me. Yet, the awareness of my naive trust in him spurred a deeper frustration. If only I had sought Ronan earlier, we might have navigated this maze of deceit more wisely. Still, the thought of sacrificing my life for the uncertain promise of resurrection was a gamble I couldn't fathom taking. It felt selfish, but the personal stakes were too high.

"Ronan," I began, the resolve in my voice masking the turmoil inside, "why doesn't the Crimson Clan seek an alliance with Valoria? Together, we could challenge Keldara."

A soft chuckle escaped him, laced with a hint of melancholy. "We're not on good terms with Valoria, Leila. You, of all people, are aware of the rift between us."

Dropping to my knees before him, I tightened my grip on his hands, seeking to convey my sincerity. "I'll talk to my father. Once I lay everything out for him, he'll surely—"

"No, Leila," he interjected, his tone firm yet fraught with an urgency that stopped me in my tracks. "It's not as simple as you think. Please, I beg of you, don't share this with anyone. The consequences could be dire for my people."

My frown deepened at his plea. "Why can't the Crimson Clan simply sever ties with Keldara?"

His response was soft, yet each word seemed to weigh heavily on him. "We've tried, but they have a tight noose around our necks. They've threatened us with harming our people who are currently enslaved in their lands."

A somber hush fell over us, my voice barely a whisper as the reality of his words sank in. "This is horrible," I murmured, a sense of despair enveloping me. The grim truth of the Crimson Clan's plight was far more harrowing than I ever imagined. "What can I—"

In the dimly lit room, the air thick with tension and unsaid promises, Ronan's strong arms encircled me, effortlessly lifting me from the floor to stand before him. "There's nothing you *can* do," he concluded with a touch of resignation. "After everything, it'd be shameless of me to ask."

His words resonated with a bitter truth I wasn't ready to confront. The sacrifice he hinted at—my life for the salvation of his people—was a price I found too steep, especially with the shadow of uncertainty that my spirit could be reclaimed from the abyss.

"I'm sorry," I replied, my voice steady yet laced with profound sadness. There was no other recourse, no other words to bridge the chasm of our dilemma.

"It's okay, Leila. I'll figure it out," he assured me, lifting his gaze to meet mine, a gentle smile gracing his lips. "As long as you can forgive me. For everything. I can't bear the thought of you being upset with me any longer. These last few days have been torture."

In a swift motion born of a mixture of frustration and a desperate need to maintain some distance, I withdrew my hands from his. "Still ... you kept the truth from me. How can I trust you again?"

"You did once before when I was your enemy. I believe you can find a way to do it again now that I'm your friend," he countered, his voice a soft but firm challenge. He grasped my arm, pulling me gently yet with undeniable strength onto the bed beside him. My breath hitched as I landed with a soft thud, his body rotating in a blink to hover just above mine, the mischievous sparkle in his crimson eyes igniting a familiar thrill. "Don't you think I should be mad at you as well?"

A frown marred my features, confusion and a burgeoning heat mingling within me. "Why? I haven't done anything."

His laughter was low, a sound that vibrated through the charged air. "Oh, no? What about when you left camp, leaving only a letter with Henry as your farewell?" His reminder sparked a memory of the last time we'd seen each other, and my eyes widened. "Remembering now? I told you to stay put," he murmured, his voice a velvet caress that seemed to stroke my skin just as his hand did, trailing a fiery path up my bare leg as he slid the silky fabric of my nightgown higher and higher with a deliberate slowness that sent shivers racing across my skin.

"What are you doing?" The question was a whisper, my voice betraying the turmoil of desire and hesitation that wrestled within me. "We can't do this. Not here."

"And why not?" he challenged, his eyebrow arching in playful defiance. "It's just you and me. No one is here to stop us this time."

My response was a gasp, a sound lost in the growing storm of our mutual desire as I squirmed beneath him, the heat of his touch igniting fires all over my skin. My hand found his once he reached my underwear, a desperate attempt to steady myself against the tide of emotions his actions unleashed.

"So tell me, Leila: am I not entitled to be upset as well?" he whispered as he slid his hand beneath my underwear.

I involuntarily spread my legs as he touched me in places I'd never been touched before. My breath hitched and I clutched the bed sheets as Ronan slowly glided a finger inside me.

"Next time when I tell you to stay put—" he murmured as he stroked his finger in and out.

"Ronan!" I gasped as I released the bed sheets and clutched the front of his shirt, pulling him closer to me. "Please," I begged, not knowing exactly what I was begging for but needing a release, and quickly.

"Yes, Leila?" he murmured against my lips, parting them as he spoke. "Tell me what you need."

"I-I—"

Slicked in my wetness, he slid another finger inside me and I gasped, clutching him tighter. I felt myself being stretched as he slowly pumped his fingers in and out of me. My eyes closed and I felt as if I teetered on the precipice before falling head-first into the abyss.

"Look at me, Leila," he commanded. When I didn't open my eyes, he stilled, forcing me to open my eyes and look at him. "When you come undone, I want you to be looking at me," he whispered.

"Don't stop," I pleaded. "Please."

I'd never felt so wound up and electric all at once. With each pump of his fingers, my hips gyrated, wanting more, wanting him to go faster. My breathing was heavy, and soft moans escaped my lips as I felt myself at the brink.

"Yes," I moaned. "Faster."

As I sucked in one last breath, Ronan's lips crashed onto mine, silencing my scream as my arms wrapped around his neck, bringing him closer to me. His kiss was all-consuming, as if he needed me to breathe. I couldn't concentrate. My thoughts were running wild not knowing what was right or left, up or down.

A whimpering moan escaped me when his thumb stroked my clit and all I could do was squeeze him tighter. Wanting more. My legs began to shake and I clenched his two fingers as he mercilessly pumped them faster and faster. I arched my back, bringing my chest to his, wanting more of his warmth.

"Ronan!" I gasped against his mouth. "I'm—"

He released my lips and stared deeply into my eyes as I

came undone beneath him. Our charged, gasping breaths were the only sounds in my chambers as I orgasmed.

"You're absolutely stunning," he whispered as his fingers slowed until he stopped once I jerked from the sensitivity. "If I could have you in my bed every night, I think I'd be the happiest man in Asteria."

My eyes felt heavy, and my breathing slowed as I gradually released him, my arms falling slack beside me. "Ronan," I muttered in a sleepy haze.

"Sleep, Princess," he whispered, placing a gentle kiss on my forehead. "I'll see you soon."

With those parting words, I closed my eyes and fell into a blissful slumber.

7

Sunlight filtered through the gauzy curtains, casting a warm glow across the room as I woke, my senses tangled in the soft embrace of my bedding. I lay sprawled across my bed in a haphazard fashion, a testament to a good night's sleep. The rhythmic knock at my door pierced the serene silence. With a voice thick with sleep, I called out, "Come in!"

Tessa, adorned in the crisp attire of a court lady entered, carefully balancing a basin filled with water and a clean cloth draped over her arm. "Good morning, Your Highness," she greeted, her voice a soothing melody in the quiet of the morning.

Greeting her with a yawn that I hastily smothered behind my hand, I managed a groggy, "Good morning," in response.

"I brought some warm water to wash your face," she offered, placing the basin on the nightstand with a gentle clink. She gestured to the other court lady who followed with a smaller basin. "As well as some water to brush your teeth." Once the court lady placed the basin down, she quickly left my chambers.

I rolled out of bed, feeling the cool floor beneath my feet as I approached the basin. The warm water was a shock to my senses, instantly dispelling the remnants of sleep as I splashed it over my face, meticulously cleaning the sleep from my eyes. Tessa handed me the cloth, which I accepted with a nod, drying off the droplets that clung to my skin. "How is everything out there?" I inquired as I moved on to brush my teeth.

Tessa hesitated and cleared her throat subtly. "Are you asking me how the court ladies are, or are you wondering about your late-night visitor?" Her eyebrow arched inquisitively, a silent acknowledgment of the unspoken words between us.

I paused, caught in the act, and then laughter bubbled up from within me. "I'm guessing there will be no secrets between us," I conceded, wiping my mouth with the cloth and tossing it aside.

"I don't believe so, Your Highness. For me and Viktor to keep you safe, it's best if there aren't any," she replied, guiding me towards the vanity. Once seated, she began to brush my hair with gentle strokes. "Are you sure you know what you're doing, Your Highness?"

I met her gaze in the mirror, a reflective pool of my own uncertainties. "Honestly? I don't know," I confessed. "Ronan and I are ... complicated. I know I shouldn't like him, but ..."

"But you do," she finished for me, a soft understanding in her voice. "Did you spend a lot of time with him in the Central Plains?"

"Not really. We only met a few months ago," I admitted with a snort, the absurdity of the situation not lost on me.

"Would you like my advice, Your Highness?" she offered, her fingers weaving through my hair as she crafted a braid.

I shrugged. "Sure."

"I think you should be careful," she murmured, her voice a whisper of caution. "I don't doubt his feelings for you, but the palace is a dangerous place where secrets are rarely kept in the dark."

Her words weighed heavily on me, a reminder of the delicate balance I must navigate. "I know. I'll be more careful," I promised, a lump forming in my throat.

"Don't worry. Viktor and I will do our best to protect you, Your Highness," she reassured me, finishing the braid with a gentle pat on my shoulder.

Rising from the vanity, I watched as she moved to the wardrobe to select the day's attire. "How is Selene?"

"She's been placed in one of your spare bedrooms here in the Eastern palace. His Highness has not come to visit her," Tessa informed, returning with a navy-blue dress.

"If he does, turn him away," I instructed firmly as she helped me into the dress. "He'll only put her in danger by showing her too much attention."

"Yes, Your Highness."

Tessa and I emerged from the sanctuary of my chambers into the opulent hallway of the Eastern palace, where Viktor awaited with the disciplined patience of a seasoned guard. His posture was a mix of rigid formality and alert readiness.

"Good morning, Your Highness," he intoned, offering a bow that was both graceful and filled with reverence as we stepped into the corridor.

"Morning, Viktor." I returned his greeting with a warmth that attempted to bridge the formal distance between us. "Is breakfast being served in the Eastern palace today?"

He shook his head, his expression solemn. "Your mother requests your presence in the dining hall."

His words sent a flutter of unease through me, stirring a nest of worries. Why would my mother summon me so early? Could she have learned of Ronan's visit last night? The thought was unsettling.

"Relax, Your Highness," Viktor interjected, his voice a soothing balm to my spiraling thoughts. "She also requested the presence of Prince Marcellus and Prince Caelan."

"Oh," was all I managed, a mixture of relief and residual tension coloring my response. "Lead the way."

The journey from the Eastern palace to the dining hall situated in the heart of the Central palace was an immersive passage through the splendor and history of the royal estate. As we stepped out of the Eastern palace, soft morning light bathed the meticulously maintained gardens in a golden hue, casting long shadows on the dew-kissed flowers and neatly trimmed hedges that lined our path. The air was crisp, filled with the gentle sounds of nature awakening and the distant murmurs of the palace coming to life.

Viktor led the way with measured steps, embodying the solemnity of our destination. Tessa and I followed, our silhouettes gliding over the cobblestone pathways that wound through the garden's heart. The scent of blooming roses and the subtle fragrance of jasmine was suspended in the air, a natural perfume that soothed the senses and momentarily eased the tension of the impending breakfast meeting.

As we neared the Central palace, the architecture transitioned from the Eastern palace's serene elegance to a more imposing, grandiose style. Towering columns and expansive windows adorned the façade, reflecting the early morning light in a dazzling display.

We finally arrived at the dining hall, a room that bore witness to countless family gatherings, political discussions, and the delicate dance of court life. Its doors stood open, inviting yet imposing.

Upon entry, the sentinels announced my arrival with a formality that felt both grandiose and suffocating. Marcellus, Caelan, and Mother were already assembled, the air thick with the weight of unspoken expectations.

"Good morning," I greeted. I took my place in the chair I'd occupied before leaving Valoria, acutely aware of the dynamics at play, with my mother presiding over us like a matriarch assessing her brood. "Apologies for my tardiness."

"Nonsense." My mother dismissed my apologies with a gesture that was both regal and dismissive. "It'll take a while until you adapt to palace life again," she mused, a hint of something unreadable in her tone. "I had the kitchen prepare your favorites. I heard you still love mooncakes."

A soft chuckle escaped me at the mention of the pastry. "Yes, I do."

Just then, the kitchen maids came out with breakfast, setting an array of plates on the table before us. With my mother at the head of the table and Caelan and Marcellus across from me, the three of us waited for my mother to eat first before we dug into our meals.

"I'm sure you missed the comfort of your own home these last ten years," my mother started. "I wanted to help you get settled in the Eastern palace, but all the ladies I sent were released from service. Were there any problems?"

Her slyness was not lost on me.

Caught mid-bite, I paused, the air charged with tension. To reveal my awareness of her surveillance would be imprudent. I chose my words with care, donning a smile that masked my inner caution. "No, Mother, no problems. I spent the day yesterday roaming the palace and made friends with some of the ladies in service. I decided to bring them on. I'm sure your ladies could be used elsewhere instead of wasting their time with me."

The silence that followed was palpable, a delicate veil over the unsaid and the understood. I glanced at Marcellus and Caelan, their expressions a mix of caution and intrigue, clearly attuned to the subtext of our carefully chosen words. The dance of diplomacy within the confines of the dining hall was a delicate one, and I had just made my opening move.

"It's no trouble at all, dear. At least accept Mary as your right hand. I'm sure she'll be much better than that Tessa," my mother scoffed. It was no surprise she already knew the names of the court ladies in my palace. The moment she suggested replacing Tessa with Mary, tension crackled through the air like a silent storm brewing. With her voice dripping with disapproval, her disdain for my preferred lady-in-waiting was evident. "I'll have her switched out by this afternoon," she declared as if the matter was already settled.

My reaction was swift, a mix of alarm and resolve. "No!" The word burst from me sharper than intended. I quickly softened my tone. "No, Mother, that won't be necessary. I really appreciate Tessa's service. She's familiar with my routines now, and I'd rather not start over with someone new."

I watched as my mother's grip on her silverware tightened, the tendons in her hand standing out starkly. "Well, if you insist," she said through clenched teeth, clearly displeased by my defiance.

Caelan intervened with a tactful cough, his attempt to diffuse the tension. "I'm sure Lyanna is not used to being pampered like she once was. Maybe *we* are the ones who should adapt to who she is now," he suggested, his voice a careful blend of respect and diplomacy.

Marcellus chimed in, his tone carrying an edge of bitterness. "Yes, Mother. Dear Lyanna is not who she once was."

My mother was unyielding. "Lyanna will quickly need to reacquaint herself with our ways. It's for the best," she stated, her tone leaving no room for further discussion.

I pressed my lips together to hold in the scoff that threatened to escape. My mother was not one to mince words. What she said was final, her expectations clear.

"Of course, Mother," I conceded, focusing on my plate to avoid further confrontation.

"If you insist on keeping those court ladies, that's fine. But I expect you to attend breakfast every morning here in the Central palace," she said forcibly. "It's the *least* you could do."

"Yes," I answered and continued to eat.

The remainder of breakfast passed in stifling silence, the earlier warmth replaced by cold formality. Once my mother excused herself, the air seemed to ease slightly, though the weight of her words lingered.

"Lyanna," Caelan started, "try not to upset your mother. You know everything she does is for your wellbeing."

I nodded but kept quiet, not wanting to argue, especially since I was almost positive my mother still had spies lingering around.

"Oh, come on, Caelan. You know *exactly* why Lyanna got rid of her maids," Marcel snorted. "You might be home, Lyanna, but you don't trust anyone here. I wonder why that is."

Marcel's sarcastic remark hit closer to home than he realized. The truth of my situation was a ponderous burden, one I hesitated to share. But as his curiosity pressed, the need for honesty outweighed my reservations.

Swallowing my food, I set my utensils down and looked up at my brother. "Do you really want to know, Marcel? Once you do, you can't unknow it."

Marcellus tensed, then narrowed his gaze before rolling his eyes. "Oh, please. What could *possibly* be—"

"The Crimson Clan wants to sacrifice me to the fox demon to resurrect him. Before the war with Keldara, they approached Mom and Dad about trading me, which was a proposition they were considering. So no, I don't trust anyone." I stared into familiar blue eyes that widened with each word I spoke.

Caelan stood abruptly; the chair screeching across the floor in his haste was a physical manifestation of the turmoil my words caused. "Lies! Your parents would *never!*" His denial was fierce, a reflexive defense against a truth too harrowing to accept. The revelation shattered the morning's fragile peace, leaving us adrift in a sea of uncertainty and betrayal.

My stance was defensive, arms crossed tightly as I challenged Caelan's righteous assurance. "Oh, yeah? And you know that how?"

He faltered. "I—I..." revealing even he harbored doubts about their capabilities.

Marcellus's reaction was softer, tinged with disbelief. "*That's* why you never returned?" he murmured, seeking confirmation.

I nodded. "It was the secret Sir Edric hid from me, and one I only recently found out."

Marcel's reaction was subdued, perhaps blurred with shame as he acknowledged the depth of our mother's ambition and what she might be capable of. His next words were barely audible, a mix of disappointment and personal affront. "So ... you didn't trust me to protect you?"

"No, that's not what I'm saying, Marcel. But I didn't want to pit you against our parents. It wouldn't be fair to you," I rushed to clarify, not wanting him to feel it was a lack of faith in him, but rather a desire to shield him from our parents' machinations. "Also, we were *children*, Marcel. You are younger than me. There was nothing either of us could have done."

He nodded and pushed his chair back. "I understand," he whispered before getting up from his chair. Despite my explanation, he exited the dining hall without another word, leaving a palpable void in his wake.

"Marcel! Wait!" I called after him.

"Lyanna," Caelan stopped me as I attempted to follow, his tone sharp. "Is this the secret Ronan was keeping from you?" he gritted between his teeth.

"Yes," I answered truthfully, though I kept the other part to myself since Ronan made me promise not to say anything to anyone.

Caelan laughed dryly as he began to pace. "Knowing all this, you're still worried about his wellbeing?"

"Caelan, you don't know everything—"

"Then tell me!" he shouted, frustration boiling over into disbelief and anger. His outburst, marked by a loud slam of his palm on the table, startled me, revealing the intensity of his emotions.

I flinched. "I can't."

His laugh was sinister as he came around the table to me. His approach was menacing, prompting me to retreat, asserting my readiness to defend myself if necessary. The fear wasn't of him, but of the potential violence his anger could unleash.

"Caelan, stop."

He froze. "Are you ... are you afraid of me?"

"No. But I believe you let your anger get the best of you sometimes. I've seen it. I've experienced it. If you try anything, you'll force me to react, and I don't think you want that," I said hesitantly.

"Lyanna—"

"Caelan, I know what you want, but I can't give that to you," I whispered. "I'm not eleven-year-old Lyanna anymore."

"I won't let him have you," he growled.

I narrowed my gaze on him. "You're not *letting* anyone have me, because I'm no one's property. I'm not yours to keep or give away."

Caelan prowled toward me, his steps slow and measured. "You may not be property, Lyanna, but you have always been mine. So no, I won't allow him to have you."

I stumbled back, trying to keep him at arm's length. "I'm not yours, Caelan."

"So what? Are you his?"

"Maybe," I admitted. "But that's none of your business."

When Caelan reached for me, I quickly held up a hand, fisting it and tightening my hold on the circulation of his blood before he could touch me. He seized before me, dropping to a knee as he clutched his chest. Gritting his teeth, spittle flying everywhere, he glared up at me. "Release ... me," he growled.

"No," I answered. "I've been patient with you because of our shared history, Caelan, but enough is enough! I won't put up with you behaving this way any longer. If you can't control your temper, I *will* stop you. And you won't like my methods," I snarled.

"Lyanna!" he roared into the otherwise empty dining hall.

I squeezed my hold, cutting off his circulation until he gasped for air. "I'm warning you, Caelan. If you wish to remain friends, don't push me."

"Lyanna!" Marcellus shouted as he ran back inside the dining hall. "What are you *doing*?" He grabbed me by the shoulders and shook me, forcing me to release my hold on Caelan.

Caelan gasped and fell on all fours, slowly getting back to his feet and charging toward me. Luckily Marcellus cut into his path and stood in front of me, pushing me behind him protectively.

"What the hell are you doing?" Marcellus exclaimed as he pushed Caelan away. "Were you really going to hit her?" he scoffed as if he couldn't believe his friend's behavior.

With his gaze locked on mine, Caelan pushed past me and Marcel and stormed out of the dining hall. My brother kept me tucked behind him until Caelan disappeared. After a beat, he turned to face me, looking me over for injuries.

"Are ... are you okay?" he asked, slightly confused by the situation.

I nodded. "I'm fine. What are you doing back here?"

"I was returning to the kitchen to take some food back when I heard the screaming." He released me and put some distance between us. "What were you thinking, Lyanna? He's our friend. How could you use your blood magic on him?"

"And what? Let him hurt me?" I scoffed.

Marcel rolled his eyes. "He wouldn't have—"

"He would," I countered, then rolled up my sleeves to show the scars that remained from Caelan's torture session back in the Central Plains. "He has."

My brother shook his head. "That was different, Lyanna. He didn't know who you were—"

"And that makes it okay?" I frowned. "He's capable of bad things, Marcel. Don't be blinded by friendship."

"I'm not," he muttered. "But—"

"But nothing. I won't put up with it." I pushed past him. Before I got too far, Marcel spun around and grabbed my wrist, stopping me.

"You're right," he muttered. "I'm sorry."

I furrowed my brows. "You're sorry? For what?"

"For everything." He peered into my eyes. "I ... I didn't know."

I sighed. "It's okay, Marcel, I don't blame you."

"I said a lot of hateful things. I didn't mean any of them."

I patted his hand. "I know. It's water under the bridge."

He nodded and released me. With nothing left to say, I left the dining hall where Viktor was waiting for me with Tessa.

"Your Highness!" Viktor quickly approached. "I saw Prince Caelan leave in a hurry. Is everything okay?"

I nodded. "Yes, it's fine. I handled it."

Viktor looked hesitant but didn't push further. "Your mother had a few choice words for me as she left."

I raised a brow. "Did she now?"

He chuckled. "Don't worry, Your Highness. I handled it," he mimicked.

I threw my head back and laughed. "Thank you, Viktor."

"Of course, Your Highness," he said solemnly. "Shall we return to the Eastern palace?"

I nodded. "Yes."

8

The cool marble of the Eastern palace echoed underfoot as we navigated its opulent corridors, the somberness of the morning's events pressing heavily upon my shoulders. As we approached my chambers, the sight of Selene poised with a mixture of patience and anxiety momentarily lifted my spirits. Her quick steps towards me and the concern etched across her features were a stark reminder of the world we'd left behind and the intricate dance of court life we now faced.

"Where were you?" Her voice carried a blend of relief and worry, a testament to the bond we shared.

"My mother summoned me," I explained, the words tinged with a resignation that came from navigating the expectations of royalty. "It wasn't something I could refuse." I shifted the topic, hoping to ease her concern. "Did you manage to have breakfast?"

She nodded, a small gesture that belied her underlying unease. "Yes, one of your court ladies was kind enough to bring something from the kitchens."

"Good. If you need anything, just tell me—" I was about

to offer further reassurance when she interrupted, her voice a soft confession of her inner turmoil.

"Leila," she began, her use of my claimed name pulling me into a moment of intimacy amidst the grandeur that surrounded us, "I feel useless here."

Her words struck a chord, although the notion that she could view herself as anything less than essential was unfathomable to me. "What do you mean?" I asked, genuinely puzzled by her admission.

Selene's sigh was encumbered with the weight of unspoken fears and uncertainties. "I thought by coming here, I could be of some help to you," she explained, her gaze dropping. "But now, I feel like I'm more of a burden than an asset."

The earnestness in her voice prompted me to dispel the shadow of doubt that had crept into her heart. Grasping her hand, I sought to infuse my words with the strength of our shared past, our struggles, and our triumphs. "Selene, look at me," I urged, waiting until her eyes met mine before continuing. "You could never be a burden. You've been my anchor, my confidante, and my friend through everything. That you would even think such a thing couldn't be further from the truth."

In the grand scheme of the palace, where every glance held a story and every whisper a potential for intrigue, the simplicity of our connection—a bond forged not in the gilded halls of power, but in the raw truth of our experiences—was my solace. As the Eastern palace loomed around us, a solid demonstration of the life into which I was born, it was Selene's presence that reminded me of the person I had become and the strength that lay in true companionship.

Her contemplation hovered between us like the early

morning fog. "But ..." I ventured further, the words trailing off into the space between us, laden with an unspoken promise. "If you wish to return to the Luminar Sea, I will escort you there myself. Don't feel pressured to stay by my side."

Selene's response, a gentle nod accompanied by a soft, "I'll think about it," resonated with a gravity that hadn't been present in our previous conversations. It was a subtle shift, yet a profound one, marking the first time she'd entertained the notion of leaving. The silence that followed was poignant, filled with the unsaid fears of separation that neither of us wanted to voice.

Retreating a step, I sought to lighten the mood and brush away the somber cloud that had settled over us. "Perhaps a walk in the gardens? The weather is perfect—"

Her grin cut through my suggestion, bright yet secretive. "I just returned from there. I saw Marcellus," she confided, her voice a whisper, a conspiratorial thread meant just for us.

Surprise flitted across my face, momentarily unguarded before I composed myself. "He was here?" The thought puzzled me; I had only just parted ways with him. "How did he—"

She waved off my confusion with an easy shrug. "It was earlier this morning. He happened to be passing by the Eastern palace. But don't worry, I kept my distance. I just hoped to see him again."

A relieved sigh escaped me and a tension I hadn't realized I was holding dissipated. "Thank the goddess," I murmured. "We must be careful, Selene. Any hint of you and Marcellus could stir a storm we're ill-prepared to weather."

Her laughter, light and seemingly carefree, did little to

ease the knot of worry in my stomach. "I promise, Leila. I'll tread lightly."

Her promise hung in the air, fragile and fraught with naivety. I couldn't shake the feeling that Selene grossly underestimated the depth of the court's intrigue and my mother's reach within these walls. The thought of her learning the harsh realities of palace life pained me. I wanted to protect her from the shadows that danced behind the gilded façade.

"Leila?" Her voice, pulling me back from the edge of my spiraling thoughts, was a lifeline.

The worry that clouded my thoughts began to dissipate as I forced a smile, though its brightness failed to reach my eyes. "Oh, sorry," I offered, a weak attempt to mask the undercurrent of concern that had momentarily seized me.

Selene, ever understanding, brushed off my lapse with a gentle, "It's fine. What do you plan to do now?" Her next question hung in the air, a simple inquiry loaded with the weight of newfound freedom.

The prospect of rest beckoned me, a siren's call to the weary. "I think I'm going to try to sleep for a bit," I confessed, the adjustment to palace life's rigorous schedule still a hurdle. "I don't remember the last time I woke up this early."

Her response, a soft murmur of contemplation, revealed the depth of her own adjustment. "I haven't had this much free time in years," she admitted, her gaze drifting. The shadows of her past, of days spent within the perfumed confines of Lomewood's pleasure house, played across her face—a stark contrast to the freedom that now lay before her.

Moved by her admission, I sought to offer comfort through familiarity. "Is there anything you'd like to do?" I asked, remembering the solace she once found in the strokes of a brush. "You enjoyed painting. We could arrange for some canvas and paints, if you'd like."

Her wish, however, was simpler, more primal. "Honestly, I just want to roam the grounds and breathe some fresh air. Is that okay?" she asked, her voice a whisper of longing.

Laughter broke from me, a light moment in the gravity of our conversation. "You don't have to ask, Selene. Feel free to explore. Just stay within the Eastern palace grounds, for your safety."

Her acknowledgment was swift, her steps carrying her past me with a promise to return. "Will do! I'll wake you for lunch," she called over her shoulder, her figure receding down the hallway with a freedom that seemed to buoy her spirit.

I lingered a moment longer and watched her disappear around the corner before retreating into the sanctuary of my room. The promise of rest, however fleeting, was a balm to the soul, a necessary pause in the whirlwind of palace life and the complexities it entailed.

~

THE TRANQUILITY of the Eastern palace gardens offered little solace to the tumult within me. Viktor, ever the silent guardian, kept his distance, allowing me the semblance of solitude as I roamed the gardens after lunch. The aftermath of the previous night with Ronan lingered as a tempest of emotions and sensations that refused to be stilled. His touch, his breath against my skin, had imprinted on me in a way that solitude and daylight could not erase. I roamed aimlessly, the vibrant hues of the flowers and the soft whisper of the breeze through the leaves doing little to distract me from replaying torrid memories of last night.

Restlessness consumed me, a fervent desire to escape the confines of my own thoughts. "I need to do something to keep my mind busy," I whispered to no one, a plea for distraction. It was then, in my aimless wandering, that I knelt before a bush adorned with roses. As I reached out, captivated by their perfection, I plucked one, only to be met with the sting of a thorn. The sharp pain was a jolt, pulling me momentarily from my reverie. I sucked on the wounded finger, the taste of iron a grounding sensation.

It was this small, inconsequential moment that sparked a realization. "The infirmary!" The word burst from me like a revelation, a beacon of purpose cutting through the fog of uncertainty.

Viktor, ever attentive, closed the distance with a few strides, concern etching his features. "Is everything okay, Your Highness? Are you hurt?" His voice, laced with worry, brought a smile to my lips despite the unrest.

I nodded, reassured by his concern. "Yes, yes, I'm fine. I just remembered I haven't visited the infirmary since I returned." The thought of engaging in something familiar, something as grounding as healing, was incredibly appealing. "Who is the resident healer now?" I inquired.

"Old Man Reeves still holds the position," he informed me, his tone carrying a note of respect for the long-serving healer. "He's been tending to the palace since your father was a child."

The information was a comfort, a link to a past that felt both distant and intimately close. With newfound determination, I decided then that the infirmary would be my refuge, a place to channel my tumultuous emotions into something meaningful, a way to reconnect with the part of me that found solace in healing others.

Exiting the lush tranquility of the garden, a figure clothed in the deep hues of royalty halted my departure. My father, clad in robes that shimmered with threads of royal blue and silver, cut an imposing yet graceful image as he approached. With a simple gesture, he dismissed his aides, ensuring our meeting would be a private affair.

His presence, both commanding and warm, enveloped me as he drew near, his smile a beacon of genuine joy. Once he reached me, he pulled me into an embrace which was one of unguarded affection—the complete opposite of my mother's touch. It wasn't that my mother didn't love me. No, I believed she did. But she was cold and calculative, and always put my brother's wellbeing before anyone else's.

"Oh, Lyanna, you have no idea how glad I am to see you again! Your disappearance was the toughest challenge I've ever endured," he confessed, his voice imbued with a mixture of relief and lingering worry. As he stepped back, his hands found my upper arms and he squeezed them gently to convey both concern and reassurance. The look in his eyes was pure fatherly love, a mirror to the affection I'd missed and a reminder of the stark differences in the way my parents expressed their care.

Where my mother's affections were measured and often overshadowed by her ambitions for my brother, my father's warmth was immediate and all-encompassing.

"I missed you too, Father," I managed, my smile struggling to mask the whirlwind of emotions his presence stirred. "You were missed at breakfast. Is everything okay?"

He nodded, a gesture of dismissal to any underlying concerns, and released my arms. "All is well. Just wanted to have a chat with young Ronan. It's been many years since I last saw him. He is all grown up now. Your generation aren't children anymore. It saddens me that I couldn't watch you grow into the woman you are today," he lamented, his touch tender as he brushed a stray lock of hair from my face.

The moment was a poignant reminder of the years we'd lost and the time that slipped through our fingers like grains of sand, leaving behind a longing for what could have been.

"You must tell me all about your journeys these last ten years. I want to hear all about it!" he encouraged, his voice a blend of eagerness and affection. His arm linked with mine in a gesture of camaraderie and paternal interest as he gently prodded into the life I had carved out for myself beyond the palace walls. As we meandered through the verdant paths of the garden, my father's curiosity about my past decade unwound like the trails beneath our feet. "I heard from Caelan that you made quite a name for yourself as a healer in the Central Plains. Is this true?"

"Yes. I delved into the realm of medicine and herbs during my time away. A local healer, wise in the ways of traditional remedies, took me under their wing, then guided me until I felt confident enough to establish my own clinic."

His follow-up question pierced the comfortable veil of our conversation, hinting at a deeper knowledge of my struggles. "Interesting. And how were you able to afford your own clinic? From what Caelan told me, you and Sir Edric faced some financial hardships after the first year of being away."

Caught off-guard by his pointed inquiry, I hesitated, wary of revealing too much. The complexities of my survival were a tapestry woven with threads of desperation and resilience. Opting for a measured response, I offered, "I sought out challenges that were beyond the scope of ordinary healers. High-risk cases became my specialty, my ...

expertise. I must confess, my blood played a crucial role in many of those cases." The admission tasted bitter, a reminder of the burdensome reliance on my unique heritage to navigate those perilous waters.

His reaction, however, was not one of judgment but of understanding. A comforting pat on my hand accompanied his reassurance. "No, no, you needn't be ashamed. You were doing your best to survive." His words, imbued with empathy, offered forgiveness I hadn't realized I needed—a recognition of the choices made, not in pursuit of glory, but simply to endure.

I cleared my throat. "Um ... Father, how is Ronan?" I asked since he had brought him up. Flashes of last night invaded my thoughts, and I flushed red at the memories.

"He's doing well. While he's not a prisoner, I don't want him roaming the grounds, so I suggested he stay in the Northern palace until the banquet when his father arrives."

I pressed my lips together to keep from laughing. Ronan was definitely not sequestering himself in the Northern palace, if last night was any indication.

"Do try to avoid going near the Northern palace, Lyanna," my father said. "I don't wish for rumors of the two of you to circulate. It's best if you keep your distance."

I stopped walking, making him halt as well. I peered up at my father and asked the question that had been nagging me since my arrival. "You know, don't you?"

He frowned. "Know what, dear?"

"About the prophecy," I continued. "About the Crimson Clan needing to sacrifice me to resurrect the fox demon."

My father sighed. "Yes. Yes, I know," he muttered. "I didn't intend to keep it from you, but I thought it was best if we kept it quiet. To keep you safe. I just never thought that when we refused, the Crimson Clan would align with Keldara to invade us."

I bit my lip to keep from talking. Ronan didn't want me to tell anyone about what hardships the Crimson Clan was enduring, even though I knew if I told my father, he might be willing to help.

My father spun me to face him, gripping my upper arms as he looked down at me. "You are the first female blood mage since the moon goddess. I will not let them take you away, Lyanna. You are too valuable—"

"But Mother would," I cut him off.

He furrowed his brows and nodded. "Yes. She would. But I won't let her. We lost ten years because of this. I won't lose any more. You have my word, Lyanna. No harm will come to you."

9

As twilight melded into the velvety cloak of night, the palace seemed to exhale, its daytime bustle giving way to a more serene, albeit still vigilant, calm. My restlessness mirrored the transition, a silent echo of the day's events and the weight of my thoughts. With a slight hesitation borne from not wanting to impose, I called for Tessa, her presence a steady reassurance in the vastness of the Eastern palace.

My lady-in-waiting appeared at the doorway, appearing every inch the epitome of readiness, her posture alert. "Yes, Your Highness?" Her voice carried the soft timbre of attentiveness.

The words left me in a gentle exhale. "I'd like to take a bath," I confessed, my voice tinged with a vulnerability I seldom allowed myself to show. "If it's too much at this hour, I can always wait until tomorrow. I'm just feeling a tad restless."

Her response was immediate, her smile a beam of understanding in the dim light of my chambers. "It's no trouble at all, Your Highness," Tessa assured me, her tone imbued with warmth. "I'll have some water warmed up for your bath."

Her willingness to accommodate and ensure my comfort regardless of the hour was a small comfort in the grand scheme of things; a reminder of the quiet acts of service that wove through the fabric of our daily existence within these walls.

As Tessa vanished to prepare my bath, the burden of the day's events seemed to lift slightly, prompting me to seek the comfort of my night attire. I glided towards the wardrobe, the soft whisper of silk a soothing promise against my skin. With deliberate movements, I donned my nightgown and robe, the fabric cascading gently around me. Slipping my feet into the welcoming embrace of my slippers, I ventured out of the sanctuary of my chambers.

The sight of Viktor standing sentinel outside my door caught me by surprise. "Oh!" I exclaimed, startled by his unexpected presence. "I didn't expect you here."

"Tessa is seeing to your bath, Your Highness," Viktor informed me, his demeanor a blend of professionalism and warmth. "Would you care for a late-night snack as well?" His inquiry, accompanied by a discreet gesture, summoned one of the nearby court ladies.

The mention of refreshments sparked a thought, a craving for a taste of home. "I heard Valoria has a famous wine called *Love in the Moonlight*. Is it available here?" I ventured, curiosity lacing my words.

Viktor's laughter was a light note in the night's calm. "We were told you liked wine," he shared, a twinkle of amusement in his eyes. "The kitchens have been well stocked in anticipation of your arrival. I'll ensure a jug of

Love in the Moonlight, along with some accompanying snacks, are brought to you."

"Thank you," I responded, a genuine smile breaking through. His steps, guiding me towards the bathing chamber, were a dance of shadows and light, the hallway a bridge between the day's end and the night's quiet promise.

The bathing chamber was a shelter of tranquility and opulence. As I stepped through the arched doorway, the warm glow from the wall sconces bathed the room in a soft golden light, reflecting off the intricate mosaic tiles that adorned the walls and floor. These tiles, a kaleidoscope of blues and greens, depicted scenes of moonlit Valorian landscapes and mythical creatures frolicking under the night sky, bringing the room to life with their vivid colors and detailed artistry.

In the center of the chamber stood a large, freestanding bathtub that could easily fit ten people, carved from a single block of marble. Its smooth, cool surface was inviting, promising a soothing embrace. Servants moved quickly to fill the tub with steaming water that seemed to dance under the flickering light, releasing gentle waves of vapor that carried the relaxing scents of lavender and jasmine, mingling in the air and inviting deep breaths and relaxation.

Beside the bathtub, a small, elegantly carved wooden table held an array of bathing oils and salts, each container more exquisite than the last, offering scents and healing properties sourced from across Valoria's lands and beyond.

Toward the back of the room, a delicate screen of frosted glass partitioned a space for changing, ensuring privacy while also serving as a piece of art, its surface etched with scenes that mirrored the chamber's mosaics. Beyond this, plush towels and a robe of the softest cotton were laid out, their crisp folds a promise of warmth and comfort to wrap around oneself after the bath.

The entire chamber resonated with a harmony of elements—water, fire from the candles, earth in the marble and tiles, and air perfumed with floral scents. It was more than a place to bathe; it was a retreat designed to soothe the weary, to wash away the concerns of the day, and to envelop its occupant in the luxury and peace that few places within the palace could offer. Here, in this secluded haven, the outside world and its demands felt a world away, allowing for a rare moment of solitude and reflection.

When the last servant finished emptying the contents of their bucket into the tub, Viktor stepped into the doorway. "I'll have Tessa bring you the wine and snacks," he said, then excused himself and left the bathing chambers. The door closed with a soft click, sealing me within this luxurious cocoon, the world beyond momentarily forgotten.

Retreating behind the frosted glass partition, its surface etched with delicate patterns that danced in the candlelight, I shed the layers of my attire, each piece a whisper against the cool air. Standing in nothing but my skin, I secured my hair atop my head with a leather cord, ensuring the strands would remain dry and untouched by the bath's fragrant embrace.

Emerging from behind the screen, I approached the marble tub, its surface gleaming under the soft lighting, an inviting beacon. The few steps leading up to its rim seemed to elevate me not just physically but mentally, preparing me for immersion into a tranquil oasis.

As I slid into the water, the heat enveloped me instantly, a gentle yet all-encompassing warmth that seemed to penetrate the very core of my being. The water, infused with oils and herbs, caressed my skin, easing the tension from my muscles and coaxing a deep, contented sigh from my lips. For a moment, within the embrace of the steaming bath, all was right with the world.

As the quiet of the chamber descended once more, the soft murmur of fabric against stone announced the arrival of Tessa, her steps measured and silent alongside two court ladies. Their presence, a gentle intrusion into the solitude of the bathing chamber, was marked by efficiency and grace as they navigated the space, setting down a tray laden with a decanter of wine and an assortment of snacks upon the wooden table beside the tub.

Observing Tessa's intention to pour the wine, I raised a hand, halting her in the motion. "Don't worry, I can do it," I offered, keen to maintain a semblance of independence even in such pampered surroundings.

"Very well, Your Highness," Tessa replied, her voice a soft echo in the marbled expanse. With a collective bow, she and the accompanying ladies retreated, their departure as unobtrusive as their arrival, leaving behind a trail of quiet respect.

Alone once again, I reached for the decanter, the crystal catching the flicker of candlelight as I poured the wine into a glass. The aroma was a bouquet of fruit and mystery, a promise of flavors yet untasted. The first sip was a revelation. The wine's complexity unfolded on my palate as layers of taste surpassed even the renowned A Thousand Roses.

With a contented sigh, I nestled back against the cool marble, the edge of the tub providing a perfect rest for both my head and the cup of wine. The warmth of the water, the subtle dance of lavender in the air, and the exquisite taste of wine coalesced into a symphony of relaxation. I allowed my eyes to close, the cup securely placed on the tub's wide ledge, as the soothing properties of the bath began to weave its magic.

Drifting, I surrendered to the embrace of sleep, the stresses and intrigues of palace life melting away into the comforting warmth and the gentle aroma that surrounded me. It was a rare moment of peace, a soft descent into slumber guided by the tranquil waters and the serene ambiance of the bathing chamber.

The peacefulness of my bath was shattered by an unexpected touch, a rough hand gliding down my neck and shoulder, snapping me out of my doze with a start. Instinctively, I recoiled, clutching my chest for modesty, only to find Ronan's familiar grin greeting me.

"Hello there, sleeping beauty," he teased, his voice a low rumble in the quiet chamber.

Panic fluttered in my chest as I scanned the room. "What are you doing here? Did anyone see you?" The words tumbled out in a hushed rush, the fear of discovery pressing down upon me.

He eased himself onto the edge of the tub, dismissing my concerns with a shake of his head. "No, Viktor has the front covered. I found a less conspicuous entry." His casual admission did little to quell my rising alarm.

"The security here is laughably lax," I retorted, my gaze sharp, seeking to mask the turmoil his presence stoked.

A chuckle escaped him, his amusement clear. "Or perhaps they're just accommodating an old friend's visit."

His teasing did nothing to soothe the tension threading through me. "Even so, you can't keep sneaking into the Eastern palace. You're going to get caught!" I whispered, the threat of my mother's wrath looming large in my mind. "If my mother—"

"She won't find out," he assured swiftly, his confidence unsettling.

I sank deeper into the water, my attempt at modesty a stark contrast to Ronan's brazen ease. "What are you doing here, Ronan? If this is about last night, we can't—"

"We can't what?" he cut me off.

"It can't be repeated," I mumbled and looked away, my face heating.

With a smirk, he began to unbutton his shirt, slowly revealing his inked skin adorned with the tales of the Crimson Clan and sending a jolt of shock through me. "Ronan!" I exclaimed, turning my back to him in a fluster.

His laughter filled the chamber, a sound too carefree for the gravity of our situation. "You've seen it all before, Leila."

"What are you *doing*?" I repeated for what felt like the hundredth time.

"I'm taking a bath. Is there a problem?"

His query, a playful challenge to the absurdity of the moment, left me incredulous. "You can't join me in here! This isn't the time or the place. Return to the Northern palace at once!" I insisted, my voice a blend of frustration and disbelief.

Ronan's presence, bold and uninvited, was a turmoil I was ill-prepared to navigate. His defiance, wrapped in the guise of nonchalance, was a reminder of the delicate balance I had to maintain—between duty and desire, caution and yearning.

The moment transformed when Ronan suddenly plunged into the tub, sending ripples through the water and a shock through my system. "Ronan!" His name escaped me in a startled gasp, my hands flying up to shield my eyes as Ronan's nude body entered the tub with me. His fearlessness escalated with each encounter, weaving a tapestry of exhilaration and apprehension within me. Each day he became more and more daring. It made me nervous. "Please," I pleaded, although I wasn't sure what I was asking for.

Ignoring my protests, he waded through the water with a predator's grace, closing the distance until only a breath's space remained between us. "Did you miss me?" His voice, a husky whisper, curled around me like smoke, his arm snaking around my waist to draw me closer, an anchor in the swirling warmth. "Because I missed you," he confessed, the timbre of his voice carrying the weight of longing, of a day spent in the shadow of separation. "I've been counting the moments until I could see you again."

Tentatively, I lowered my hands, opening my eyes slowly as I allowed myself a glimpse of the man before me. Ronan, in the flickering candlelight, was a vision of ethereal beauty—his hair, a cascade of midnight, parting to reveal intricate braids that framed his face, a testament to his heritage. His eyes, a deep, mesmerizing crimson, bore into mine, soft yet intense, brimming with an emotion that tethered me to the spot. The sight of him so vulnerably majestic ensnared my gaze, rendering me incapable of looking anywhere else.

In that moment, the world beyond the steam-filled chamber ceased to exist—there was only Ronan, the warmth of the water, and the burgeoning realization of the depth of our connection.

As Ronan's declaration hung in the air between us, a profound silence enveloped the chamber, thick with unspoken promises and the weight of our reality. My fingertips, barely grazing the canvas of his ink-streaked skin, felt the subtle rise of his muscles under the intricate tapestry of tattoos that adorned his body. The sensation of his breath, sharp at my touch, reverberated through me, a tangible marker of our closeness.

Confession spilled from me, a whisper lost in the steam and warmth. "I don't know what's right or wrong anymore." My voice was barely audible above the sound of water lapping against marble. The admission of my longing for him, mingled with the knowledge of the impossibility of our union, left me adrift. "I want you. Desperately. But I know we can never be. I don't know what to do."

His question, soft and insistent, cut through the fog of my hesitation. "Why?" He searched for logic in my denial, a reason within the confines of our desires. "Why is it impossible? Why is it wrong? Nothing has ever felt more right."

As our gazes locked, the moment seemed to be suspended in time as the depth of our predicament unfolded within the span of a heartbeat. "Do you honestly believe your father will give up on abducting me? Your people are desperate to resurrect the fox demon and you need me to do it," I countered, the reality of our situation a barrier as tangible as the walls of the palace that trapped us both.

Ronan's vow, fervent and unwavering, enveloped me like a cloak. "I won't let you get hurt, Leila," he assured, his hand cradling my face with a tenderness that belied the strength within. "Even if I have to go against my father I will ... *for you*."

The gravity of his pledge, a promise of defiance for my sake, left me breathless. "You shouldn't have to," I murmured, a plea for him to understand the magnitude of his proposed sacrifice. "Your priority is—"

"*You're* my priority," he interjected, his voice a beacon of resolve in the uncertain waters of our future. "Nothing else."

Before I could say anything further, his lips descended

onto mine. With my senses heightened, I felt his hands on my body, the parting of my lips by his, the sensation of his tongue on mine. I was lost in a sea of awareness so deep that when he pulled away, I felt lightheaded and he had to hold me steady.

"If you say no, I'll leave this instant. So tell me, Leila," he whispered. "What do *you* want?"

My heart beating like a hundred war drums, all I wanted was to feel his touch just one more time. Without hesitation, I wrapped my legs around his waist and hoisted myself up, draping my arms around his neck and slamming my mouth onto his. Kissing him with a hunger I'd never felt before, his hands engulfed me and he spun us around until my back was against the edge of the marble tub.

His lips slid down my neck to my chest, until he latched onto my breast. I moaned as he sucked and nipped, the throb at my core growing with each practiced flick of his tongue. I felt his hard length stroke my core and I gasped at the sensation as he rubbed against me.

"Ronan..." I moaned his name like a prayer, my eyes rolling into the back of my head as I closed my eyes, absorbing all the sensations. Biting my lip and wanting more, so much more, I reached down between us and grabbed onto his length. He hissed and bit down on my nipple at my touch. Slowly, I stroked him and rubbed against him.

"Leila," he moaned against my breasts. "You're driving me crazy."

I couldn't hide the satisfied smirk that spread across my face as I stroked him faster and faster. I *wanted* him to go crazy. I wanted him to be lost in my touch as much as I was in his. At this point, I didn't know where we started or ended. All I knew was that I wanted this feeling to last forever.

A whimpering moan escaped me as my legs began to quake and I felt myself teetering on the edge. Rubbing faster, I gasped when I saw stars float across my vision as shuddering waves of ecstasy consumed me. Soon after, Ronan tensed and shuddered as he placed his head in the crook of my neck, biting down hard as he came into my hand. As our breathing slowed, we held onto each other as if we were the other's life raft in a turbulent sea.

"Ronan?" I whispered. "I don't know how much longer I can do this. I don't know how much longer I can hold out before I give you my all."

He shook his head, which was still in the crook of my neck. "There's no rush, Leila. We have plenty of time. The prophecy—"

"I don't care about the prophecy," I blurted.

"You're not thinking clearly." He pulled away from me. I unhooked my legs from his waist and slid down his body. "You don't know the repercussions—"

"I don't trust anyone but you," I said adamantly. "I don't *want* anyone but you."

Ronan caressed my face and planted a soft kiss on my forehead. "I know. But we're in no rush. *I'm* in no rush. I want us to take our time. I want you to make your decision with a clear head."

I nodded in understanding. "I will. I promise."

"Good girl," he said with a grin as he brushed the loose strands of hair away from my face. "I should probably go before someone finds us."

I wanted to beg him to stay. I wanted to beg him to follow me into my bed chambers and spend the night with me, but I knew realistically, it wasn't possible. At least not yet.

"When will we see each other again?" I inquired, already desperate for our next meeting.

"I'll visit you tomorrow night. And the night after that, and the night after that," he promised. "I'll find a way."

"Be careful," I whispered as I stood on my tiptoes and placed a gentle kiss on his lips. "I look forward to tomorrow."

10

The next couple of nights, Ronan found every way possible to see me; whether by sneaking into my bedroom, finding me in the kitchens, or coming to see me in the bath chambers. He didn't miss a night, just as he promised.

The night before the banquet, it was nearing midnight and he still hadn't arrived. I grew anxious with each hour ticked by, as many of our guests had already started trickling in. From what Viktor told me, Chief Aryan of the Crimson Clan arrived in the capital earlier that day.

There was a knock on my door and Tessa came in with warm tea. "Some chamomile with valerian root to help you sleep," she announced as she placed the tray on my bedside table.

"Thank you, Tessa." I crawled to the edge of the bed as she poured me a cup. "Do you know if—"

"He has not arrived yet, Your Highness," she said, giving me a knowing look. "Viktor is on the lookout for him. He just left for the Northern palace to see if he's still there."

I snapped my mouth shut and nodded. It hadn't taken

long for Viktor and Tessa to realize what was happening, but they promised to keep it a secret. That was all Ronan and I could ask of them.

"Do you think he's in trouble?" I asked, worry lacing my voice. I believed in Ronan's promise and knew he wouldn't break it unless he had no choice.

"I don't know, Your Highness. He's been very careful. I can't imagine him getting caught," she said as she urged me to sip some tea.

I drank some of the tea and paused, then took a sniff. "Why is there so much valerian root? Are you trying to knock me unconscious?" I joked.

Tessa chuckled. "No, Your Highness, my apologies! This was my first time making tea and I wasn't sure of the ratio. I should have gone to the palace healer. Next time, I will."

Dismissing Tessa's concern with a wave, my restlessness refused to be quelled by the mere presence of tea. "Don't worry. Thank you for trying." I set the tea aside, its warmth untouched.

"Your Highness—"

The plush bed offered no solace to my unease, prompting a sudden decision. "You know what?" I interjected before Tessa could voice her worries. "I think a night stroll in the gardens is just what I need." I swiftly shrugged off the covers and leapt from the bed, propelled by a need for movement and the fresh embrace of night air.

Tessa's laughter, light and understanding, filled the room as she handed me my robe, a shield against the coolness of the night. Perched on the edge of the bed, I slipped into a pair of sturdy shoes and left the softness of my slippers behind. "Come on, Tessa, let's breathe in some fresh air," I invited. Together, we ventured out into the gardens.

The garden paths, bathed in a subtle glow from the

moon, wound before us, a labyrinth of shadows and silhouettes. The night bloomed with the heady scent of roses, their fragrance intensified by the cool air to guide us as much as the faint trail underfoot. My steps, aimless yet purposeful, kicked at the pebbles along the path, their soft clatter a companion to our nocturnal wanderings.

Seeking a diversion from my tumultuous thoughts, I turned to Tessa's steady presence. "Tell me about your time in the army, Tess," I prompted, genuinely curious to hear her story rather than dwell on my own.

Tessa's response was modest. Her hands were clasped loosely behind her back as we walked. "There's not much to tell, Your Highness. I joined the Mage quadrant when I turned seventeen and have been there ever since." Her words were simple, yet they hinted at a depth of experience hidden beneath the surface.

My curiosity piqued, I probed further. "But what made you join? Not all mages choose the army. Wasn't there anything else you dreamed of doing?" The question lingered in the air between us, an invitation to share more about herself.

Her denial was gentle yet firm. "No, I can't think of anything else. My mother was a mage, too, in the Valorian army, until ..." Her voice trailed off and the sentence was left hanging, laden with unspoken history.

"Until the war," I finished for her, the weight of her legacy a silent echo in her words.

"Yeah," she whispered, her voice barely audible against the backdrop of singing frogs from the fountains nearby. In her admission, there was a sense of continuity and loss, a story of service and sacrifice that spanned generations. We continued to walk, the night around us a cloak of shared understanding that bridged the gap between past and present, a princess and her protector.

"I'm so sorry, Tessa," I muttered, feeling incredibly guilty. While deep down I knew the war wasn't my fault, I was still one of the reasons for the attack. At least for the Crimson Clan's part. Keldara just wanted our lands.

"Lyanna!" someone called out from behind us.

Tessa and I turned to see who it was and my stomach dropped when I saw Caelan striding across the garden. Even in the dark, his silver hair shone like a beacon. I tensed. Noticing the change in my demeanor, Tessa stood slightly in front of me, partially blocking me from his view.

"I just want to talk," he said, holding his hands up in surrender. "I promise."

I moved out from behind Tessa and nodded. "Go ahead, then. Talk," I said unflinchingly.

He prowled toward me and stopped a few feet away. "Tomorrow's the banquet. I don't know if your father has showed you the guest list, but—"

"He hasn't and I don't care," I cut him off. "Is that why you came looking for me? To discuss the guest list?"

He shook his head. "No. Not really. I just didn't want you to be surprised when you saw a contingent from Keldara here."

I frowned. "Keldara?"

Caelan nodded. "Your father invited all who may be important in Asteria, including Keldara."

I didn't want to believe him, but at the same time, what was his motive to lie? There was no reason I could think of.

"Fine. Is that all you wanted to tell me?" I said, pretending I wasn't bothered by his news when I clearly was.

"No," he answered. "I want you to stay by my side tomorrow. For your safety."

I scoffed. "My safety? Who would harm me in my own home?" Admittedly, *home* was relative, because I hadn't felt at peace since I'd arrived in Valoria.

"You were the one who told me about the Crimson Clan's plans. You really think they won't try something tomorrow night?" he asked incredulously. "Don't be naïve, Lyanna."

He was right. I *was* being naïve. But I also wanted to believe Ronan wouldn't let anything happen to me. For that, I needed to put my trust in him.

"I received your message loud and clear." I looked over his shoulder to see Viktor approaching. "You can go now."

Caelan furrowed his brows and followed my line of sight, peering over his shoulder to see Viktor. He turned his attention back to me. "If you're waiting on a certain someone, I wouldn't hold your breath. His father summoned him as soon as he arrived in the capital, and he hasn't returned to the palace since."

I hated how obvious I made my feelings known. If I was going to survive in the palace, I needed to learn to hide them better. I rolled my eyes and looked away. "If that's all you came to say, you can be on your way ..." I offered nonchalantly. As I spun on my heels to leave, Caelan took ahold of my wrist. I whirled around and saw Tessa grip Caelan's wrist at the pressure point, forcing him to release me.

He glared at Tessa but released me at once. "Tomorrow won't be easy, Lyanna. Your father thinks it's a celebration, but the other nations will view it as a power move. You must be careful. You don't understand everything that's going on in Asteria—"

"Then explain it to me!" I interrupted hotly. "What do I need to look out for? How can I protect myself?"

His eyes were earnest. "Just stay by my side, Lyanna. I'll protect you."

I scoffed. "Of course you will, because that's what you want: for me to be a wilting flower who's dependent on you. Sorry to break it to you, Caelan, but that's not me. I can protect myself."

His eyes glittered. "You may *think* you can, but you can't. You've been in hiding so long, you don't know what your return means to the world." He stepped closer. "The return of a female Blood Weaver brings a change that no one expected, Lyanna. Your power—"

"A power I don't even know how to use!" I exploded, instantly regretting my vulnerable protest.

"And it's best if you don't," Caelan admitted. "It'll keep you safe."

My mouth fell open in shock. I couldn't believe what he was saying! Would staying ignorant keep me alive? It was a contradiction. I never asked to be this so-called Blood Weaver; I just wanted a normal life – the one I had before I was discovered. The normal life Sir Edric tried to give me. But now it was gone.

I knew I could no longer stay hidden in the shadows. If I wanted to survive, I needed to be strong. I needed power.

"I won't hide," I growled. "So you can forget about it."

Caelan sighed. "Fine. But at least promise that you'll try to blend in tomorrow night. Stay by my side for now. Please, Lyanna."

"I won't make promises I can't keep," I said. "Good night, Caelan." Gripping Tessa's arm, I wheeled us toward where Viktor was waiting.

Viktor bowed as we approached. "Your Highness," he

greeted, then leaned in to whisper. "Sir Ronan is not at the Northern palace. His father—"

"I heard," I cut him off. "Thank you, Viktor." And with that, I returned to the Eastern palace to sleep.

∼

UNFORTUNATELY, instead of slumber, Marcellus was waiting for me outside my chambers. With furrowed brows, I cleared my throat and caught his attention. "Hey ... what are you doing here?"

He scratched the back of his head. "I was just taking a walk around the Eastern palace and thought I'd, uh ... come say hi."

I snorted and rolled my eyes. "In other words, you came to see Selene." I pushed past him and into my bedroom while Tessa stayed outside to give us privacy.

Quickly, Marcellus followed me inside. "No I didn't. I came to see *you*."

My steps faltering, I turned to face him. "Is that so? May I ask why?"

"I wanted to ... apologize." He looked down at his booted feet. "I, uh, ... know I haven't been the best brother, and I'm truly sorry."

I watched him for a moment; the way he nervously fiddled with his fingers, how he scuffed his boot against the floor, and how he avoided eye contact. I wished I could say I knew my brother's mannerisms, but too much time had passed. I didn't know who he was anymore. Still, I wanted to believe his motives were pure.

I sighed heavily. "It's okay, Marcel. I don't blame you ... not entirely. I understand why you were upset."

He slowly lifted his head and looked at me with a frown. "Really?"

"Really," I repeated. "Maybe we can start over?" I held out a hand for him to shake.

A slow smile spread across his face before he took my hand in his. "Definitely," he replied eagerly.

"Good." I chuckled as we shook hands. "Then maybe you can do me a favor tomorrow." I winced as the words came out of my mouth.

He nodded. "Sure. Anything."

"Do you think you can escort Selene to the banquet?" I asked as if I didn't already know the answer.

He frowned again. "Me? Why?"

"I know I told you to stay away from her, but honestly, there's no one else I'd trust with her safety," I said. "I can't escort her myself, and Caelan …"

"You don't trust Caelan?" Marcellus asked, slightly confused.

I shook my head. "No. I don't."

His eyes widened slightly as he absorbed my answer. "Oh. I thought … never mind. It doesn't matter what I thought. Of course I'll escort her."

I smiled up at him. "Thank you, Marcel. I guess I owe you one."

11

The evening of the banquet arrived, a night to mark my long-awaited return to Valoria. In the privacy of my chambers, surrounded by the soft glow of candlelight, the process of dressing felt more ceremonial than routine. Tessa, along with two other ladies from the court, laid out a gown that had been arduously created for the occasion—a true masterpiece of Valorian craftsmanship. Its fabric, a cascade of deep emerald silk, shimmered with threads of gold, mirroring the lushness of the palace gardens under the moonlight. The gown was adorned with intricate beadwork along the bodice, each bead a testament to the meticulous dedication of the palace's seamstresses.

As Tessa carefully laced the back of the dress, I couldn't help but marvel at the transformation reflected in the mirror before me. The gown fit perfectly, accentuating my form while the rich color complemented my complexion, making my skin glow with a radiant warmth. My hair was styled in an elegant updo; the strands were artfully arranged to frame my face with a few loose curls cascading down my neck. The finishing touch was an exquisite necklace, a family heirloom of emeralds and diamonds that lay gently against my collarbone, its green hues a perfect match to the dress.

"You're a vision, Your Highness," Tessa remarked, her voice warm with genuine admiration as she adjusted the fall of the fabric to ensure it draped perfectly.

Feeling like a true Valorian princess for the first time in years, I took a deep breath to calm the flutter of nerves in my stomach. This was more than a mere celebration; it was a declaration of my presence, a reaffirmation of my identity in the land in which I'd once lived.

"Is this really me?" I murmured half to myself as I admired my reflection.

"It's you, Princess. Tonight, Valoria will see its daughter in all her splendor," Tessa affirmed, her smile reflected in the mirror.

With a deep breath, I readied myself for the walk to the Grand Hall. Viktor and my court ladies formed a royal escort that felt more like a procession of old. The palace corridors, illuminated by the soft glow of torchlight, seemed to watch in silent anticipation as we passed.

Viktor, maintaining a pace that was both protective and respectful, glanced back. "You're ready for this," he said, a statement more than a question, his voice steady.

"As ready as I'll ever be."

The walk from the Eastern palace to the Grand Hall was a journey of its own. Viktor, ever the protective guardian, led the way. My court ladies followed in a graceful procession, their gowns a flurry of pastel hues that created a picturesque scene as we traversed the palace grounds. The path was lined with torches that cast golden light upon the marble, guiding our steps through the maze of corridors and archways that made up the heart of the palace.

As we approached the Grand Hall, the sound of music and revelry filtered through the air, a lively melody that quickened my pulse. The massive doors, carved from ancient oak and bound in iron, stood open, welcoming us into the opulent space beyond.

Sentinels were poised, waiting to announce my arrival. Their voices were loud and clear as they rang throughout the Grand Hall. "Her Highness, Princess Lyanna of Valoria!" they called out. Hushed silence fell.

Stepping over the room's threshold, I felt the weight of countless eyes upon me as a sea of faces turned in unison to mark my entrance.

The space was bathed in the warm glow of countless candles, a spectacle of Valorian splendor. Tapestries depicting scenes of legend and lore adorned the walls, while the high vaulted ceiling gave the room an air of boundless space. At the far end, my parents' thrones sat elevated on a dais, a symbol of the enduring legacy of the Valorian crown.

As I made my way down the center aisle, leaving Viktor and the court ladies outside, I felt a mixture of curiosity and admiration in the gazes of the assembled guests. Each step was a statement of the journey I had undertaken, a path that eventually led me back to the heart of Valoria, to a home that was both familiar and wholly new.

My parents, Valoria's King and Queen, sat enthroned in regal splendor, embodying the strength and grace of Valoria. Drawing near, I bowed deeply, an homage to tradition and respect. "Mother, Father," my voice echoed softly in the Grand Hall, "I have returned."

In a moment that seemed to stretch, capturing the weight of years and the depth of our separation, my mother rose. Her movements were deliberate, a portrait of royal poise. A court lady, with practiced reverence, presented a tiara—a symbol of my status and the responsibilities it entailed—on a pillow of the richest burgundy velvet.

Plucking the tiara from the pillow, my mother approached me. The air between us was charged with unspoken emotions and the significance of the act about to unfold. With a grace that spoke of countless similar ceremonies, she crowned me. The tiara's weight settled upon me as light as a whisper, yet loaded with meaning. Her hand then rested on my shoulder, a silent command for me to rise.

The gesture was simple yet profound, marking not just my physical return but the reclamation of my place within the royal family and Valoria's heart. Standing, I faced the assembled nobility, the tiara a gleaming testament to my journey and the path that lay ahead.

My father, resplendent in his ceremonial attire, met my gaze, a beacon of pride and joy. "My daughter," he announced, his voice carrying through the hall, "has returned to us. Let the festivities in her honor begin!"

The swell of applause and exuberant cheers momentarily startled me, a stark reminder of the many eyes fixed upon my every move. As the Grand Hall buzzed with renewed energy for the celebration, I felt their weighty expectations pressing in from all sides. The assembly's attention, though momentarily diverted, returned to me with palpable curiosity.

Caelan, ever the embodiment of courtly grace, was the first to bridge the distance between us. He bowed with a flourish, his gesture a blend of respect and something more elusive. As he lifted my hand to press a kiss against the back of it, his voice, barely above a whisper, carried a hint of challenge. "Welcome back, Lyanna," he said, his smirk betraying his confidence. "Would you honor me with the first dance?"

Caught in the intensity of his gaze, I was momentarily ensnared in indecision. Our recent history, fraught with tension and unresolved conflicts, urged me to decline. I was about to when my mother's voice, authoritative and expectant, pierced the hesitation. "Lyanna, let Caelan escort you onto the dance floor."

Her directive, non-negotiable in its delivery, left me with little choice but to acquiesce. With a tight nod, I extended my hand towards him as a silent concession to the evening's public demands.

Caelan's grip was sure as he led me to the center of the floor, an island amidst the sea of onlookers. The quartet, seizing the moment, wove a melody that filled the space between us, a tangible expression of the evening's splendor. As his hand found its place at the small of my back and drew me into the dance's embrace, our proximity dissolved the remaining distance between us.

We swayed to the music, our eyes locked on one another, never missing a step, though I was the first to look away. Scanning the crowd, I searched for a familiar face. For anyone other than Caelan.

There were many unfamiliar faces in the crowd, but I recognized a few. Caelan's brothers from Eldwain were in attendance, no doubt as representations of their infirm father who couldn't attend. Some elders from Ellyndor, if their pointed ears were any indication. Marcellus and Selene were cloistered in a corner, away from prying eyes. As I continued to search, I saw them—the Crimson Clan.

My eyes first landed on Ronan where he stood stoically next to his father, Chief Aryan. His hands were fisted at his sides and his jaw clenched in frustration as he watched us dance. I wanted to go to him but knew I couldn't. Silas was close by, along with a few more clan members I recognized by face alone. Unlike the rest of the guests who were dressed in their finest silks and satins, the Crimson Clan wore their battle leathers, showing off their tattooed skin and muscled physiques.

"If you continue to stare at him, others will take notice," Caelan murmured as he whipped us around, forcing me to give Ronan my back.

I dug my nails into his shoulder, but he didn't so much as flinch. "You're doing this on purpose," I gritted between my teeth.

He shrugged. "So what if I am? I've told you before and I'll tell you again: the two of you are impossible. Your parents will never let you marry into the Crimson Clan."

I scoffed. "Who said I wanted to marry?"

His eyes snapped to me. "You mean to tell me ..."

"Yes, Caelan, that's *exactly* what I'm saying. I have no desire to get married, because I don't need to," I whispered.

"We'll see about that," he murmured into my ear before twirling me around and dipping me. "We don't always get what we want." He grinned as he lifted me and then released my hand. "Don't stray too far, Lyanna. The night has just begun."

The instant he left me alone on the dance floor, I was engulfed by the clapping crowd. Strangers approached, seeking only to touch my arms, dress, and hair. I felt like a spectacle. I tried to talk to everyone, but it was hard keeping track of all the questions thrown my way. Each person clamored for a moment with me, their questions and touch insistent, until I couldn't breathe. I gasped for air and whirled around with wide eyes, trying to find an exit route, but saw nothing but smiling faces that stretched across tight faces. It was a scene out of a nightmare.

Suddenly, someone gripped me from behind and said, "Everyone, let's give Princess Lyanna some space, hmm?"

Slowly, my savior escorted me out of the crowd of nosy guests. Once we were in a more secure location, I looked up to see who he was. Startled, I gazed up at Orion. I exhaled in relief. Despite my feelings for the irksome fae, I could have kissed him.

"Thank the goddess." I held onto his arm to steady myself. "Where have you been?"

He smirked. "Once I learned you were on your way to Valoria, I returned to Ellyndor for some ... business. I figured you would be safe now that you had been found by your people."

"Why didn't you free Selene?" I whispered. "We made a deal—"

"And I would have kept my word if your brother hadn't beat me to it," he whispered back. "I'm assuming she's in his care?"

"No. He promised to give her the slave release documents, although he hasn't done it yet." I glanced around for any eavesdroppers. "Did you come with the elders from Ellyndor?"

He nodded. "All of Asteria is here to see the lost princess. No one would dare miss this spectacle."

I snorted. "I bet."

"Tell me, Princess, is there any gossip you'd care to share?" He raised a mischievous brow.

I pushed him lightly on the shoulder. "No. Life has been relatively ... boring since I arrived," I lied. I had no intention of divulging my affair with Ronan to him. Especially not in front of everyone. I didn't know who was listening.

A court lady came by with a tray of wine and I flagged her down. Grabbing a cup, I chugged it all in one go and slammed the cup back on the tray. "Apologies," I offered sheepishly. The lady nodded and scurried away. I needed some liquid courage if I was going to get through the night.

"I'm assuming all is *not* okay," Orion hinted as he carefully watched me, seeing how my hands shook.

I blew out a breath. "Please don't remind me," I muttered. "My mother is overbearing as usual, Caelan has something up his sleeve, and my poor father is oblivious to it all. I've been home for all of ten days and I already miss the Central Plains."

"Well, then," Orion sighed. "Maybe you should drink some more." He flagged down another court lady with a tray of wine.

Without a second thought, I grabbed another cup of wine and drank it in one gulp. Setting the cup back on the tray a bit more gently than before, I turned my attention back to Orion and took a deep breath. "Is there anything I should know? Caelan hinted that tonight would have a completely different meaning than what my father intended."

"Is that so?" Orion raised a brow. "I can't say much, but I *will* say you're in for a surprise tonight because—"

Orion was cut off by the sound of trumpets coming from the entrance to the Grand Hall, snaring the attention of the crowd. Two sentinels marched into the room to announce the latest visitor.

"Commander Mykal Kaiser of the Kingdom of Keldara!" the sentinels announced.

The commander strode in with a full entourage. Dressed in the finest clothing, he strolled into the Grand Hall with a smirk playing on his very handsome face.

Caelan wasn't lying; my father *did* invite everyone from Asteria. Of course, it would be strange for the King of

Keldara to cross the border to Valoria, so sending Mykal in his stead made sense. Unfortunately I still harbored a grudge against Mykal for concealing the truth about Ronan's intentions. He instigated our fallout by twisting the truth, because he knew the simple truth wouldn't turn me against Ronan.

Orion snorted. "Of course he would show up late and upstage the arrival of the princess," he mumbled as he rolled his eyes. "What a diva."

"Who cares?" I turned away from Mykal, but Orion stopped me by tugging on my wrist.

"Lyanna, there's something you should know—" Orion started, but his words stalled when my father cleared his throat and stood.

"Thank you all for your attendance tonight," the King's voice boomed. "It's a blessing from the goddess that our Lyanna has returned. I prayed for many years that I would see her once again, and the goddess answered my prayers." He placed a hand over his heart. "Tonight, I would like to thank someone very special who made this all happen. His relentless efforts in finding the lost princess did not go unnoticed. Please, let's all welcome and thank ... Prince Caelan of Eldwain!"

Caelan stepped out of the crowd to the center as everyone clapped and cheered the so-called savior of Valoria. His expression was cocky as he soaked in the applause.

"Caelan, you are like family to us. If there is any request you have, any at all, I will do anything in my power to make it happen to thank you for all your hard work," my father continued. "If—"

"Your Majesty," Caelan interrupted. "I *do* have one request."

My father's smile broadened. "Of course!" he laughed. "Anything. What is it?"

"Leila," Orion whispered. "You—"

"I would like to ask for Princess Lyanna's hand in marriage," Caelan announced.

A chorus of startled gasps rang out in the Grand Hall, not least of which was my own.

"The fuck?" I muttered as I dropped the cup of wine in my hand with a loud clatter.

Orion sighed. "I was *trying* to tell you," he mumbled.

I glared up at the fae. "Well you could have tried harder!"

My father's expression tightened as he attempted to maintain the smile on his face, but it was obvious he was having difficulty.

"Well ..." he started, but his words were cut off by my mother.

"That's a wonderful proposition!" my mother declared cheerfully. "How joyous, and a magnificent prize for Valoria's savior!"

If looks could kill, my mother would be dead from the force of my glare. Marry Caelan? No fucking way!

I quickly searched the crowd for Ronan and found him standing stoically beside his father and Silas across the room. The veins in his neck bulged as Silas held him back from bursting through the crowd to throttle Caelan. I wanted him to look my way so I could reassure him that I would never marry Caelan, but he was too distracted. Too angry.

"Uh ... well ..." my father faltered, a tight smile on his face as he attempted to play the diplomat.

"Father!" Marcellus emerged from the crowd to the center where Caelan stood, leaving Selene behind. "This isn't a decision that can be made *here*." He glared at Caelan, then turned back to my father. "Lyanna's input matters, and I don't think—"

"As her parents, *we* make the decision on her marriage," my mother chimed in. "Lyanna's thoughts do not matter. She will do as we say."

"Mother!" Marcellus pleaded, but she sent him a look that shut him up quickly.

My father cleared his throat. "While Derinda is technically correct," he glanced toward my mother sheepishly, "I agree with Marcellus on this. This decision isn't one to be made on a whim, or in a public forum. Especially since Lyanna has just returned to us. I don't know if I'm ready to part ways with her just yet." He chuckled.

I breathed a relieved sigh. Thank the goddess for my father and oddly enough, Marcellus.

Petulant, my mother crossed her arms over her chest and plopped down onto her throne in muted anger. My father tried to regain control of the situation.

"We will continue this conversation some other time. For now, let's continue the celebration!" he said.

The crowd awkwardly clapped and mingled as if they hadn't just witnessed the biggest news of the century. Softly at first and then gradually increasing in volume, the musicians began to play.

"That Caelan is absolutely mad!" Orion murmured as he grabbed a cup of wine from a passing servant. "After all he did, he has the *audacity* to actually ask for your hand in marriage?"

I peered over at him. "How did you know he was going to request it?" I asked suspiciously.

Orion shrugged and offered a smirk. "Call it intuition."

But I wasn't buying it. He knew more than he was telling,

which made me wonder if Caelan had some dealings with Ellyndor that we weren't aware of.

"Well, Lyanna, it's been lovely, but I must mingle. Be safe!" With a wink tossed over his shoulder, Orion disappeared into the crowd.

I rolled my eyes. There really was no telling what was going on in that fae's mind. I still wasn't sure if he was friend or foe. Casting my eyes over the crowd for Ronan, I saw him standing in the same space as before. I'd taken three steps in his direction when I was stopped by Mykal.

The commander grinned as he intercepted me. "Congratulations are in order, Princess. Who would have thought you'd end up marrying the Prince of Eldwain?"

I scoffed and crossed my arms over my chest. "I'm not marrying anyone."

He smirked. "Is that so? Could have fooled me. Your mother all but agreed on the spot."

"Don't believe everything you see or hear," I snapped. "What do you want, Mykal?"

He chuckled and brushed a strand of my hair away from my face. I quickly slapped his hand away and stepped back. "Touchy!" He held his hands up in mock surrender. "I thought we had a connection," he whispered as he leaned toward me. "I mean, we *did* kiss ..." He let the sentence linger.

I glared. "I never kissed you," I gritted between my teeth.

He shrugged. "If you say so, Princess. It was very memorable for me, in any event," he offered cheekily. "Since Eldwain is entertaining thoughts of marriage alignments with Valoria, maybe I should throw my hat into the race as well. I think we'd be lovely together."

I pushed him away. "Don't even think about it!" I growled. "I would rather marry Caelan than you."

Mykal's expression darkened, and he took a step toward me. "I wouldn't be so quick to reject me, Princess. You never know what the future holds."

"*I* am the master of my future and you're not in it!" I whispered back. "Don't think for a second that I've forgotten your part in all of this."

Mykal's face softened. "Apologies, Princess," he murmured. "I should not have taken advantage of you in that manner. Unfortunately, unlike you, some of us are not the masters of our future."

I frowned at his admission, wondering what he could possibly mean. According to everyone, he enjoyed a very good relationship with the King of Keldara. He was practically an adopted son since the king had no heirs. But his words hinted that he lacked freedom. I wanted to pry, but that would mean I was interested in his fate, which I certainly wasn't.

I rolled my eyes and tried to step around him when Mykal quickly took ahold of my wrist. "Lyanna," he whispered, "I'm not your enemy. Contrary to popular belief, I don't want to hurt you, much less see you get hurt. I know you must feel safe at home, but trust me, you're not safe anywhere. If you're ever in need of aid, know you can count on me."

I furrowed my brows and peered up at him. His expression mirrored his deadly serious tone. "Why? Why would you help me?"

He sighed and released my wrist. "Sadly, you're a victim in all these political games and I don't think you deserve it. You're too good to be involved in this mess."

"How do you know I'm good? I could be a horrible person." I lifted my chin defiantly.

Mykal smirked. "I have eyes and ears everywhere, Princess. I would know."

Tired of this circular conversation, I pushed past him and stomped away. He was the last person I wanted to speak to right now. The farther I was from Mykal, the better.

12

I searched the crowd for Ronan but couldn't find him anywhere. In the meantime, I was stopped by almost everyone in attendance. I politely excused myself from one fawning group before I turned around and saw Adler, the third prince of Eldwain standing next in line.

"Princess Lyanna." He took my hand in his and gave it a light kiss as he bowed. "It's been a long time." He lifted his head with a smirk and a wink. "You've grown into quite a woman."

I quickly snatched my hand back, feeling oily and unclean under his touch. "Adler. It's been a long time." I stared up at the silver haired half-fae with barely disguised unease. His hazel eyes, so much like Caelan's, glinted back at me with the knowledge of how I felt about him.

"It really has. I thought you were all but dead. Had I known you were still alive, I would have made an effort to find you myself. Maybe then it would be *me* asking for your hand in marriage instead of my little brother."

I rolled my eyes. "As if you would have bothered. You

were never interested in me before, why would you be now?"

He shrugged. "You never know, Lyanna. Things could have been completely different—"

"But they're not," I interrupted. "You're just mad because Caelan's attempt at a marriage alliance could earn him Eldwain's throne," I declared confidently. "I might have been gone ten years, but I haven't been living under a rock," I retorted.

Adler snorted. "Well, then you must know King Malik would never agree to a marriage between you two."

I shrugged. "You never know, Adler. You heard my mother. She's very keen on this marriage."

I wasn't normally this petty, but Adler had irked me since we were children. He had a tendency to pick on Caelan since he was the youngest of the five princes, and since Caelan and I were such good friends, that meant he picked on me as well. He had a cruel streak that must have bled into Caelan's personality over the years. Once when we were young, he flung Caelan into the lake before he knew how to swim and watched him indifferently as he gasped and almost drowned. If Marcellus and I hadn't been around to fish him out, Caelan would have surely died that day.

Adler rolled his eyes. "You might have fooled me ten years ago with that lie, Lyanna, but not now. The two of you have been apart for a very long time, and it shows."

I wanted to argue, but I'd made my feelings known all night. There was no use refuting them now. "I'm not interested in joining your family's political strife—"

"Good," Adler interrupted. He grinned wickedly. "Then stay out of it, because I will never allow an alliance with Valoria ... At least not through my brother."

I stepped toward him and lifted my chin to look up into

his smug face. "That's not up to either of us, so move out of my way, asshole," I growled. Pushing my shoulder into him, I almost knocked him over as I stormed around him.

I was tired of so many ... *men* getting in my way, thinking they knew better than I did what I wanted in life. There was only one man I wanted to see, and he was nowhere in sight.

Lifting the skirt of my dress, I bustled out of the Grand Hall and angled toward the gardens, hoping I would catch him outside. The air was cold and winter's early chill was making itself known in the north. My skin prickled with goosebumps as I searched the area for Ronan. Relief swam through me when I found him in the garden maze with Silas.

"Ronan!" I yelled and hurried toward them. Silas and Ronan turned around, and to my surprise, young Henry was with them.

His eyes were as bright as the stars in the sky when they caught sight of me. "Miss Leila!" Henry shrieked as he pushed past the Crimson Clan warriors and ran toward me. Meeting each other halfway, Henry wrapped his arms around my mid-section without a care in the world. "Miss Leila, I've been so worried!"

I squeezed him tightly. "By the goddess, Henry! Where have you been?"

He lifted his head from my mid-section and grinned up at me. "I've been with Silas," he announced proudly, showing a bright smile that was missing several teeth.

I brushed the hair back from his face and kissed the top of his head. "Your teeth!" I giggled.

He nodded with a laugh. "My baby teeth are falling out."

I hugged him even tighter and took in his freshly bathed scent. "What are you doing here? How did you get in?"

Ronan and Silas approached and answered my question.

"We smuggled him in," Silas admitted. "It's nice to see you again ... Your Highness," he said with a bow.

I bit my lower lip, feeling awkward around Silas. The last time we saw each other was on the battlefield after Ronan had been taken hostage. It wasn't on good terms.

"No need for formalities," I murmured. "It's nice to see you as well."

"Are you getting married?" Henry asked, gaping up at me while hugging my stomach. "That prince doesn't seem like a very nice person," he admitted with a frown.

"Don't worry, Henry." I met Ronan's eyes. "I would never marry him."

Ronan snorted. "As if you'll have a choice. You heard your mother when—"

"My mother does not dictate who I get to marry," I interrupted. "I'm no longer the same princess I was ten years ago. *I'm* in control of my life. No one else."

Ronan gritted his teeth and looked away, running a hand through his long, dark hair. "Leila, I can't—"

"I know," I said. "Don't worry. I'll handle it. Just ... relax."

"Is ... is everything okay between the two of you?" Silas glanced between us. "The last time I saw you together, you were boiling his blood."

Henry released me and darted his eyes between the three of us, wholly confused. Embarrassed, I scratched the back of my neck.

"That was a ... misunderstanding," I muttered sheepishly, "that has since been resolved."

Silas, still unsure, continued to look between me and Ronan. "Well ... I guess that's good."

I chuckled awkwardly. "Yeah ..."

Henry grabbed my hand and then Ronan's, bringing

them together. "You two should get married," he said innocently as he clasped our hands together. "Then you can both adopt me. Right, Miss Leila?"

My mouth fell open, and I looked away to hide the tear that slid down my face. I quickly wiped it away and turned back to Henry with a watery smile. "That would be ideal." I brushed his hair back with my free hand.

"Yes ... it would be," Ronan said to Henry, but his crimson gaze was locked on mine.

"Ronan—" My words faltered, cut short by an unexpected interruption. The sound of someone clearing their throat echoed behind us, a signal that our solitude had been breached. Ronan and I disentangled ourselves and turned to face the newcomer.

With a start, I realized it was Ronan's father, Chief Aryan of the Crimson Clan. His presence was commanding and imposing. The resemblance to Ronan was unmistakable—those same piercing crimson eyes set beneath furrowed brows; long, dark hair that cascaded down his back, braided at the sides in a show of tradition and strength. His skin, a canvas of intricate crimson tattoos, spoke of battles fought and victories claimed. Adorned in battle leathers that hugged his muscular frame, he bore the aura of a warrior born, albeit unarmed as per the palace's strict regulations regarding weapons.

"Well, look who we have here!" Chief Aryan announced, stepping forward with a confident swagger that filled the space between us. His hand instinctively reached for a sword that wasn't there. All weapons had been taken at the gate. "Your Highness," he greeted with a stiff bow. "It is a pleasure to finally meet you."

I felt Ronan's presence behind me in a protective stance

as his father held out a hand for me to shake. Tentatively, I took it and his grip tightened on mine in a knowing manner. "The pleasure is all mine," I managed, even as his grip intensified, signaling a challenge rather than a mere formality.

The moment stretched, charged with unspoken tensions, until he finally released me, a wide grin unfurling across his features. "I've heard much about you from Ronan. A healer, is that right? I heard you're among the best in the Central Plains. No surprise, given your blood mage heritage."

I mustered an awkward smile, downplaying the compliment. "I wouldn't go that far, but thank you."

"Oh, don't be modest, Your Highness. Little Henry hasn't stopped raving about you since he came to the Grasslands." His gaze drilled into me, carrying infinite layers of meaning. "Although I will say I'm a bit disappointed that you didn't come visit us when you were relatively still unknown. We would have welcomed you in the Grasslands with open arms."

I swallowed the snort that threatened to escape. "Right," I murmured, my voice laced with skepticism I couldn't fully hide. I was sure they would have welcomed me ... and then they would have sacrificed me to the fox demon right after. Except he didn't know I knew the truth. At least, I didn't think he did.

"Father." Ronan emerged from behind me, his tone laden with a blend of surprise and caution. "What brings you here?"

Chief Aryan's eyebrow arched, a hint of amusement in his gaze. "Is a man not permitted to seek a breath of fresh air? The confines of the hall have become rather ... oppressive with all the ... strategic discussions underway." His glance towards Ronan carried an unspoken message, one that seemed to stretch beyond mere words.

"I assure you, Father, everything is handled," Ronan said. I peered over my shoulder at him with an arched brow.

"I'd hope so," Chief Aryan remarked, his voice carrying an edge of expectation. "Well ... I guess I should return before anyone notices I'm missing." Turning towards me, he added, "It was a pleasure, Your Highness. I anticipate our paths will cross again soon." With a final nod, he departed, his silhouette merging with the shadows as he made his way back to the Grand Hall.

Silence enveloped the garden in his wake, leaving me with more questions than answers. "Everything is handled?" I echoed Ronan's earlier assurance, my frown deepening. "You and I both know that's far from the truth."

Silas' eyes widened in surprise. "She—she *knows*?"

Ronan bit his lower lip and nodded without looking at Silas. "I can't tell him the truth, Leila. I don't know what my father would do if he knew. He might even be foolish enough to start a war by kidnapping you from your own home. I can't take the risk of that happening."

Frustrated, I ripped the tiara from my head and was about to run a hand through my hair before I remembered it was in an updo. I gave an irritated growl. "I won't do it, Ronan," I whispered.

"Wait!" Silas cut between us. "If you know about the fox demon, then you know Ronan's plan. You won't stay dead! He'll bring you back—"

"I know," I interrupted, narrowing my gaze at Silas. "But I can't take the risk that something will go wrong."

Silas stumbled backward, deflated that I'd shot down all

their plans to resurrect the fox demon. "Then we're doomed."

I sighed, the weight of their predicament bearing down on me. "I told Ronan that if we explained to my father what was happening to the Crimson Clan, I'm sure he would help. But—"

"No," Ronan said. "I'll figure it out." His determination, while noble, left us entangled in a complex web of duty, loyalty, and the desperate search for a peaceful resolution.

"What's going on?" Henry interjected innocently. "Is there anything I can do to help?"

I smiled down at him and squeezed his bony shoulder. "No, Henry, there's not. Thank you, though. We appreciate your offer."

"We should return to the festivities before we're found out here together," Ronan suggested. "It wouldn't look good if you're found with us," he said with a bit of anger.

I wanted to argue and say I didn't care, but truthfully, I *did* care. If rumors spread about us before I could lay the foundations of our relationship, it wouldn't end well for any of us.

"Leila?" someone whisper-yelled. We all turned around to see who was coming. Selene emerged from around the orderly row of bushes, holding up the hem of her maroon dress. "By the gods, Leila!" she said in relief once she spotted me. "Everyone is looking for you. There's trouble inside the Grand Hall."

"What?" I frowned. "What's going on?"

She looked between me and the two Crimson Clan members and whispered, "Someone is claiming you're not the lost princess. That no proof has been given other than the crescent moon birthmark on your forehead."

My eyes widened as I gasped. "What? Who would dare make such a claim?"

"From what Prince Marcellus said, it was a prince. Prince..." She furrowed her brows and attempted to remember the name. "Ah! Prince Adler."

I rolled my eyes and snorted derisively. "Of course it would be Prince Adler."

"Do you know who he is?" she asked, confused by my nonplussed reaction.

I nodded. "He's the third prince of Eldwain. One of Caelan's older brothers."

"We should hurry. They're looking for you and if they find you out here ... with *them*, it won't look good," Selene insisted.

"You're right." Lifting the hem of my voluminous dress, I turned back to Silas and Ronan. "I have to go and see about this disturbance."

"We'll go with you—" Ronan attempted, but I held up a hand to stop him.

"No. If we go in together, it'll look suspicious," I said quickly. "Just wait a few minutes after I leave before you go back in." With hurried steps, I followed Selene out of the garden maze and back to the Grand Hall. I could hear the tumult before the doors were even opened. The instant the sentinels opened the doors, everyone turned to see who had entered. A hush fell over the crowd. "I heard someone was looking for me?" I said loud enough for everyone to hear.

The crowd parted as I walked down the center of the room where Adler was standing in front of the king and queen's thrones, with Caelan standing protectively in front of my parents. I didn't think Adler was stupid enough to attack my parents in front of so many witnesses, but I wouldn't put it past him.

Adler spun on his heels and faced me as Selene and I walked toward him. "Ah, there she is!" he said with a grin. "The girl of the hour."

"The *woman* of the hour," I corrected. "I stopped being a girl a long time ago."

Adler snorted. "Apologies. I was just telling the king and queen how lovely it is that you've returned, even though most of us here have the same question."

I cocked a brow. "Which is?"

"Are you *really* the lost princess?" he asked with a smirk. "The birthmark doesn't really tell much, besides that you're Valorian." He turned to face the crowd, raising his voice to captivate the audience with his foolish theory. "We all know the lost princess is the only female blood mage since the Goddess. Isn't it within our rights to ask for a demonstration? To ease our worries, of course."

"Of course," I said sarcastically. I held an arm up in front of Selene to stop her from following, then walked to the front of the aisle where Adler and Caelan stood.

"Lyanna, you have nothing to prove," Caelan argued. "We know who you are—"

"Obviously your brother doesn't. Seems he's a bit skeptical that I am who I claim to be," I said loudly enough for all to hear. "Let's ease his worries, shall we?" I turned to face Adler. Lifting my hand, I seized the blood circulating in Adler's veins and flicked my wrist downward, forcing him to his knees.

Caelan's brother sucked in a pained breath and dropped to the marble floor, eliciting a startled gasp from the crowd. Adler scratched at his skin as I boiled him from the inside.

"I'm sure you're feeling a bit ... warm, right about now," I taunted, then turned up the heat. "Why don't I beat you to death and then bring you back to life with my blood? Would that be proof enough for you and anyone else who doubts my claim?" I fisted my hand, seizing control of his body.

Adler collapsed to his side and curled into a fetal position. "S-Stop!" he gritted between his teeth. "P-Please!"

I snorted. "Sure. Why not?" Relaxing my hand, I dropped it to my side and relaxed my stance, gazing out at the crowd that watched in open fear. "Hopefully that's proof enough for you all!" Spinning on my heels, I faced my parents and bowed to them in respect. "Apologies for the spectacle."

My father waved me off. "No, no, no trouble, Lyan—" He didn't have time to finish saying my name before there was a guttural scream behind me. My father's eyes widened in fear.

I spun around in time to see Adler stagger to his feet with a dagger in hand, heading directly for me. Stunned, I was about to lift my hand up again when a hand intercepted the dagger, catching it by the blade. I gasped in horror as blood dripped from Ronan's palm as he gripped the blade, forcing it back toward Adler.

"You *dare* attack the Princess of Valoria in her own home? In front of all these witnesses?" Ronan growled loudly enough for all to hear. His crimson eyes were the darkest maroon as they glared at Adler. The muscles in his arms stiffened as he grappled against Adler's assault. He held the dagger so tightly, I worried there would be permanent damage to his palm.

"Stay out of it, you barbarian!" Adler shouted as he ripped the dagger out of Ronan's hand, cutting his palm even deeper.

"Ro—" I attempted, but Caelan held me back with a tight grip on my wrist. I whirled on him, but he only shook his head in warning.

"*I'm* the barbarian?" Ronan scoffed. "Yet here you are, attacking a defenseless woman from behind. I don't believe anything is more barbaric than that."

"For someone who wants my hand in marriage, you're certainly not trying to defend me," I hissed at Caelan as I ripped my wrist out of his hand. "Don't try to stop me!"

I raced to Ronan just as Marcellus appeared with a cloth for Ronan's wound. I took Ronan's hand in mine and wrapped it. The crowd watched in awed fascination.

Adler laughed. "Why are you savages so serious? This was just a test. I wasn't actually going to hurt her! Do you think my own brother would stand by idly while I killed his bride to be?"

"Yes. I think he would," Ronan answered tersely. "Because unlike me, Caelan is afraid of you and what you're capable of. That cowardice would compel him to stand by while you stabbed his *potential* bride."

Adler's expression darkened as he squared off with Ronan. Silas burst from the crowd to stand beside his friend, turning the situation to four against ... *two* ... as Caelan stepped past me to stand beside his brother.

"Please don't start any rumors, Ronan. The relationship with my brother is solid." Caelan looked between us. "I would never let him hurt Lyanna, nor would he dare to do so."

Ronan laughed. "Right. Because what we all witnessed here was merely an illusion," he said sarcastically.

My father bolted to his feet and cleared his throat, catching the attention of everyone in attendance to this spectacle. "Enough! Whether intentional or not, weapons of any kind are not allowed within the palace walls. And you, Adler, know that very well." Snapping his finger for the guards' attention, they quickly disarmed Adler and searched him for more weapons.

Adler bowed to my father. "Apologies, Your Majesty. The guards must have missed this one."

I snorted and looked away, but my thoughts were clearly written on my face. If you dumped a million Glint at my feet, I still wouldn't believe Adler's claim that it was merely a demonstration.

13

After the commotion from the banquet finally settled, the night ended fairly early. But due to my father's request, they celebrated my return for three full nights with enough food and drink to feed a whole nation. I made my nightly appearance, but never stayed long. The feigned smiles and the endless cycle of introductions to faces and names I would soon forget became increasingly wearisome. By the time the festivities drew to a close, I was relieved, tinged with a fatigue born not from physical exertion but from the emotional labor of constant pretense.

By the fourth night, many started to return to their lands while some stayed to explore Valoria and all it had to offer. I was surprised when my father allowed Ronan to stay, even after his father and Silas announced they were returning to the Grasslands. It seemed my father was very appreciative for what Ronan did the first night of the celebration, when he saved his only daughter's life.

"I leave him in your care," Silas said as he handed Henry off to us. "He's been such a good little spymaster; I hope he can stop for a bit and enjoy his time in Valoria." Silas ruffled Henry's hair as he smiled at the boy. It seemed they had grown close over the last few weeks.

"We'll take good care of him," Ronan reassured Silas. "Thank you for all you've done."

Silas turned to me with a voice tinged in regret. "Your Highness, I wish we'd had more time to get to know one another. But I trust you will watch over my brother while he's on your lands."

His words elicited a sincere promise from me. "Of course," I said. "I won't let anything happen to him."

Ronan rolled his eyes and patted Silas on the shoulder. "Go on now, before my father leaves you behind."

We watched Silas mount his horse and ride through the palace gates, a lone figure that gradually disappeared into the distance. The sight, though simple, marked the close of one chapter and the tentative beginning of another, leaving us to navigate the complexities of the days to come in the quiet aftermath of celebration.

After Silas vanished, I lowered to one knee, aiming to meet Henry at his level and create a space where he might feel more at ease to express his wishes. "Alright, Henry, what's on your mind? Hungry for something special? Whatever you desire, consider it yours," I offered, my smile aimed to coax him into sharing his thoughts without reservation.

The boy's hesitation was palpable. His cheeks flushed a deep shade of crimson as he wrestled with his request. "Well ..." he started, his voice barely above a whisper.

Ronan, ever the encourager, chimed in with a playful tone. "Ah, come on, Henry! You weren't this shy back in the Crimson Clan camp. You boldly requested a feast back then!" he reminded him, tousling the boy's hair affectionately.

Henry's response came with a roll of his eyes, a gesture that carried a weight of consideration. "Yes, but this is Miss Leila. I can't just ask her—"

"Of course you can," I cut in, eager to assure him of his place here. "You can ask me for anything, Henry."

In a move that warmed my heart, Henry embraced me, his small arms encircling my neck. "Can I be your spymaster?" he ventured, the question hanging between us like a vow. "I promise to be loyal only to you, Miss Leila."

Ronan and I couldn't contain our laughter at his earnest request. "Henry," I replied, drawing him closer for a hug, "is that really all you wish for? Not a grand feast or to dive into a bathtub filled with gold coins? Because I can make both of those things happen," I added, joining in the lighthearted jest.

His reply came with a playful snort. "Of course, I expect payment," he stated, "but I don't want handouts. I wish to earn my keep, Miss Leila."

I looked deeply into Henry's eyes, now clear of the shadows of sadness that once lingered there. "Alright, then." I rose to my feet and extended my hand in a gesture of agreement. "If becoming a spymaster is your ambition, then so be it. But know it won't be an easy path," I warned, half-hoping to sway his resolve.

Henry's handshake was firm, his determination unwavering. "I don't expect it to be easy, Miss Leila. I promise to serve you for the rest of my life."

The notion of 'service' weighed heavily on me. The last thing I wanted was for Henry to view his life as one of obligatory servitude. I yearned for him to experience the freedom and joy of childhood, a gift I wanted to offer freely. Yet, his insistence on earning his place and not accepting charity was a stance I had to respect—at least for now. In the back of my mind, I acknowledged that this arrangement would require re-evaluation in the future.

Freedom, not lifelong obligation, was what I truly wished for Henry.

∼

AFTER ENSURING Henry was comfortably situated in his new quarters within the Eastern palace, I accompanied Ronan to his temporary residence in the Northern palace—a decision graciously approved by my father. Our path through the palace grounds was shrouded in the cool, enveloping cloak of evening, our hands nearly touching, nearly intertwining, yet refraining—a silent concession to the eyes that might be upon us.

"Ronan," I breathed, a whisper meant only for him, even as we paced a discreet distance ahead of my ever-watchful guards, Viktor and Tessa. "Can I ask you something?"

"Anything," he responded, his gaze fixed ahead, a testament to the gravity of the moment.

My gaze drifted to his hand, carefully tended and bandaged by the palace's healer, a visible sign of the tumultuous events that had transpired. The urge to comfort, to connect, was palpable, yet restrained by circumstance. "I feel somewhat foolish for this," I admitted softly, "but I need to understand ... what exactly is *this* ... between us?"

Ronan's stride halted abruptly and he turned, the intensity of his gaze piercing the twilight. "If clarity is what you seek, then let it be clear. You are mine and mine alone, Leila. I cannot, and will not, entertain the thought of you with Caelan—or anyone else, for that matter. If marriage is not your desire, I accept that. But should you choose it, know that it must be with me. Because just like you're mine, I'm yours, Leila. And I don't want anyone else but you."

His declaration, fervent and unwavering, left me momentarily speechless. My heart raced at the sincerity and depth of his commitment. "Eventually you'll have to return to the Grasslands. You can't stay with me in Valoria forever," I countered, the practicalities of our situation weaving a complex web of uncertainty. "What will we do if—"

Ronan closed the distance between us, a gesture both tender and bold. "Let that be my concern," he assured me, gently tucking a wayward strand of hair behind my ear. "But know this—I have no intention of leaving your side."

A mix of frustration and affection bubbled up at the evidence of my own vulnerability. "I feel stupid. I don't know why I'm worried."

"It's only natural to feel this way, Leila. The odds are stacked against us in so many ways. But as long as you don't give up, neither will I," he soothed, his touch a balm against the chill of the night, his fingers tracing the contours of my face with a care that spoke volumes. "We can make this work ... I promise. Do you trust me?"

Locking gazes with the Crimson Clan warrior who'd stolen my heart, I realized I stood at the crossroads of emotion and reason. Trust ... that fragile, intangible thread had frayed under the weight of unspoken prophecies and past actions. My heart yearned to leap and affirm my unwavering faith in him, yet the shadow of doubt cast long by the events woven around the prophecy that entwined our fates, held me back.

"Yes." I finally allowed the word to escape, a whisper of hope amidst the storm of my hesitations. "I do."

Ronan's acknowledgment was a mirror to my inner turmoil. "I know this isn't easy for you, Leila. I haven't always made the wisest decisions when it comes to us. For that, I'm eternally sorry and will spend the rest of my life making up for it," he professed, the sincerity in his voice attempting to bridge the chasm my reservations had created.

How I wished to dissolve into that promise, to tell him that understanding and forgiveness had already paved much of the path towards healing. That I understood it was all for his people. His people who continued to suffer under Keldara's cruel thumb. A situation that painted Ronan not as a villain, but a leader caught in an impossible-to-win situation. Yet words failed me, choked by the complexity of emotions and the reality of our situation.

Ronan cradled my face and his lips tenderly met my forehead, a fleeting sanctuary from the world's prying eyes. I couldn't help but whisper a caution. "Ronan, we must be careful. The walls, the shadows, they all have eyes," I reminded him, my voice a hushed echo of our precarious reality.

His sigh, laden with a blend of regret and longing, marked his reluctant retreat. "I'm sorry," he whispered in return. "I guess I just got caught up in the moment."

I peered over my shoulder at Viktor and Tessa, who had given us their backs for privacy.

A mischievous idea took root, spurred by the temporary privacy their vigilance afforded us. "Let's go get caught up in the moment elsewhere," I suggested, a playful lilt in my voice that invited Ronan to entertain the notion of a clandestine escape.

His laughter, a rare sound that wove warmth through the cool night air, followed me as I led the way, silently beckoning him to join me in finding our secluded haven. My call to Viktor and Tessa to resume their protective roles was met with immediate compliance, their presence a constant reminder of the delicate balance we navigated between duty and desire.

As we navigated the intricate tapestry of moonlit pathways that connected the Eastern and Northern palaces, silence settled, a reflective space where unspoken thoughts and lingering doubts danced in the shadows. The night air, cool and fragrant with the scent of late blooms, whispered secrets to the ancient stones under our feet, bearing witness to the complexity of emotions that swirled around us.

As we reached the shadowed archway that led into the Northern palace, an unexpected figure emerged from the dim light, grounding our steps to a halt. Caelan, unmistakable in his posture of impatient expectation and silver hair, pivoted toward us, his surprise unmistakable.

"What are *you* doing here?" he demanded, his steps quickening as he closed the distance to where we stood, a storm brewing in his eyes.

Instantly, Ronan and Viktor positioned themselves defensively before me, a living barrier to Caelan's advances.

Caelan's frustration peaked. "What is this? I have no intention of harming her!"

Ronan's response was laced with cold sarcasm. "You mean no more than you already have?"

The color in Caelan's cheeks deepened, a silent testament to his anger. "Whatever has happened is between me and Lyanna."

Ronan took a step toward him. "Her body is still covered in scars from your so-called love," he growled. "Those marks will never go away."

Before the tension could escalate further, I intervened by stepping forward to diffuse the brewing confrontation. "Enough!" I shouted. "What are you doing here, Caelan?"

His retort was immediate, tinged with accusation. "What about *you*? You should be secure within the Eastern palace, not here ... with *him*."

"I'm not a prisoner in my own home," I replied, striving for a tone of measured calm. "I'm free to roam the grounds as I wish, with whom I wish."

Caelan, visibly struggling to contain his frustration, seemed on the verge of an outburst, yet restraint held his words at bay. I could tell he wanted to scream and shout and tell me I was wrong, but somehow he managed to hold it all in, as evidenced by the vein pulsing at his temple. I'm sure there was much he would like to say, but he remained quiet.

Viktor stepped in, aiming to placate the situation. "We are keeping an eye on her, Your Highness," he attempted to reassure Caelan. "She is safe."

Undeterred, Caelan confronted Viktor with a fierce glare. "She should not have crossed the threshold of the Northern palace. Should you dare to neglect your duties ..."

"Apologies, Your Highness," Viktor interjected with firm respect, "but I don't take orders from you. You are but a visitor on our lands. I take orders from the princess and the king only. Your status grants you no command here."

Caelan's reaction, a mix of shock and righteous indignation, mirrored the tension of the moment. As for me, the effort to suppress my amusement at Viktor's bold declaration was a battle. Indeed, Viktor more than earned my esteem in that moment, proving himself to be a true guardian amidst the crossfire of royal complexities. He deserved a raise.

Caelan's ire was palpable. He jabbed a finger in Viktor's direction, his voice a rumble of barely contained fury. "You! I would advise against such arrogance—"

His challenge was cut short by my interjection. "And

why should he? Viktor is correct," I asserted, my voice steady. "If you care to argue, you can take it up with my father."

A grieved sigh escaped Caelan, and his posture deflated slightly in resignation. "Lyanna, please ... just listen to me for once. As your future husband—"

Unable to contain his mirth, Ronan barked a laugh. "By the gods, Caelan! You'll *never* be her husband. King Malik's reaction should have told you enough."

Caelan's retort was swift, a sharp edge to his words. "And you think *you* will? Because I vow that'll never happen."

Ronan shrugged and stepped toward him, invading his personal space, and whispered, "Maybe not, but I'll be the one warming her bed at night."

The tension snapped. Caelan's fist flew, connecting with Ronan's face in a burst of anger. "If you touch her, *I'll kill you!*"

My voice rose above the chaos, a command for peace. "Enough! Caelan, leave now. You have no place here."

With a parting glare, Caelan retreated, his departure leaving a charged silence in his wake. I turned to Ronan, frustration boiling over. "What was *that* about?" I demanded. "Why would you taunt him like that? I thought this was supposed to be a secret!"

Ronan's stance was defiant, a mixture of protective fervor and anger. "He needed to be put in his place, Leila. He can't go around claiming to be your future husband!" Ronan shouted before licking the blood on his cut lip. "I'm sorry if it offends you, but when it comes to him, I won't keep quiet."

Ronan stomped back to his rooms in the Northern palace. I started to follow, only to be halted by Tessa's cautioning hand. "Your Highness, you shouldn't enter the Northern palace. Others are watching."

Glancing around, I caught the curious stares of a dozen courtiers, their presence a stifling reminder of the palace's ever-watchful gaze. The realization that our confrontation would fuel tomorrow's gossip over breakfast trays settled heavily upon me.

"Let's go before anyone else sees me," I whispered, urgency lacing my words. With Tessa and Viktor by my side, we retreated to the safety of the Eastern palace, away from prying eyes and whispered judgments.

14

The struggle to rise the next morning was monumental, a battle against my body's demand for rest after a tumultuous night of restless thoughts and fragmented sleep. Tessa, in her infinite pragmatism, deemed it necessary to employ a rather startling wake-up call, resorting to drenching me with water to ensure my punctuality for the family breakfast. The echoes of last evening's confrontations, particularly the unresolved tensions between Ronan and Caelan, left a palpable shadow, casting dark circles under my eyes as silent witnesses to my internal turmoil.

Sure, I knew Ronan was angry and he had every right to be. Especially when it came to Caelan. I'd forgiven him one too many times in the Central Plains. As I looked back on those days, even I was frustrated with myself for giving him the benefit of the doubt. But things were different now. He had to know they were different.

Shuffling along, I let Tessa dress me while half asleep. Once she was done arranging my hair, I was promptly escorted to the dining hall in the Central palace where my mother, Marcellus, and Caelan were undoubtedly already waiting to have breakfast.

When I entered the dining hall, I was surprised to see my father seated at the head of the table.

"Good morning, Lyanna!" His voice, warm with the joy of reunion, greeted me as I settled into my designated seat, surrounded by family yet isolated by the silent undercurrents of recent events. "I thought I'd join you all today. I have much to do, and I didn't know if I'd have time to see you otherwise."

While he wasn't consistent, my father did try to see me often and spend time with me. Out of everyone at this table, he was the only one I truly thought had missed me over the last ten years.

"No worries." I offered a broad smile and sat down, taking the napkin and spreading it across my lap. "I didn't sleep well last night, so it was a bit difficult to wake up this morning. Apologies for my tardiness," I said honestly.

My father frowned. "Are you unwell? Has this been recurring? I'll have the palace healer send you some valerian root at night to help you sleep."

"I'm fine, honestly. I just think with all the celebration from the recent days, I'm just fatigued," I lied, attempting to deflect his worry. "The valerian root should help."

My father nodded. "Good, good. You would know more about that than I do," he chuckled. "I heard you might be interested in working in the infirmary—"

"Absolutely not!" my mother interjected, her glare cutting through the morning's tentative peace. "A princess, working with the ill? No. We cannot have that."

I looked over at my father, who sighed in resignation. "Well ... we can discuss this more later. We don't have to make decisions right away—"

"Malik!" she yelled.

He slammed his fist on the table hard enough to make the silverware rattle. "Enough, Derinda!" he shouted, his voice booming throughout the dining hall. "I said enough," he said softer, lowering his voice.

I peered over at Marcellus beside me, but he only shrugged. Our parents never used to fight, and I'd like to assume that ten years later they still didn't. My father generally gave in to my mother's whims to avoid conflict, but it seemed he'd had enough of her in recent days.

My mother cleared her throat. "All I was saying," she said a bit gentler, "is that Lyanna should not risk getting sick. She's only just returned to us." She looked over at me from across the table knowingly. She wanted me to agree with her.

"Mother might have a point," I conceded as I stared down at my empty plate. Breakfast hadn't even been served and we were already at each other's throats. "For now, I'll avoid the infirmary unless it's necessary."

My father sighed. "If you wish, Lyanna." He glanced at Caelan, who sat beside my mother. "Caelan, I know what you want. I'm just not sure I can give it to you."

Caelan turned his shrewd gaze to my father and smiled politely. "No decisions need to be made right away. I would be content with an engagement for now."

My father cleared his throat. "Well ..."

"She doesn't like you, Caelan. Why are you forcing the issue?" Marcellus barked abruptly.

"Marcellus!" my mother chided. "Mind your tongue!"

"Marcel is right," my father said. "We need to take Lyanna's feelings into consideration. I refuse to force my children into political marriages."

My mother turned her icy stare my way. "Of course this

is what Lyanna wants. Isn't that right, dear?" She stared me down and willed me to agree with her once more.

I knew the answer she wanted from me. She wanted me to agree with her as I always used to do to please her. But not this time. No. This was something I couldn't agree to. This was marriage. A lifelong commitment. And even if that wasn't the case, too much unpleasantness had passed between me and Caelan in the Central Plains. If I turned around and married him, what would that make me? For the first time, I understood Ronan's train of thought.

"No," I said clearly. "I do *not* want to marry Caelan, nor will I ever."

My mother slammed her palm on the table, making everything rattle once again. "Nonsense! You don't know what you want!"

"And you do?" I countered with a raised brow. "You've been my mother for only half of my life. You don't know me."

She scoffed, clearly offended. "I am your mother! Of course I know you!"

"Do you really? What's my favorite food? How do I like my baths? What's my favorite color? Do you know what my passions are—"

"All of that is irrelevant." She waved me off. "I know what's important, and that's for you to enter into a proper marriage with someone at the same level as you. Not some riff-raff from the Grasslands."

My brows shot up at the mention of Ronan. "I never said I wanted to marry anyone from the Grasslands."

My mother laughed dryly and fixed me with a calculating glare. "As if we haven't heard the rumors? Lyanna, we weren't born yesterday. Please don't insult our intelligence."

So the rumors had spread, just as I predicted. Maybe it

was for the best. Eventually I would have to make my feelings known. Ronan and I couldn't sneak around forever.

"So?" Marcellus shrugged. "So what if she wants to marry into the Grasslands? Ronan is a son of a Chief; he's no riff-raff, as you say. This could be a good alliance—"

"Enough, Marcellus!" my father barked. "No one is marrying into the Grasslands." He looked away nervously.

I frowned and worried if they were afraid of the prophecy. Sir Edric did mention that they knew about it because Chief Aryan contacted them to make a trade. It was one of the things Sir Edric feared the most – that eventually my parents would give in.

"Father," I started, but he glared and cut me off.

"I'm sorry, Caelan, but if Lyanna does not agree to a marriage with you, I fear I won't be able to either," he said.

Marcel and I deflated in relief. I peered over at my brother, wondering when he'd become a fan of Ronan. The last time we were arguing in the Central Plains, I distinctly remembered him calling me a Crimson whore. Oh, how the tides had changed.

Caelan nodded. "I understand, Your Majesty. But I hope you won't reject me so quickly and will give me time to court Lyanna in the hopes of changing her mind."

"Hmm ... I can agree with that," my father said. "It'll give you both some time to think things over."

Just then, the servants entered the dining hall with our breakfast, quickly bustling to set the table as we waited in awkward silence. Once they left, the silence continued as we ate. I nibbled on a plate of eggs, wishing for a mooncake instead.

Marcellus leaned into me and whispered, "Are you really going to try with him?"

I snorted. "No way. But it'll look bad if Father continues

rejecting him, so I guess he has to accept it for now," I whispered back.

Marcellus shook his head. "This is crazy. After everything Caelan did to you, I can't believe he has the nerve ..."

I furrowed my brows at him. "Isn't he your friend? Didn't you use to hate me?"

He rolled his eyes. "Water under the bridge, sis. And of course I'm going to take your side over his."

"You know what the Crimson Clan wants to do with me." He nodded grimly. "Would you really be okay with me marrying into the Grasslands?"

He scoffed. "Of course not. The last thing I want is for you to be in their grasp. But ..." he sighed. "I know how you feel about Ronan. It's obvious to everyone. And I think he feels the same in return, which means he wouldn't let anything happen to you."

I chuckled and covered my mouth when my mother looked over at me. "You're quite trusting," I said once she looked away.

"Don't let my handsome face fool you," Marcellus said. "If he were ever to sacrifice you as you said, I'd lay waste to the Grasslands without hesitation."

I smiled at my brother. Our relationship now was decidedly different from just a few days ago when he thought I was the absolute worst. Now ... I didn't know what he thought of me, but at least it wasn't hatred.

"What are you two whispering about over there?" my mother asked with a frown.

"Nothing," Marcellus and I answered at the same time.

Our father laughed. "Derinda, leave them be. It's good to see them bonding."

Our mother huffed but didn't say a word. Marcellus and

I shared another mischievous look as if we were in on some secret.

"All right, I think I've eaten enough. Are you ready, Derinda?" my father asked as he tossed his napkin onto the table and pushed his chair back, standing.

My mother sighed. "I suppose." She gently patted the corners of her mouth and set her napkin aside before standing.

Without another word, our parents left the dining hall, leaving me alone with Marcellus and Caelan.

"I hope you'll give me a chance, Lyanna," Caelan murmured, leaning forward. "All I want is a chance."

I sighed and rolled my eyes. "It's not like I have a choice."

"Ronan can't give you what I can," he insisted. "If what you said is true, then being with him is even more dangerous. You can't risk—"

"I'll make my own decisions," I said quickly as I threw my napkin on the table. I'd had more than enough of this conversation already. Pushing my chair back, I stood. "I said I'd give you a chance because my father agreed to it. But don't expect me to like it."

I hurried out of the dining hall with Marcellus calling after me. I didn't want to ignore him, but I also didn't want to keep repeating the same old song and dance with Caelan. No matter how many times I said no, he still didn't understand.

Viktor and Tessa were waiting for me outside the dining hall. We quickly departed the Central palace and headed back to the Eastern palace.

When I entered my chambers, I should have been surprised to see Ronan lying on my bed, but of course I wasn't. His boots were lined up in front of the footboard, his ankles crossed and his hands tucked behind his head. A smirk splayed across his face the instant I stepped through the door. It was absolutely irresistible and brightened my mood considerably.

I chuckled. "What are you doing here?"

His grin widened. "I thought we could explore beyond the palace grounds today. Maybe take a stroll in the capital and get some of those mooncakes you love so much."

It was as if he read my mind. "I was just thinking about a mooncake! I was going to tell Tessa to ask the kitchen to make some."

Ronan sat up and gave a devastating grin. "Why ask, when we can venture to the capital where they've already been made? Come on, Leila. Let's explore Valoria. I'm sure things aren't the same as when you were eleven."

I walked toward him and perched at the edge of my bed. "I'll have to ask permission to leave the palace," I groaned. "And after the breakfast I just had, I doubt my mother would allow it."

He frowned. "Everything okay?"

I shook my head. "Caelan keeps insisting on the marriage alliance, and my mother is all for it. Luckily Marcellus and my father are not, but Caelan requested an opportunity to court me in the hopes he can change my mind."

Ronan rolled his eyes and muttered, "Well, he's persistent, I'll give him that much."

I attempted to ease his worries. "I won't change my mind, no matter what he does."

He nodded. "Still, his persistence is worrisome. I don't know why, but I sense he has something up his sleeve."

"Possibly, but I don't want to think about him now," I said. "Is there anything else we could do besides leaving the palace grounds?"

Ronan raised a mischievous brow. "Well Leila, I'm sure we can think of *something*." He slid closer, then grabbed my waist and flipped me onto my back until he hovered over me. "Why don't we …?" he trailed off as his fingers glided down to the buttons that ran down the front of my dress.

"Ronan…" I moaned as he began to unbutton my dress. "We can't keep doing this, or we'll eventually get caught."

He brought his lips to mine, effectively shutting me up. Our mouths melded into one another and I wrapped my arms around his neck, pulling him closer. His hard body pressed against mine and I couldn't resist roaming my hands over his skin. He was utter perfection, his beauty unmatched.

"I wish we could stay in bed all day long," Ronan murmured, trailing a fiery path of kisses down my neck to my chest. He unbuttoned the top of my dress and exposed my breasts, kissing them gently before taking my nipple into his mouth.

I worried others outside my room would hear the moan of ecstasy that erupted from me. My hands dug into Ronan's hair, needing to take ahold of something as his tongue licked, swirled, and sucked on my breasts.

My eyes rolled to the back of my head. "I want you, Ronan. Desperately."

He paused and peered up at me. "Leila," he whispered, his mouth hovering just above my breast. "If I go any further … it might complicate things."

"Like the prophecy?" I grinded against him. "I don't care. I just want you. *All* of you. *Now*."

He shook his head. "You're not thinking clearly, Leila. If we do this, it'll ignite the prophecy."

"No one has to know," I protested, and he quieted.

He knew I was right. His father wouldn't find out unless one of us told him.

I slowed my feverish movements and opened my eyes. "Wait. What is it that we'll cause?"

"Taking your virginity allows me to possess the sole wish granted by the fox demon if he's resurrected. My father has always wanted me to be the one, but after seeing us together at the banquet, I'm not sure if he feels the same way," Ronan whispered.

Without giving him another second to overthink it, I flipped him onto his back and straddled him. The front of my dress splayed open to expose my breasts.

"I don't care what your father thinks." I slowly lifted his shirt up and over his head. "What matters is what *we* want. And what I want is *you*."

I feathered my fingertips across the defined planes and curves of his hard abdomen, tracing the ridges of muscle that tensed under my touch. Slowly, I inched closer to the button of his trousers with a mischievous smile. With eager anticipation, I pulled down his pants, releasing his throbbing member from its confines. I wrapped my hand around his shaft and stroked him, reveling in the way he hissed and clutched at the bedsheets.

"Leila ... are you sure?" he asked once again, a hint of hesitation in his voice. "Once we cross this line, there's no going back."

A grin spread across my face as I looked down at him. "That's exactly what I want," I replied confidently. "I don't want you to hold back anymore." Without another word, I lowered myself down his body and took the tip of his cock into my mouth. His hand tangled into my hair, holding me steady as he guided me up and down his length with gentle motions.

As I took him deeper into my mouth with each stroke, Ronan let out a low groan and closed his eyes in bliss. But it didn't take long until he lost all sense of control. With a tight grip on my hair, he started thrusting into my mouth with more force and urgency.

"Fuck, Leila!" he moaned. Unable to restrain himself any longer, he pushed me off him and lifted me onto the bed, quickly discarding his pants before readying himself between my legs. "I won't hold back," he murmured, staring deep into my eyes as he positioned himself at my entrance. "This is your last chance to turn back."

But I was already too far gone to even consider it. "Don't hold back," I whispered, wrapping an arm around his neck and bringing his lips toward mine. "I'm yours."

With a deep breath, he slowly pushed into me. The intense pressure and his girth made me gasp in a heady combination of pain and pleasure. I lifted my hips to take more of him in, determined to handle it all.

Once he was fully sheathed inside of me, my core pulsing with sensation, he started to move. A cry escaped my throat, but Ronan swallowed the sound with a passionate kiss as he pumped in and out of me at a slow pace before gradually picking up speed.

"You're incredible," he gasped between kisses. "By the gods, Leila, you have no idea how many times I've thought about having you ... *all* of you."

I met his thrusts eagerly, reveling in the feeling of being completely consumed by him. "I'm all yours," I promised.

"And I'm yours," he repeated, the look in his eyes telling me that he meant every word.

As he continued to drive into me with increasing intensity, my body trembled with anticipation. He spread my legs wider and took me even deeper than before, hitting a spot that sent a wave of sensations washing over me, making my vision blur slightly.

"Oh, gods!" An explosive orgasm ripped through me, my legs shaking from the force of it.

Ronan slowed his movements, mindful of my overstimulated body. As he eased down and kissed me softly, I basked in the perfectness of the moment.

"You're beautiful," he whispered against my lips. "I never want to leave this room."

A grin spread across my face as I returned his kiss. "Then don't."

As the passion between us intensified, Ronan's crimson eyes locked onto mine. His gaze was filled with a love I'd never seen before; the intensity sent shivers down my spine. He moved faster, his rhythm almost frantic. I wrapped my legs around his waist and pulled him in deeper.

The room was filled with the sound of slapping bodies, groans, and heavy breathing. It was as if we'd left the world we knew and had been transported to another realm where we were the only two people who existed.

As he continued to thrust into me, I felt my body building up to another climax. I moaned his name, my voice echoing in the room. He groaned and matched my rhythm as he thrust into me harder and faster. My body shivered with every stroke and heightened pleasure built within me. I gasped, my breaths becoming shorter and heavier as my climax neared.

Ronan's muscles bulged with each movement, a feast for

the eyes. I reached up and ran my hands over his broad, sculpted shoulders and back, feeling the sweat that beaded on his skin. His breaths became ragged, and his eyes locked onto mine as he reached the edge of his own pleasure.

With a final thrust, Ronan cried out my name, his body shuddering as he released himself inside me. I felt his warm release filling me, and I knew it was only for me. The feeling of being so connected to him was overwhelming.

As we lay there, both panting heavily, I traced my fingers over his skin. His eyes met mine and I saw unbridled love and devotion swimming in their depths.

"I love you, Leila."

Those words were monumental, but something stopped me from saying it back. Instead, I smiled up at him and caressed his face.

We lay there for a moment, basking in the afterglow, our hearts beating in sync. The room was filled with the scent of our sweat and arousal. We finally broke apart and I rolled onto my side, pulling him close to me.

"Stay with me?" I asked, my voice barely a whisper.

He grinned and pressed a soft kiss to my lips. "There's nowhere else I'd rather be."

And so we lay there in the aftermath of our lovemaking, listening to each other's heartbeats and the gentle sounds of our breaths mingling in the air. The world outside the door could wait. For now, we were content in our own universe.

15

We spent the day in bed doing the kinds of things that would make a lady blush. I was voracious, and almost didn't want to leave until Viktor knocked on the door, informing us that dinner had been served. Unwilling to allow the bubble we'd built around us to pop, I took Ronan up on his offer to explore the capital.

Escaping the confines of the palace felt like shedding a second skin, one made of lofty expectations and responsibilities. As Ronan and I slipped through the ornate gates, disguised in cloaks that blended with the crowd, a sense of liberation enveloped me. The capital of Valoria, with its bustling streets and vibrant marketplaces, was a stark contrast to the silent, echoing halls of the palace.

"Where to first?" Ronan asked, his voice low, almost blending with the murmur of the crowd.

I pulled my cloak tighter around me, the fabric whispering against my skin. "Let's just walk. I want to see everything. It's been ten years since I last roamed the capital."

As we meandered through the cobblestone streets, the

cacophony of the capital surrounded us—a symphony of haggling voices, laughter, and the distant melody of a lute player. The air was rich with fragrant spices and freshly baked bread that mingled with the slightly cooler breeze that promised the onset of evening.

"Look at that!" I exclaimed, pointing to a stall adorned with vibrant fabrics from distant lands. The colors were a feast for the eyes, patterns dancing in the fabric as if alive.

Ronan leaned closer, his interest piqued. "You have an eye for beauty, Leila. Shall we get one as a keepsake?"

Before I could respond, the scent of something sweet and warm tugged at my senses. "Mooncakes," I murmured almost to myself, drawn to a nearby stall where a kindly old man was displaying an array of the delicacies under a sign that read, "Moonlight Delights."

"Ah, mooncakes," Ronan echoed, a smile playing on his lips. "Just what we were looking for! Let's get some. How many do you think we should buy?"

I approached the stall, mesmerized by the wide array of mooncakes, each imprinted with delicate patterns. "Maybe a dozen? Some for now, and some to share with Henry and Selene."

The old man behind the stall caught our attention and beamed, his eyes crinkling at the corners. "A dozen it is. Would you like to try the lotus paste or the red bean? We also have a special filling made from the sweetest dates."

Ronan looked at me, a silent question in his gaze. "Your choice, Leila."

"Let's try a mix of all three," I decided, excitement bubbling within me. "And could we have two of each to eat now?"

The old man nodded, carefully packing our selection into a box adorned with images of the moon in various phases. As he handed the box to us, I couldn't help but feel a connection to this place, to these moments of simplicity and joy. I thanked the man and Ronan handed over the coins as payment. We each took a mooncake and slowly bit into the sweet, rich filling that seemed to melt on the tongue.

As we continued our exploration of the capital, mooncakes in hand, the sights and sounds of the city felt like a vibrant tapestry unfolding before us. The laughter and chatter around us seemed to echo the lightness in my heart—a lightness born from the simple pleasure of sharing mooncakes with someone who understood the value of these moments, away from the shadows of the palace.

"Today is absolutely perfect," I said, my voice barely above a whisper, afraid to break the magic of the moment.

Ronan glanced at me. His crimson eyes were soft under the hood of his cloak. "It's not over yet, Leila. There's so much more to see, and I'm right here with you."

Just then, I believed him. The capital, with its endless possibilities and hidden corners, felt like a promise of more days like this—days filled with discovery, laughter, and the shared sweetness of mooncakes under a vast, unjudging sky.

"By the goddess, I can't believe this is still here!" I hurried over to a children's toy store, one in which I'd whiled away many hours as a child. I gazed up at the storefront. "My father would take me and Marcellus here whenever we managed to sneak out of the palace."

"I'm almost certain you would have caused your father to go broke," Ronan chided, and I lightly punched his arm. "Come on, let's keep walking."

The allure of the city's heartbeat drew us further into its embrace, leading us to a cozy tavern tucked away on a side street, its warm light spilling out onto the cobblestones.

"Why don't we try some of the Love in the Moonlight wine here?" Ronan suggested, a playful challenge in his eyes.

The tavern's name, The Crescent Pour, was painted in elegant script above the door, a nod to Valoria's belief in the moon goddess. As we stepped inside, the lively melody of a string quartet greeted us, music weaving through the air like threads of silver moonlight.

The atmosphere inside was buzzing, a vibrant mix of locals and travelers alike, all drawn in by the promise of good music and finer drinks. We found a table near the back, a small, intimate space that felt removed from the hustle of the tavern.

A server approached, her smile as welcoming as the tavern itself. "What can I get for you this evening?"

"We'll have a jug of Love in the Moonlight, please," I replied, my excitement for the wine evident.

As we waited, a troupe of performers took to the small stage at the front of the tavern. Their act was a mesmerizing blend of dance and acrobatics, each movement in perfect harmony with the music, as if the melody itself guided them through their performance.

Our wine arrived, served in delicate glasses that caught the light, making the liquid within shimmer like its namesake. "To us," Ronan toasted, raising his glass.

"To us," I echoed. The wine was sweet and fragrant on my lips, a perfect complement to the joy of the evening.

As we drank our wine, the performers continued to captivate the audience, their finale a breathtaking display of skill that earned them thunderous applause. The energy in the tavern was infectious, a reminder of the world's beauty and the simple pleasures that made life worth savoring.

"Did you enjoy the performance?" Ronan asked, his eyes reflecting the tavern's warm glow.

"I did. I wish these moments could last forever," I confessed, the bustling energy of the tavern and the day's earlier adventures mingling into a perfect memory.

"Then let's make more memories, Leila. Not just tonight, but every chance we get," Ronan proposed, his hand finding mine across the table.

In The Crescent Pour, surrounded by laughter, music, and the taste of Love in the Moonlight on our tongues, the world outside faded away. It was just Ronan and me, finding solace and excitement in the hidden corners of Valoria, away from the weight of crowns and familial duties. Tonight, we were simply two souls intertwined by the magic of the moment, eager to explore all the wonders that lay waiting in the shadow and light of the moon.

I couldn't stop the grin that spread across my face. Thank the goddess I was wearing a cloak and it wasn't visible. Unfortunately, we had to stay hidden. With his startling eyes and tattoos, it was obvious Ronan was a Crimson Clan member, and if they saw him with me, a mage from Valoria, it would raise eyebrows and possibly start trouble due to our fraternization.

"What do you want to do next?" Ronan asked. "I'm sure there's much more to see and do. The night is still young and I'm all yours."

"For starters, I want to finish this jug of wine!" I poured myself another cup. "Then, maybe we can go on a boat ride on the river that cuts through the capital. It'll be a great way to see everything."

Ronan chuckled at my plan, the low timbre of his laughter blending seamlessly with the tavern's ambient sounds. "That sounds like a perfect plan. But let's make sure we can still find our way to the river after this jug of wine," he teased, raising his glass in a half-toast before taking another sip.

The wine, Love in the Moonlight, lived up to its name. Each sip was a poetic symphony of flavors that seemed to dance across the palate. It was easy to get lost in the moment, as the rich notes of the wine were a perfect accompaniment to the lively tunes played by the musicians in the corner of the tavern.

We savored our drinks and enjoyed the performances, each act as captivating as the last, weaving an enchanting tapestry of art and entertainment that held the tavern's patrons spellbound. It was a testament to the vibrant culture of Valoria, a city that pulsed with life and creativity at every turn.

We were listening to a wonderful singer when the conversation at the table beside us caught our attention.

"Did you hear?" one of the men at the table asked. "The lost heir has returned."

The other man nodded. "Yes; didn't you see all the guests who came to the capital these past few days? They were here to see her return for themselves."

"What do you think King Malik will do? Is there any hope?"

The other man shrugged. "With the queen in his ear, I doubt it," he said. "She's never been warm toward the lost heir. There are many who say she despises her."

The man sighed. "What a shame. If the Crown Prince takes the throne, dark times will come to Valoria. He's nothing but a child."

"There's rumors he didn't even lead the army down to the Central Plains. They say it was Prince Caelan of Eldwain who took charge!"

"Exactly. It's why..." he lowered his voice and glanced

around the tavern for anyone who might be eavesdropping, assuming Ronan and I couldn't hear, "...the scholars are petitioning for the lost heir to take his place."

I frowned. *Who are they talking about?* And what kind of reputation does Marcel have if Valoria's people speak about him in this manner?

"Ronan," I whispered as I leaned toward him. "Are you listening?"

He nodded.

"Who is the lost heir?" I asked, feeling a knot form in my stomach.

"I've never heard of a lost heir ... but I assume they're speaking about you," he whispered in return.

My eyes widened and for the second time tonight, I thanked the goddess that part of my face was obscured by the cloak's hood. I flagged down the server and requested another jug of Love in the Moonlight.

"Leila!" Ronan attempted to stop me. "I think one jug is enough—"

The server returned in minutes and placed a fresh jug on the table. "Wait here," I said.

Without taking time to think through what I was about to do, I grabbed the jug and sauntered over to the table where the men were gossiping. I slid into an empty chair and tossed my cloak's hood back to expose the crescent moon birthmark on my forehead. The same one the men had, which let them know I was one of them. Thankfully, no one in Valoria knew what the princess looked like, so I was able to blend in as a commoner.

"What is this about the lost heir?" A smirk curled across my lips as I poured them a drink from my wine jug.

One of the men raised a brow, surprised by my audacity

to interrupt a conversation they thought was private. "Who are you?"

I shrugged and offered my most charming smile. "I don't mean to startle you, but I overheard your conversation and it piqued my curiosity. I've never heard of a lost heir. Are you referring to the lost princess?"

The men took a drink and their eyes widened.

"Is this Love in the Moonlight?" the other man asked in shock.

I nodded and my grin widened. "Just sharing with friends."

They each took bigger gulps, then poured more of the free wine. The very expensive, free wine.

One of the men leaned forward and whispered, "The lost heir is the lost princess. For over a decade, the mages of Valoria have petitioned that the line of succession be altered and she be made Crown Princess instead of her younger brother, which the king has refused."

My eyes widened. "Is that so?" I poured them some more wine. "Why do the mages want her to be the Crown Princess?"

One of the men leaned in conspiratorially, warming up to the topic. "Well—"

"Shh!" the other man stopped him. "We cannot speak of this. If anyone else overhears …"

The man brushed him off. "No one's listening, mate!"

I fought the urge to laugh because they'd obviously forgotten I had eavesdropped on them and was sitting with them now. But the wine made it a distant memory.

"You know the lost princess is the first female blood mage since the moon goddess, right?" the man whispered and leaned forward.

I nodded.

"Well, they say she's the reincarnation of the moon goddess." His eyes widened with barely contained excitement.

I frowned, not believing this so-called theory for a second. "Really? How so?"

The other man shrugged. "I mean, the only other female blood mage in history was the moon goddess. That means it has to be true, right?"

Not necessarily, I thought, but I didn't want to mess with their illusion or make them start asking me questions. I remained quiet as they continued to ramble about the lost heir, who happened to be sitting in front of them. I wondered if the moon goddess theory was a well-known one that I just never knew about.

I poured them some more wine. "Didn't the moon goddess refuse to enter politics? Didn't she want to stay neutral and protect Valoria without interfering with the monarch?" I asked curiously, hoping I'd remembered history correctly.

One of the men nodded. "True. But from what I heard, it wasn't that she didn't want to, but more like the king at the time refused her."

The other man nodded eagerly as he chugged his wine. "I heard a rumor she had an affair that the king was completely against, and that was his way of punishing her. But we all know the moon goddess was the *true* heir to the throne. We only survived Keldara because of her."

"That's why the lost princess needs to become Crown Princess," the man closest to me added, beginning to slur his words. "She's the oldest child of the king and the rightful heir, as the reincarnation of the moon goddess. She'll be the one to save us from Keldara again."

I cleared my throat. "Does everyone believe this theory about the lost heir being the moon goddess?"

The man closest to me shook his head. "Only in Valoria. I don't believe any outsiders know."

"Oh ..." I stood, then topped off their cups with more wine. "Well, thank you for the information. I appreciate your time."

"Of course!" the men said, waving me off before clinking their cups together to celebrate their good fortune.

On leaden feet, I stumbled back to our table where Ronan was waiting for me.

"So?" he asked as I sat. "What did they say?"

"It's just as you predicted. They're talking about me," I mumbled in a daze. "They believe I'm the reincarnation of the moon goddess."

Even though I couldn't see his expression within the darkened folds of his cloak, Ronan tensed. "And what do *you* think?"

I shrugged. "I think it's rubbish. There's no way I'm the reincarnation of the moon goddess. I'm my own person."

Ronan nodded. "Yeah, I don't think so, either," he muttered uncertainly.

I sighed and tossed back the rest of my wine, then tipped the empty jug. Warmth from the last bit of wine spread through my limbs and left me with a pleasant buzz that made the world seem a bit brighter, even after my unsettling conversation.

"Alright, I think we've finished it. Let's head to the river. I remember the night views being something you can't miss."

After paying, we made our way out of the tavern, the cool night air a refreshing contrast to the warmth inside. Valoria's streets still bustled with activity, and the city basked in a gentle luminescence that seemed to guide our steps toward the river.

"Winter is coming." I wrapped the cloak tighter around me and pulled the hood back over my head. "I can feel it in the air."

Ronan nodded. "Yes, it's getting chilly. Do you want to head back? We can always come back another time."

I shook my head. "No. I want it to be tonight." With an affirmative nod, we continued walking. I didn't know when we'd have this opportunity again. I was sure once my mother learned about me sneaking off to the capital, she'd make sure I never got another chance to leave again.

The river was a serene sight. Its waters reflected the moonlight and the city's twinkling lights. We found a boat ready for hire; its keeper was a jovial man who seemed ready to sell us on the boat ride.

"Taking a ride under the moon, are we?" the boatman asked with a knowing smile as he helped us aboard. "You've picked a beautiful night for it."

Taking my hand in his, Ronan helped me onto the vessel and then followed, taking a seat beside me.

"Are you both travelers?" the boatman asked. "I've never seen anybody look so mysterious around these parts."

Ronan and I laughed. "It's really cold," I said as I rubbed my arms. "We're just trying to stay warm."

The boatman nodded and pushed off the bank. Though he seemed unconvinced by our story, he knew better than to bite the hand that paid him. As the boat glided through the water, the city's beauty unfolded before us in a new light, the reflections on the water adding a layer of magic to an already mesmerizing view. Gently lapping waves against the boat provided a serene soundtrack to our journey, a peaceful interlude in the bustling life of the capital.

"There's something truly special about Valoria at night," I mused aloud, captivated by the illuminated buildings and bridges we passed.

Ronan nodded, his gaze fixed on the same enchanting views. "There is. And I can't think of anyone I'd rather share this moment with."

In that tranquil boat ride, the complexities of our lives seemed to drift away, leaving behind a moment of pure, unadulterated beauty. It was a reminder of the simplicity at the heart of happiness, a simplicity found in shared experiences and the quiet majesty of the world around us.

"But," Ronan started, "you've never seen the night sky until you've seen it in the Grasslands. Stars glitter the skies and the full moon shines brightly overhead. Stealthy animals silently sing in the stillness. It's ... it's truly the best, and one of a kind."

I gave him a tight smile. The Grasslands was one place I didn't think I could ever go without risking my life. Especially after what we did today. While I loved every single minute I spent in bed with Ronan, I knew there would be repercussions for our actions. In the moment, I didn't care about any of them. Even now, I needed him more than I needed to breathe, and I didn't regret a second of it.

As the boat gently rocked beneath us, guided by the silent strokes of the boatman, I felt the weight of Ronan's words settle around us like a comforting cloak. The city lights danced on the water's surface, providing a mesmerizing backdrop to our conversation.

"Ronan," I whispered and reached for his hand. "Do you think—"

"Nothing those men said were true," he interrupted, his voice firm yet tender, cutting through my hesitation with a calm reassurance that warmed me to my core.

"They might consider you the lost heir, but you're just Leila to me."

I couldn't help but smile at his steadfast declaration, highlighted by the moon casting a soft glow over his features. "You never call me Lyanna … Why not?"

Ronan offered a shrug, a simple gesture laden with meaning. "I've met Lyanna, and she was lovely … but I fell in love with Leila. And *that* is who you are."

I furrowed my brows. "You met me as the princess before? When?"

His laughter was soft, carrying across the water. "You may not remember. You were around eight years old, I think. It was during the fifth wedding of the Eldwain King."

My furrowed brows deepened as I tried to remember. I remembered going to Eldwain, but I didn't remember meeting anyone from the Grasslands. I spent most of the time playing with Marcellus, Caelan, and his brothers. I was usually the only girl in the group. The scattered, hazy fragments of my childhood failed to conjure the image of a young Ronan in my mind. Yet, his assurance that the memory held value for him filled me with a curious warmth.

"It's okay if you don't remember. What matters is that *I* remember." He brought my hand to his lips. "And it's a memory I cherish dearly."

"Yet you fell in love with Leila … not Lyanna," I clarified.

He nodded. "Correct. Leila the healer was nothing like the pampered princess I met back then … although I have to say I never got over the fact you stood me up," he smirked.

My brows shot up. "What?"

Ronan chuckled. "We met earlier in the day and made plans to meet again at midnight to see the stars, but you never showed."

I frowned and tried to remember that night. I couldn't remember Ronan, but I did remember something... "You said the fifth wedding of the King of Eldwain?" Ronan nodded. "If I remember correctly, I got sick that night. A fever. My family and I had to leave Eldwain early."

Ronan nodded, slowly processing my words. "So you didn't stand me up," he chuckled. "You were the only one to show me kindness that night, which made it a night I would never forget."

His words, so full of sincerity, sparked laughter within me. Lightness bubbled up and over, carried away by the river's gentle flow. In that moment, floating under the Valorian sky, I was just Leila—a woman defined not by her lineage or duty, but by the connections she forged, by laughter and love, shared under the watchful gaze of the moon.

16

It was around midnight when we returned to the palace. The moon hung heavily in the sky, illuminating Viktor's anxious form, a shadow against the dimly lit entrance. His expression, taut with unease, foretold a brewing storm within the palace walls.

"Viktor!" I called out. "What's wrong? Did something happen?" My voice sliced through the quiet, a ripple in the still night as we drew near.

He bit his lip nervously. His reply, laced with apprehension, struck a chord of alarm. "The queen requested an audience with Selene. I attempted to stop her, but it was no use."

The timing of such a request seemed ominously precise, orchestrated during our absence. "When was this?"

"About an hour ago," Viktor confessed, distress evident in his restless movements. "Apologies, Your Highness."

"No, no, it's not your fault, Viktor. There's nothing you could have done without getting yourself into trouble. Do you know why she was called?" I asked as we passed through the palace gates and entered the palace.

"I sent someone to be our eyes and ears, but I haven't heard back."

I nodded. "Very well. Go to the Western palace and retrieve Marcellus. Inform him of the situation." I turned to Ronan, whose presence would only complicate matters further. "It's probably best if you head back to the Northern palace. It wouldn't bode well for either of us if you came with me."

Ronan nodded. "Be careful."

"Always."

With our paths set, we diverged, each to our own duties. My steps hastened towards the Grand Hall, where the echo of my name announced by the sentinels filled the space. Passing through the doors, the sight brought me to a screeching halt. A tableau of power dynamics laid bare—Selene, vulnerable and on her knees before my mother's imposing figure, ignited a fire within me.

"What's going on?" I demanded as I rushed toward my friend. "Selene?" I attempted to help her up.

"Lyanna!" my mother yelled. "I did *not* give her permission to stand!"

I looked over at my mother in shock. "Why is she here? What could you *possibly* need to discuss with Selene in private? At this hour?"

My mother snorted and looked around in mock surprise. "Is the mermaid off limits? I wasn't aware of this. I wasn't aware that there was something I, the Queen, could not touch."

I sighed. "That's not what I meant, Mother. But—"

"But nothing!" she spat. "I'm merely having a friendly chat with the young mermaid."

With a frown, I glanced down at Selene to see an expression filled with fear. This was far from a friendly conversation. With no other option, I dropped to my knees beside Selene and faced my mother.

"Whatever you need to ask her, you can ask me. There's nothing about her I don't know."

My mother smirked. "Is that so?"

I nodded.

"Very well. Then answer me this: where does this young woman come from?" she asked, as if she already knew the answer.

Her confidence made my frown deepen. "She comes from the Luminar Sea off the coast of Keldara."

"No, Lyanna. I mean *where* has she come from most recently?"

My eyes widened at the implication. There was no way she knew or could have found out that Selene worked in a pleasure house. Not without someone telling her.

Selene sighed. "In the Central Plains, I resided in a pleasure house," Selene relented. "I was sold into servitude by my father at the age of twelve. I've been at the Rose Petal Lounge since then."

Silence encompassed the room before my mother scoffed and turned her attention to me. "And yet you *dare* bring a prostitute onto palace grounds?" she shouted.

My face bloomed an angry shade of red and I gritted my teeth. "She's not a prostitute, she was a courtesan. But not anymore. And even if she was, why would that matter? She's a good person and she's helped me a lot in the last five years."

"I don't care if she's the goddess herself.!" my mother fumed. "She's a danger to those in the palace. I want her out!"

"A danger?" I scoffed. "How?"

My mother's eyes widened and her mouth fell open. "Do

you *dare* the risk of her seducing Marcellus, or worse, your father?"

I felt sick to my stomach. I could only imagine how Selene felt hearing such shameful accusations being thrown her way. But I didn't dare look at her. I was embarrassed to even face her.

The doors to the Grand Hall burst open before an announcement could be made. I whirled around to see Marcellus storming inside with a thunderous expression.

"Mother!" His eyes widened at the sight of me and Selene on our knees before the throne. "What are you *doing*?"

"What should have been done days ago, Marcellus. Getting rid of the trash." Our mother looked away dismissively.

"Who is in your ear?" Marcellus demanded.

Our mother gasped. "You think someone has fed me this information?"

"Yes!" Marcellus and I shouted in unison.

"How *dare* you!" she yelled as she stood from her throne. "My own children *dare* disrespect me, all for ... all for a prostitute!"

Selene's shoulders slumped and she lowered her head in shame. The sight of her like that only angered me further. This was all my fault. Since I arrived, I'd neglected her and wasn't around to protect her. All because I was absorbed by Ronan's presence.

Fueled by anger, I shot to my feet and balled my fists. "I don't care what you say, Mother. The ruler of the Eastern palace is *me*, and I say Selene stays. And I won't abide you calling a guest in my palace a prostitute!"

My mother's eyes slowly widened. "You ... you would defy me ... for *her*?"

I raised my chin defiantly. "Yes."

My mother stormed down the aisle toward me and lifted her hand to slap me, but before she could, my hand darted into the air and I seized the blood flowing through her veins.

She froze in place, and I couldn't imagine her eyes growing any bigger. "Lyanna!" she gasped.

Marcellus turned to me with startled eyes. "Lyanna," he whispered. "You can't use your powers on our mother ... She might be wrong, but ... she's still our mother!"

"I. Don't. Care," I gritted. "I've been on my own for the last ten years. I refuse to be controlled by anyone!" I tightened my hand into a fist and squeezed, watching as she crumbled to the marble floor.

"Lyanna!" Marcellus shouted and ran toward me, grabbing my fist and trying to open my hand. "This is our *mother*!"

I relaxed my hand and Mother collapsed, gasping for air. When Marcellus gaped at me in shock, I knew I made a mistake. I went too far. Horrified, I glanced down at my hands and wondered what the hell had come over me.

"You went too far, Lyanna," Marcellus whispered. "She won't let this slide."

Just then, Father stormed into the Grand Hall with purposeful steps. When he saw the scene before him, his steps faltered and angry red circles bloomed on his cheeks.

"What is going on?" he shouted. "Who did this?" He offered Mother a hand and gently helped her stand.

"Father—" I started, but I was promptly cut off.

"Malik!" my mother gasped. "This child just tried to kill me!" In a turn no one expected, she pointed a trembling finger at Selene.

"What?" Marcellus and I shrieked.

"No she didn't!" I countered. "It was *me*. I used my powers on her."

"You never would have attacked me if it wasn't for that mermaid!" my mother accused.

My father switched his glare to Selene, who was frozen on her knees. I quickly stood in front of her, blocking her from my father's ire. "If you're going to throw Selene out, then you might as well throw me out, too," I said.

"Me too!" Marcellus stood beside me in solidarity. "Selene did nothing wrong."

My father's face looked pained. "Lyanna," he started, "I don't know what's going through your mind, but to do this to your mother over an ... *outsider* is unacceptable."

I frowned. "She's not an outsider. She's my family."

"She's a prostitute!" my mother screamed.

My father's eyes widened at Mother's declaration. "What did you say?"

Still leaning on him for support, my mother's eyes glinted vindictively. "She's a—"

"She's a courtesan," I interrupted. "Or at least, she was until Marcellus freed her."

My father visibly relaxed, but his shoulders were still tensed. "Well, since she's free, maybe it's best if she goes elsewhere."

"If she leaves, I leave," I retorted, crossing my arms defiantly. "That's the deal."

"Fine. Leave then!" my mother shouted.

"Derinda!" my father scolded. "We just got her back! How could you say that?"

To emphasize the point that our family squabbles were never private, the doors to the Grand Hall opened and the sentinels announced Caelan's arrival. I rolled my eyes. This honestly couldn't have gotten any worse.

"Apologies for my interruption," he said as he strode toward us. "But I heard about the situation and thought I could be of aid."

He heard? Or was he the one who informed Mother of Selene's past? Something about this didn't add up, and I had a feeling it was all being orchestrated by Caelan. He was a master puppeteer and we were all his puppets.

He bowed to my parents and stood beside Marcellus. "If Selene's presence is such an issue, then why not have her work in the palace? Have her earn her keep."

"Fuck, no!" I exclaimed. "She just got her freedom and you want her to be sold into servitude again? Are you insane?"

Caelan shrugged. "I don't believe Marcellus has actually given her the slave release documents, so technically, she was sold by the Rose Petal to Marcellus, making her his property to do with as he wishes."

My eyes widened and my mouth fell open in shock. Caelan knew how much Selene meant to me and how ardently I strived to gain her freedom. For him to do this – to offer such a heartless suggestion – only confirmed that he was the one whispering in my mother's ear.

"Caelan, I swear to the goddess, I will kill you," I threatened.

The bastard raised his hands placatingly as if soothing a wild beast. "It was merely a suggestion, Lyanna. No need to get hostile. It's up to Selene." He looked down at her. "What do you say, Selene? Get kicked out of the palace, or become a court lady?"

Up until now, Marcellus had been quiet. But his anger had steadily grown with Caelan's appearance. He cleared his throat and glared at his former friend. "I don't see how any of this is your business, Caelan, but since you commented, let me clarify some things. First, Selene is not my *property*, as you called it. I've already had the release documents written up; I just haven't had the opportunity to give them to her. Secondly, the option to become a member of the house or be expelled from it is a threat, and I don't appreciate you getting involved in a family matter. If you're that bored, you should return to Eldwain and handle your own family squabbles." He leaned closer to Caelan's face and sneered, "In any event, stay out of ours."

I was shocked at the suddenness of my brother's aggressiveness toward Caelan. As young boys they were inseparable, and he'd always considered Caelan like an older brother. I saw their bond had only deepened over time when they were in the Central Plains. But right now, it felt as if Marcel was severing all their ties. Selene must truly mean a lot to him.

"Marcellus?" Caelan started, surprise evident in his voice.

Marcel turned his attention back to our father. "It seems Caelan has been whispering nonsense into Mother's ear, hence her audacious reaction and threats. Selene is a free individual, and if anyone," he glared at Caelan pointedly, "tries to take that away from her, they'll have *me* to answer to."

I leaned down beside my friend. "Selene," I whispered. "Come on, stand. You don't need to kneel before anyone."

My mother scoffed. "Excuse me?"

"Enough, Derinda!" my father boomed. "Lyanna is correct. We are not the type to abuse our power against those who are weaker than us."

Slowly, Selene stood on wobbly legs as I supported her arm. Turning to my father, I announced, "Selene is a guest of the Eastern palace. If there's ever a problem with that, you can take it up with me. There's no need to speak to my guests in private."

"Understood, Lyanna. You can take her back to your palace," my father said. "You're all dismissed ... except Caelan. Stay back for a moment."

Marcel and I helped Selene out of the hall. We let out a collective breath when the heavy doors closed behind us.

Viktor's silhouette emerged from the inky shadows, a beacon of concern and loyalty. "Is everything all right, Your Highness?" he inquired, his voice laced with unease.

I managed a small nod, an attempt to convey a sense of calm I didn't feel. "All is well. Thank you, Viktor," I replied, the lie bitter on my tongue.

"All is *not* well!" Marcel interjected, his gaze sharp. "Did that bastard really tell Mother Selene came from a pleasure house?"

My laughter was hollow, a sound of scorn rather than amusement. "What do *you* think? Of course he did, and I know exactly why." I met my brother's puzzled look with a hard stare. "He's sending me a message. I bet his little spies told him Ronan and I snuck out of the palace and were walking around the capital. This was a warning."

"Leila?" Selene reached for my hand and gave it a gentle squeeze. "Please don't get into trouble because of me. I'm not—"

"Don't you dare say you're not worth it!" I turned to her, my voice fierce. "If anything, you're caught in the middle of something that has nothing to do with you. This is my fault."

"I never thought Caelan would go to such extremes," Marcellus murmured, then frowned. "But ... you went to the capital?"

Affirming with a nod, I admitted, "Yeah, I, uh ... needed to get out of the palace for a bit."

"With Ronan?" His eyebrow arched in mild amusement.

"Correct," I confirmed a bit defensively.

"Right. No problem there," he mused, a light chuckle escaping him.

"It's fine!" I insisted, feeling the weight of their gazes. "But ... I did hear something strange while we were there."

"What did you hear?" Selene asked.

I turned to my brother. "Marcel, have you heard anything about a lost heir?"

His demeanor shifted in an instant, and a storm seemed to brew in his eyes. "What of it?"

I kept my tone carefully neutral. "I just learned about it, and it seemed to be a big secret that everyone in Valoria was in on, except for me."

Marcellus gave a resigned sigh. "From what I understand, some have been petitioning for you to be named the Crown Princess. It died down when you went missing, but now that you've returned, the capital is all abuzz with those hoping that Father will change the line of succession."

I searched his eyes. "And you don't hate me for it?" I sought assurance, wary of unseen rifts.

Marcel shook his head. "No. Why would I? It's not like it's your doing. Truthfully, I'd step down if this was something you'd like to pursue. You know I never wanted to be king."

His declaration, though generous, left me exasperated. "That's because you're lazy, Marcel, but honestly, you would be an amazing king. Don't give up just yet."

He sighed. "I guess. It's not like I have a choice." Shaking his head, he turned to Selene. "Are you okay, Selene?"

Her response was timid, a mere murmur. "Yes, I'm fine, Your Highness."

"Good, good." He nodded. "Listen, if anything like that ever happens again and Lyanna's not around, I want you to come to the Western palace." He eyed her carefully. I could tell from the worry frowns on his forehead that he was concerned for her safety.

"She'll be well taken care of in the Eastern palace," I reassured them both. "Nothing like this will ever happen again. Rest easy, brother."

Marcellus nodded before taking one last look at Selene and heading back to his palace.

After he disappeared, I turned my attention to Selene, who was wringing her fingers nervously. "I know Marcel already asked, but are you really okay?"

She cleared her throat. "I'm fine. Truly."

I sighed. "It's okay if you're not, Selene. What you just went through … Well, I can't imagine what you're feeling right now."

"Your mother didn't mistreat me … she just asked a lot of questions," Selene whispered as she leaned into me. "She asked me questions about you and Ronan."

I furrowed my brows. "What?"

Selene nodded. "I found it odd that the instant you arrived, she brought up where I came from, because we weren't talking about that at all."

I nervously nibbled my lip and wondered out loud. "She's in league with Caelan. I just know it. She jumped at the chance of a marriage alliance … but *why*? What does she gain from it?"

"I don't know, but she hounded me for an hour and was getting frustrated when I couldn't answer. I think she believes I was protecting you, but truly, Leila, I don't know what *is* going on between you and Ronan."

I exhaled loudly. "Maybe that's for the best."

"Just be careful ... he's still from the Crimson Clan."

Her worries were warranted, but in the same token, no one outside the Grasslands knew what was going on between the Crimson Clan and Keldara. If they did, they probably wouldn't think they were such a threat.

"Come on, let's head back. Henry is probably worried."

17

The Eastern palace was shrouded in darkness when we arrived, the only light coming from flickering torches that lined the stone walls. To my surprise, Ronan was waiting for us with Henry by his side.

"What are you doing here?" I asked, noting the slight tension in Ronan's posture.

"You left the mooncakes with me," he said, holding up the box. "I thought you wanted to share them with Selene and Henry."

"I do," I replied, taking Selene's hand and leading her towards them.

Ronan's gaze flickered between us before he spoke again. "Is everything okay?"

I forced a smile and tried to ignore the knots in my stomach. "It will be." I turned to face Henry and raised an eyebrow at the young boy. "And what are *you* doing up so late?"

Henry squirmed beside Ronan. "I heard some commotion and came out to investigate," he admitted sheepishly.

I ruffled his hair fondly. "Come on, it's time to go back to bed now. Everything is under control."

"Can I at least have a mooncake before bed?" he pleaded, his eyes wide and hopeful.

I laughed. "Of course. Selene, would you mind escorting young Mr. Henry back to his room?" I asked, gesturing towards their direction.

Selene nodded, her eyes cautiously meeting Ronan's before she led Henry back inside.

Once they were gone, I took Ronan's hand and pulled him into my bed chamber, shutting the door behind us. "You're becoming bolder," I commented dryly. "Did anyone see you come here?" My heart raced at the thought of being caught together, but I couldn't resist him any longer.

"I was careful," he whispered.

My hands trembled as he guided me towards the bed. We sank down onto the soft blankets and for a moment, all worries faded away in his embrace. Our breaths mingled in the hushed chamber, the tension between us palpable yet exhilarating. Ronan's touch ignited a fire within me, a fire that threatened to consume all reason and restraint. I leaned in and captured his lips with mine in a fervent kiss that spoke of longing and desire.

His fingers traced patterns along my skin, setting every nerve aflame as we succumbed to the intoxicating dance of passion. The world outside faded away as we lost ourselves in each other, our hearts beating as one in the darkness.

I sighed contentedly as Ronan trailed his lips down my neck, sending shivers down my spine. His touch was electric, igniting a hunger within me that I had suppressed far too long. The room grew warmer with each passing moment, the air thick with anticipation.

"I want you more than anything," Ronan murmured

against my skin, his voice husky with desire. "Now that I've had a taste, I can't seem to get enough."

I met his gaze, my eyes filled with a silent plea for him to continue. "I want you," I whispered, my voice hardly more than a sigh.

With a hunger that matched my own, Ronan's hands roamed my body, worshipping every curve and dip as if he was committing them to memory. The exquisite sensation sent waves of pleasure coursing through me.

As our bodies moved together in a dance as old as time, an overwhelming rush of emotions flooded through me. Desire mingled with love, creating a potent elixir that bound us together in an unbreakable embrace.

Ronan peppered kisses down my body, leaving a fiery path in their wake. His lips stopped as he removed my cloak and roughly pulled my dress apart, revealing my bare skin to the moonlit room.

I trembled under his gaze, feeling exposed and vulnerable in his arms. The desire in his crimson eyes was all-consuming, making my heart race with fear and curiosity.

With a gentle caress, Ronan lifted me onto the bed, our bodies pressing together as we indulged in our desire. The air was filled with a haze of lust and longing.

We moved together in a frenzied dance, our bodies syncing with the rhythm of our hearts. Each touch and kiss were a testament to our deep connection, a bond forged in the heat of passion and burned into our souls. But just as the embers of our love blazed brighter, a sudden noise shattered the tranquility of our stolen moment. Shouts outside my bed chambers jolted us apart with wide-eyed panic.

I held my breath, praying an unwelcome visitor hadn't discovered our secret liaison. Ronan's hand tightened around mine, his expression a mix of concern and determination as he moved to block me from anyone who might barge into the room.

When I heard the sound of steel against steel, I quickly grabbed a sheet and wrapped my body, afraid of what was to come. Ronan deftly slid into his trousers and barely had time to fasten them before the doors to my bed chambers burst open and Caelan stormed in.

"I knew it!" he growled. His expression was murderous as he glared daggers at the shirtless Crimson Clan warrior standing beside my bed. "How *dare* you touch her!"

The few days of privacy Ronan and I had shared was long gone.

Ronan tensed and fisted his hands. "You must not have realized it yet, but I'll break it down to you here and now in very simple terms. Leila is mine. Always has been and always will be. No matter what you try, she'll never be yours!"

Caelan swung his sword at Ronan, who easily dodged his sloppy strike. Unarmed, Ronan was forced to rely on his instincts and evade Caelan's vicious attacks.

"You have no right!" Caelan shouted, each word punctuated with wild sword swings. "This woman is *my* prize! *My* birthright! I will *not* allow you to take what's *mine*!"

I watched in horror as my one-time friend attempted to murder the man I loved. I started to step between them to break up the fight, but Ronan gripped my arm and prevented me from interfering.

Viktor ran inside, his eyes wide at the scene before him. "I'm sorry, Your Highness! I tried to stop him, but—"

"Stop *me*?" Caelan scoffed. "You should have stopped *him*! He's an animal!"

When Caelan stepped forward to attack Ronan again, I ripped my arm out of his grasp and held it up, seizing

Caelan's blood. He froze as I slowed his circulation, and he stumbled as if he was drunk.

"S-stop this," he stuttered. "Lyanna!"

"I can't do that," I said. "You crossed the line, Caelan. I don't know how far you're willing to go, but I bet I can go further. So don't test me." Closing my fist to tighten the noose on his veins and emphasize my point, I released my hand and flung him out of my chambers. He crashed against the hallway wall hard enough to dislodge a portrait, the glass shattering as it hit the floor.

Ronan cut into my view and gently gripped my shoulders. "Leila, stop," he pleaded. "I'll handle him. Don't worry."

I glared up at him. "*You'll* handle him?" I repeated. "How? You're not even armed! Or dressed, for that matter. If he hurts you—"

"He won't," he promised. "I just don't want you involved. If your family ever questions us about what happened here, I want the fault to lie with me, not you."

"Who cares whose fault it is?" I shouted in frustration. "He's going to tell everyone about us!"

Ronan furrowed his brows. "And? Do you have a problem with that?"

I didn't know how to respond. The proper answer would be *of course I don't mind*. But the truth was different. I *did* have a problem with it. If our relationship was made public, we would be criticized and cursed by all of Valoria. The Valorians still held deep-seated prejudices against the Crimson Clan. Prejudices that wouldn't disappear overnight.

Noticing the turmoil within me, Ronan's grip on my arms softened. "Leila?" he said softly, his eyes searching mine. "Whatever comes our way, we'll face it together. I'm not afraid of Valoria's judgment or what anyone else thinks. My only fear is losing you."

His words, sincere and fearless, sparked a courage within me I didn't know I possessed. "Ronan," I whispered, "I ... I'm scared. Not of being with you, but of what the world will say when they find out about us. Of the wedge it might drive between my family and me."

He lifted my chin and forced me to meet his gaze. "Leila, love is a force far stronger than any prejudice or opposition we might face. If we stand together, there's nothing we can't overcome."

Viktor, who had been a silent witness, finally spoke up, "Your Highness, if I may, your happiness is what truly matters. Those who care for you will see the truth of your hearts."

Ronan nodded in agreement. "Exactly. And if Caelan or anyone else tries to harm you or tarnish your name, they'll have to answer to me."

I looked between Ronan and Viktor, their unwavering support forming a shield around me. It was then I realized that whatever battles lay ahead, I wouldn't face them alone. With newfound resolve, I turned my attention back to Caelan, who was slowly regaining his bearings, his face a mask of confusion and fury.

I stepped forward, mustering as much dignity as I could while still wrapped in a bed sheet. "Caelan, this ends now. My heart belongs to Ronan, and nothing you say or do will change that. If you have any respect left for the friendship we once shared, you'll stop this madness."

Caelan scowled angrily. "You don't know *what* you want, Lyanna. You're obviously confused!"

"No, *you're* the one who doesn't know," I said calmly. "Leave now, before I truly feel like ending you."

Dusting himself off, he stormed out of the Eastern palace just as Henry crept inside. "Miss Leila?" he whispered as he took in my disheveled room. "Are you okay?"

I tightened my grip on the sheets wrapped around me and gave Henry a reassuring look. "Everything is fine, Henry. I'm sorry if we woke you up."

He shook his head. "Do you ... do you want me to follow him?" he offered quietly.

"No," I said adamantly. I had no desire to put the child in any danger. "Caelan is unstable and dangerous. I don't want you anywhere near him."

"She's right, Henry," Ronan concurred. "I know you want to be Leila's spymaster, but some things are best left alone."

Henry nibbled his lower lip. "Okay." With a nod, he turned and headed back to his room.

Once he was gone, I looked at Viktor. "Keep an eye on him. I don't trust that Henry will leave it alone."

"Yes, Your Highness." Viktor bowed and exited my room.

Alone now, with the silence of the night wrapping around us, I turned to Ronan. His presence was a comforting constant in the whirlwind of events that had just unfolded. The room felt smaller somehow, the echoes of the confrontation still lingering in the air.

"I think it's best if you return to the Northern palace," I said, avoiding eye contact. "Everything's about to change."

He nodded. "Why don't I have lunch with you here in the Eastern palace tomorrow? If we come out in the open before Caelan says anything, it'll be less scandalous."

"You're right." I nodded. "Let's do that."

With those final words, Ronan leaned forward and placed a soft kiss on my forehead. Slipping back into his shirt and shoes, he left and closed the door with a soft click.

18

Breakfast the next morning was a quiet affair. A little too quiet, if I really thought about it. My mother didn't offer any snarky remarks or comments about what happened in the Grand Hall last night; nor did either of my parents question me about Ronan, which I fully expected, given how angry Caelan was last night when he stormed out of my room. I expected him to go running straight to my mother to tell her what happened. But everyone was so ... *calm*. It was unsettling. Luckily Caelan wasn't here to fuel the flames.

I cleared my throat and turned to where my father sat at the head of the table. "I have a request."

He nodded. "Sure. What is it, Lyanna?"

I bit my lower lip and said the words in a rush before I could chicken out. "I want to learn blood weaving."

The already quiet dining hall turned deathly still. Marcellus was the first to break the tension.

"Blood weaving?" he repeated. "I've never heard of that. I want to learn, too!" he said giddily.

I rolled my eyes. "You want to learn, yet you have no idea what it is?"

He shrugged. "It sounds interesting."

Our father coughed into his hand. "Lyanna ... where did you hear that term?"

I frowned at the rising tension that permeated the room. "Sir Edric told me. He said it was one of the abilities I have, but I haven't learned how to do it."

"Gods damn that bastard!" my mother shouted as she tossed her napkin on top of her full plate.

"Excuse me?" I felt as if I'd just been slapped. "What did you say?"

"You heard me clearly," she scoffed. "That bastard kept you hidden for years and *still* couldn't keep his mouth shut!"

"And it's good he didn't, because who knew what could have happened to me if I'd returned to Valoria!" I shouted. "You might've decided to send me to the Grasslands on one of your whims."

My mother gasped. "I would never!"

I smiled at her condescendingly. "Sure, Mother."

"Enough!" my father interrupted. "Lyanna, do you know what blood weaving entails?"

I nodded. "Slitting my wrists," I answered confidently. Sir Edric had given me a brief overview when I contacted him using the Crimson Clan's witch doctor.

"Whoa!" Marcellus turned his attention to me. "What exactly is blood weaving?"

I chuckled. "Something only I can do."

He sighed and rolled his eyes. "Of course it is."

"From the moon goddess, we've learned that blood weaving takes a toll on the practitioner that goes well beyond physical scarring, Lyanna. Are you sure you want to do this?" my father asked.

I paused, weighing his words and the implications behind them. "I understand the risks," I said, meeting his gaze firmly. "But if it's a part of who I am, part of the power I possess, then I need to learn. To not only protect myself, but those I care for."

My mother snorted and rolled her eyes. "Interesting to hear you say that, although I'm guessing I'm not included in those you care for, since you so attacked me last night."

I winced with the realization that my comment came back to bite me in the ass. Still, I refused to back down. "Let's not pretend, Mother. You and I both know you've never liked me much."

She was about to counter when my father interrupted, ignoring our squabble completely. "Lyanna, are you sure about this? Blood weaving can be dangerous."

I turned my attention back to him. "I'm positive. I think it's for the best."

My father nodded slowly, though lines of concern were etched deeply on his face. "I can't say I'm thrilled with this decision, but I trust you know what you're doing. We'll need to find you a suitable teacher; someone who can guide you without putting you in unnecessary danger."

"That's just it, isn't it?" my mother interjected, her tone cutting. "Who in Valoria knows about such dark arts? You're inviting trouble, Lyanna, meddling in powers better left untouched."

I scoffed. "If it was dark arts, how come the moon goddess was a Blood Weaver? Are you saying the moon goddess was—"

"Lyanna!" my father stopped me before I could go further.

Tension rose as the breakfast that was meant to be a quiet family gathering turned into a battleground of wills.

"It's not about inviting trouble, Mother. It's about being prepared for it," I countered. "Sir Edric believed I was capable, and I trust his judgment."

Marcellus, ever the peacekeeper, tried to lighten the mood. "Well, if Lyanna turns into a powerful Blood Weaver, I guess I'll have to up my game, as well. Can't have my big sister outshining me."

His attempt at humor did little to dissolve the tension, but it did bring a small smile to my face. I was grateful for the levity in his words. "Thank you, Marcellus. I appreciate the support."

My father cleared his throat, drawing our attention back to him. "We will discuss this further and find the best way forward. If this is truly your path, Lyanna, then we will ensure you have the support and guidance you need."

The rest of the breakfast passed in strained silence, with each family member lost in their own thoughts. As the meal concluded and we stood to leave, I couldn't help but feel a mix of determination and apprehension. I was about to embark on a journey that could change everything. And yet, despite the uncertainty, I felt a sense of purpose, a calling to embrace my heritage and the powers that came with it. Especially if it could help me with whatever was to come. I was convinced Caelan had something up his sleeve.

As we parted ways, my resolve hardened. Blood weaving might be considered a dark, dangerous art, but it was part of me and the gift I'd been given. And with the right guidance, I believed I could master it; not for power or prestige, but for the protection of those I loved.

"Lyanna!" Marcellus called out to me as I walked out of the dining hall on my way back to the Eastern palace. "Wait up!"

I turned around with a raised brow. "Yes?"

He looked around to make sure no one was close enough to listen before whispering, "I heard something happened after we left Mother's display in the Grand Hall last night."

So rumors *had* spread, just not through Caelan. Interesting. "Caelan paid me an unexpected visit last night ... and Ronan was around."

"Oh ... *oh!*" he gasped as he caught on to my insinuation. "Lyanna, you haven't ..."

I rolled my eyes. "Marcellus, this is *not* a conversation I want to have with my baby brother," I sighed. "We can talk about anything but this."

He nodded. "Deal. So what did Caelan do?"

"He wanted to fight Ronan, what else? I expected him to run straight to Mother and tell her all the sordid details, but she didn't mention anything at breakfast. It was ... strange, don't you think?"

"Do you think Caelan is planning something?" Marcellus asked carefully.

"Definitely. Which was why I brought up the blood weaving. I need to prepare for whatever is to come," I admitted. "Being a blood mage will only take me so far. I need to get stronger, more powerful."

Marcellus rubbed his lower lip. "Hmm ... I'll be honest, Lyanna, I don't think Father is planning to help you learn anything. Especially with Mother being so against it."

I shrugged. "I figured, but I thought I'd ask anyway. I guess I'll just have to figure it out on my own."

My brother's eyes widened. "Oh, can I help? I want to see what blood weaving is about!" he said eagerly.

I chuckled. "You want to help me learn?"

He nodded. "Yeah, why not?"

I eyed him for a moment, wondering if he had some

ulterior motive. When I couldn't find any indecision or manipulation in his gaze, I nodded. "Fine. Meet me in the Eastern garden after lunch. We'll start today."

His eyes lit up with excitement, and I saw a spark of his usual mischief. "Are you serious? This is going to be epic!" He clapped excitedly. "But, uh, you *do* know how to start, right?"

I paused as the weight of his question sank in. Sir Edric only had time to provide a broad overview of blood weaving, nothing more. "We'll figure it out," I assured him, though I felt a twinge of uncertainty myself. "I'm sure there are some books in the library we can check out. We'll start there."

"Books? I was hoping for something more hands-on," Marcellus grumbled, but the curiosity was evident in his tone. "Alright, count me in. This will be far better than any lesson at the Mage Academy."

The Mage Academy. Yet another experience that was stolen from me when I had to disappear and go into hiding.

Marcellus bounded off, excited for our new venture. I smiled at his enthusiasm. It was a rare moment where the Prince of Valoria seemed more like an eager child than the heir to the throne. But his reaction reminded me of the seriousness of the path on which I was about to embark. Blood weaving wasn't a game or a mere curiosity to be explored on a whim. It was a potent and potentially perilous art that could very well change the course of our lives.

∽

I SPENT the morning in the library, pouring through a stack of books longer than my arm. When I returned to the Eastern palace with another mountain of books, I was surprised to find Ronan waiting for me. I asked Tessa to bring the books to my chamber so I could greet my guest. She grabbed the books out of my hand and headed down the corridor.

I walked over to Ronan, who was seated at a table in the gardens, the top covered by a brightly colored tablecloth and silver place settings. "What are you doing here?" I raised a brow and waved at the table. "And what is all this?"

He frowned. "Did you forget already? We're supposed to have lunch together."

"Oh! By the goddess, I forgot all about it!" I sat across from him with a sheepish expression. "I'm sorry, my mind has been elsewhere all morning."

"Did your father bring us up during breakfast?" Ronan asked carefully.

I shook my head. "No. No one mentioned a thing. It was odd," I mumbled. "But I'm sure Caelan is up to something. I can almost guarantee it."

"And you're most likely right." He waved for one of my ladies-in-waiting to bring over our lunch. "I took a little trip to the capital this morning and thought you'd enjoy some wine," he smirked.

"Love in the Moonlight?" I gasped. "You sure know the way to my heart."

"Of course I do!" he laughed.

The ladies made quick work of setting the table with an array of fragrant dishes. As they worked, my gaze settled on Ronan, a mix of gratitude and affection warming my heart. The fact that he remembered my fondness for wine made this moment even more special.

"I can't believe you went all the way to the capital just for this." I picked up the jug and uncorked it, taking a deep whiff of the fruity aroma.

"If it's for you, I'd traverse the uncharted North. Nothing

is impossible," he said, his tone and expression as serious as I'd ever heard it.

The area North of Valoria and Keldara was known as the *uncharted North*, where civilization hadn't settled. The lands were vast and largely unknown. Many went on expeditions there and never returned. As such, the area was shrouded in mystery to all those in Asteria.

"I would never ask that of you," I said as I poured myself a cup of wine.

"But for you, I would," he said, his crimson gaze intense.

His declaration stirred something deep within me, a mix of awe and fear at the lengths he was willing to go for me. The uncharted North was a place of legends and unknown dangers, yet here Ronan sat, ready to face it all for my sake if I asked.

I reached across the table and clasped his hand. "Let's hope it never comes to that." I squeezed his hand gently. "I couldn't bear the thought of you in danger because of me."

Ronan's grip tightened, his thumb caressing the back of my hand. "I know. I feel the same way. If you were ever to get hurt because of me, I ... I don't know what I would do. I would lose my mind."

"That won't ever happen. I'm going to get stronger. More powerful. Just wait and see."

Ronan frowned. "You're already powerful, Leila. You don't need to push yourself just to—"

I shook my head lightly. "I'm not. I simply have some untapped potential that I want to learn how to use. It's no big deal." I offered a broad smile. He smiled in return, but I sensed his uneasiness. "I'll be fine, Ronan. I promise."

He eyed me carefully. "If this is because of last night, you don't have to—"

I shook my head again. "It's not because of that. Caelan

is getting out of hand, and I should have put a stop to it back in the Central Plains. I can't sit back and wait for him to escalate things anymore."

I knew he wanted to give me a big fat 'I told you so', but he valiantly restrained himself. There was a lot I should have listened to Ronan about that I now regretted. All I could do at this point was move forward and find solutions.

"Your Highness?" Tessa approached after the ladies finished placing the last plate of food on the table. "Before you start eating, please let me test the food."

I frowned. "Pardon?"

"For poison," Tessa clarified.

I knew people tested our food for breakfast, but I had no idea Tessa was doing it for lunch and dinner. I waved her off. "There shouldn't be any problems, Tessa. I—"

"Your Highness," she interrupted, "I have to."

Ronan cleared his throat. "Let her do it, Leila. It's her job."

I reluctantly nodded as Tessa approached with a small plate and utensils. She picked at every dish, eating a portion of each and tasting them for poisons. The whole situation made me uneasy. I didn't want to put Tessa in any unnecessary risk.

After a moment, she stepped back and nodded. "Everything is fine, Your Highness."

"Thank you, Tessa," I mumbled as she excused herself to give us privacy.

Under the midday sun, we enjoyed lunch and stayed to innocent, light topics. He didn't broach the subject of Caelan further, nor did I explain that I planned to learn blood weaving. I didn't know what Ronan's reaction would be; I preferred to find out once the damage was done.

Throughout our meal, Ronan reached for my hand and

held it, cementing our status and making our affection obvious to any who passed by. Soon there would be gossip, and that gossip would spiral back to my parents. Then, we would wait and see what happened.

As we finished our meal, a bevy of court ladies whisked our empty plates and jug of wine away, leaving us alone. Ronan cleared his throat. "Leila ... there's something I have to tell you."

My brows raised at his grave tone. "What happened?"

He shook his head. "Nothing serious, but I received a letter from my father. He wants me to return to the Grasslands as soon as possible."

My brows shot up to my hairline in surprise. "Why? Did something happen?"

Ronan shrugged. "I don't know. He didn't say."

I bit my lip and tried to suppress the worry that bubbled inside me. "You're going back, aren't you?" The thought of being apart from Ronan, especially now, felt like a punch to the gut.

He took a deep breath, his gaze locked with mine. "I have to, at least long enough to find out what he wants. But I promise you, Leila, I will return."

My heart sank, but I understood. Ronan had responsibilities, just as I had mine. "I know. It's just ... with everything going on with Caelan, and my parents soon learning of our relationship ... it feels like the world is against us."

Ronan reached out and cupped my face gently. "The world might be against us, but we have something stronger than any of them—our love for each other. That's not easily broken."

His words offered a semblance of comfort, but the fear of the unknown lingered. "Just ... be careful, okay? I don't trust your father, and I don't want you caught in the middle of a dangerous political scheme."

"I will," he assured me, his thumb brushing away a stray tear that escaped. "And I want you to promise me something in return."

"What is it?"

"Promise me you'll stay safe while I'm gone. Don't take any unnecessary risks, especially when it comes to Caelan. Wait for me to come back and we'll figure it out together."

I nodded, the lump in my throat making it hard to speak. "I promise. When do you plan to leave?"

"In three days," he answered solemnly.

Three days would go by in the blink of an eye. As we stood to leave the garden, Ronan held my hand tightly, almost as if he was afraid I'd disappear if he let go. Our walk back inside the palace was silent, each of us lost in our thoughts of the future and the challenges that awaited us.

As we reached the entrance to the Eastern palace, Ronan pulled me into a tight embrace. "I promise to spend as much of the next three days with you as I possibly can."

I wrapped my arms around him, holding on for a few moments longer. "You better," I snorted.

"I have a few things to take care of before I leave. Mainly, I need to send word to my father that I received his message and will return. When I'm done, I'll find you. Okay?"

I nodded.

With a gentle kiss, he turned and walked away, his figure disappearing out of the Eastern palace. As I watched him go, I made a silent vow to myself. I would become stronger for him, for us. And when he returned, we would face whatever came our way together, as one.

19

"Are you scared?" Marcellus asked.

We stood in the gardens, books splayed out on the ground while I tentatively held a dagger to my wrist. I scoffed and tried to pretend I wasn't scared shitless. "Me? Scared? No way."

Marcel crossed his arms over his chest and smirked. "I think you are. We've been standing here for thirty minutes, and you still haven't made a cut."

He was right. I was nervous. But I couldn't keep stalling much longer. "Okay. Here I go..." I pressed the dagger to the soft flesh of my wrist and made an incision no bigger than an inch. Blood slowly dribbled down my hand, the sight causing a wave of lightheadedness to sweep through me. I wasn't afraid of blood. I'd pricked my finger many times to save a life, but *this* ... this felt dangerous.

Marcellus stepped closer; his previous smugness replaced by concern. "Are you sure you want to do this, Leila? This isn't like healing someone. This is... different."

I looked up at him, stubborn determination setting in. "I

need to learn, Marcel. If not for myself, then for everyone I care about. Including you."

As the blood pooled in my palm, I focused and tried to recall what little was mentioned about blood weaving in the books I found in the library. According to them, blood weaving was all about intent, focus, and control. The incision stung, a sharp reminder of what I was attempting to unleash.

Closing my eyes, I concentrated on the droplets of blood, feeling their warmth and imagining them as more than just part of me, but as extensions of my will. "It's about connecting with the essence of life," I whispered, echoing the words I had just read.

Marcellus watched silently, though his worry was evident. "Leila, be careful," he said softly.

I nodded and opened my eyes. The world seemed sharper somehow, the colors around me more vivid. The droplets of blood quivered, and for a moment, nothing happened. Then, slowly, they began to move, coalescing into a small orb that floated just above my palm.

"By the goddess!" Marcellus whispered, his eyes wide with a mixture of fear and awe.

I couldn't help the smile that stretched my cheeks, even as the blood orb dissipated and settled into droplets. "I did it!" Relief and excitement coursed through me. "I actually did it."

Marcellus rushed to my side with a cloth to wrap my wrist. "You did something, I'll tell you that much, but it's far from what you're capable of, Leila. Please promise me you'll be careful."

I nodded, feeling the weight of his words. "I promise, Marcel. This is just the beginning. I have so much more to learn."

For the next hour and a half, I practiced making anything more or bigger than the orb of blood. I sweated profusely as I attempted something grander, to no avail. It was a miracle I made it that far on my first try. But Marcel was right; I shouldn't get *too* excited.

"Let's call it a day," Marcel suggested. "If you keep going, you're going to pass out from blood loss. Maybe you should get some rest." He changed the cloth to a new one to stop the bleeding.

As we packed up the books, I knew that the journey I was embarking on would be filled with unknown variables and potential dangers. But the payoff would be worth it. I was sure about that much.

As Marcel and I were leaving the gardens, we ran into Ronan, who was returning after completing his errands. His eyes went straight to my wrapped wrist, which had splotches of blood stains. His crimson eyes went wide and he rushed over, taking my arm and inspecting it carefully. "What happened?" he demanded.

I ripped my arm out of his grasp and hid it behind me. "Nothing! Just a little scratch. I wasn't being careful." I smiled brightly. Marcel peered over at me as the lie easily rolled off my tongue. A little *too* easily.

Diverting the attention away from my bandaged wrist, Marcel stepped forward and extended a hand to Ronan. "I don't think we've formally met."

Ronan watched me, worry evident in his gaze before I nudged him. He turned his attention to Marcel. "Oh, right," he mumbled as he took my brother's hand.

"I hope we can let bygones be bygones," Marcel offered with a raised brow.

Ronan frowned. "It's not *you* I have an issue with."

Marcel nodded. "Yes, but I'm not an innocent bystander,

either. I admit I've hurt Lyanna in more ways than I'd care to admit."

"That's all in the past now," I said as I attempted to cut through the tension.

Ronan nodded and released Marcel's hand. "For Leila's sake, we can move past it. But I'm still concerned about this 'scratch' of yours." His gaze shifted back to me, filled with an unspoken question.

I waved the hand not wrapped in the cloth dismissively. "Honestly, it's nothing. Just got a bit too enthusiastic with some gardening."

Marcel gave me a look that said he wasn't buying the gardening excuse any more than Ronan was, but he played along. "Yeah, she decided to take on a rose bush single-handedly. You know how stubborn she can be."

Ronan's expression softened and a small smile played on his lips. "Yes, I'm well aware. Do you want to see the palace healer to treat the wound? I could go with you," he offered.

"No, I should be fine," I assured him, feeling a mix of gratitude and guilt for the lie. Ronan had always been there for me and hiding the truth about blood weaving felt wrong. But I knew if I managed to master it, it would be worth it.

"Well then, I guess I should go," Marcellus muttered as he moved to the path that led out of the garden. "I'll see you tomorrow, Lyanna."

I waved and we watched him leave and amble back to his Western palace. Once he was gone, Ronan turned his gaze to me.

He raised a brow. "Now tell me: were you *really* gardening?"

I nodded and smiled brightly. "Of course!"

He sighed. "If you're going to lie to me, at least make it

believable. You have the cleanest hands for someone who has been working with soil."

My eyes widened as I looked down at my slightly red, but otherwise clean hands. Right ... maybe I should have put a bit more effort into the lie. With a grin, I looped my arm in his. "Aww, come on, Ronan. I promise it was nothing bad."

He peered over at me as if he didn't believe a single word I said, but instead of arguing, he simply nodded. I wasn't sure if that was preferable to him hounding me about it.

"Did you send word to your father?" I asked, changing the subject.

"Yes. But I plan to spend every waking minute with you until I leave." He leaned down and brought his lips to within a whisper of mine. "Think you can handle that?" He raised a brow in challenge.

I scoffed and gave him a devilish grin. "Piece of cake."

"Good. I've already told your court ladies that I'll be having lunch with you every day until I leave."

Grinning, I stood on my tippy toes and gave him a quick kiss. "Perfect."

Ronan wrapped his arms around me, bringing my body flush against his. "I don't know how I'll manage to be away from you while I'm in the Grasslands," he muttered as he brought his lips closer to mine.

I wrapped my arms around his neck to bring him closer. "I guess that means you'll have to hurry back." In the next instant, Ronan slammed his lips onto mine with an all-consuming kiss that forced all other thoughts to flee.

Our hearts raced as the world around us faded into a blur of colors and sensations. Ronan's touch sent shivers down my spine, igniting a fire that threatened to consume every inch of my being. The intensity of our kiss deepened, our breaths mingling in a passionate dance.

With each moment that passed, I realized I was falling deeper and deeper for him. His presence was intoxicating, and his touch set my soul ablaze with desire. The taste of his lips lingered on mine, imprinting itself on my very essence.

As we finally pulled away, our eyes locked in a silent promise of what was to come. The connection between us crackled with energy, drawing us together like magnets unable to resist their pull. In that moment, I knew that no matter how much physical distance separated us, our love would endure.

Ronan smiled, and the tenderness in his crimson eyes made my heart swell. "I will return to you, I promise," he whispered.

"You better, or I'll go to the Grasslands looking for you," I joked.

His expression turned serious in a blink. "Whatever you do, do *not* come to the Grasslands. My father is full of all kinds of tricks. If he captures you, he's not above keeping you there against your will," Ronan admitted.

I frowned. "You really think he'd do something that foolish, knowing Valoria would call for war to get me back?"

"If he's able to resurrect the demon fox, the Crimson Clan would be unstoppable. A war with a neighboring kingdom would mean nothing in the grand scheme of things," Ronan said. "Promise me you'll wait here for me."

"I promise," I said. "Just return quickly."

"I will."

20

I spent the next few days wrapped up in Ronan, which was fortunate since Selene was secretly meeting Marcellus. Occasionally Ronan and I would come up for air and wander the grounds, and on those occasions, Henry was our little shadow. As I predicted, the days went by in a blur and the third day was upon us sooner than we liked. Ronan would leave for the Grasslands after lunch.

The morning of his departure was charged with unspoken sorrow. We both tried to keep the mood light, laughing and reminiscing about our time in the Central Plains and Valoria, but the impending goodbye loomed over us like a dark cloud.

Before lunch, we decided to take a walk through the gardens, a place that had become our sanctuary in the past three days. The flowers were in full bloom, their colors vibrant against the pale backdrop of the palace. It was beautiful, yet I couldn't fully appreciate it knowing that in just an hour, Ronan would be on his way back to the Grasslands.

"Leila," Ronan said, breaking the silence between us, "you know I wish I didn't have to go."

I squeezed his hand tighter, suddenly finding it hard to swallow past the lump in my throat. "I know."

He stopped walking and turned to face me, cupping my face in his hands. "Remember, no matter where I am, my heart remains with you. I'll return as soon as I can."

I nodded, my eyes brimming with unshed tears. "I'll be waiting," I managed to say, my voice barely above a whisper.

We sat at a table nestled in the gardens and waited for the court ladies to finish serving our meal. When Tessa came over with her tasting plate and spoon, I rolled my eyes. "Tessa, you really don't have to check my food every day. No one wants to poison me!" I chuckled and reached for a piece of bread.

Tessa stopped my hand and scolded, "Your Highness, *please*."

Letting out a deep sigh, I patiently waited as she tried everything. She nibbled a piece of bread, tested the salad, and ate a bite of the meat course. But when she took a spoonful of the soup, she paused for a moment and suddenly dropped the spoon with a clatter. Tessa's eyes bulged and she clutched her throat as foam trickled at the corners of her mouth. She dropped to her knees before us, her face going beet red as she gasped for air.

"Tessa!" I shrieked.

"Viktor!" Ronan shouted for my guard, who was standing outside the garden to give us privacy. "Call for the healer!"

Sensing the urgency in Ronan's voice, Viktor ran off.

I gathered Tess's convulsing body in my arms and Ronan dropped to the ground beside me. "Hang in there, Tess," I murmured. "Just ..." A thought crossed my mind and my eyes widened. "Ronan! Pass me a knife!"

He frowned in confusion, but leaned up to the table and

grabbed a knife. With it, I quickly pierced the tip of my finger and applied pressure to stimulate blood flow. Once a scarlet drop of blood welled up, I squeezed several droplets into Tessa's gaping mouth.

"Leila," Ronan started, "I don't think your blood can cure poisoning—"

"My blood can cure anything!" I shrieked. "It has to! It cured Caelan when he was poisoned!"

Tessa's body convulsed as I desperately tried to feed her more of my blood, hoping beyond hope that it would save her. Her eyes locked with mine for a fleeting moment, filled with fear and agony, before they rolled back into her head. Seconds stretched into minutes as we waited for any sign of improvement, for a miracle that seemed increasingly out of reach.

But nothing changed.

"Tessa?" I whispered, shaking her lightly. "Tessa, stay with me."

Her body grew still and cold in my arms, the last breath escaping her lips in a soft sigh. The garden fell silent all around us, the vibrant colors fading to dull shades of gray as grief washed over me like a tidal wave. I searched the garden for a lady-in-waiting or anyone who could possibly help, but Ronan and I were alone.

Ronan placed a comforting hand on my shoulder, his eyes filled with sorrow. "I'm so sorry, Leila, but she's gone."

Tears streamed down my cheeks as I cradled Tessa's lifeless form, feeling a crushing weight settle in my chest. "No. She can't be!" I wailed. "Why ... why would someone want to poison me?"

"I don't know," Ronan answered truthfully. "But we'll find out. Your father won't let this slide, I can guarantee that."

Before I could respond, someone screamed my name.

"Miss Leila!" Henry rushed through the gardens to reach me. He hadn't come from the Eastern palace. Where had he been? Henry gasped for air as he took in the scene before him. "No," he muttered, horror-stricken. "I'm too late."

I frowned. "What do you mean?"

He nibbled his lower lip. "Miss Leila, I overheard Prince Caelan. I know his plan."

Ronan shot to his feet. "What did you hear, Henry?" he asked urgently.

"I told you not to go near him, Henry!" I chided. I clung to Tessa, afraid to let her go. If I did, it would make this real.

"Henry!" Ronan shouted, trying to get the boy to focus. "What did you hear?"

Henry cleared his throat. "Prince Caelan told the Queen he was going to frame you for poisoning Miss Leila to get you out of the way. He's already sent word to King Malik. The guards will be here any moment."

"What?" I gasped as more tears streamed down my face. "That can't be! He was trying to kill me?"

Ronan scoffed. "Caelan knows your food gets tested every day. He knew *you* wouldn't get hurt. This was it, Leila. This was the ace up his sleeve. If I don't leave now, I won't leave here alive."

I gently laid Tessa on the ground. "Henry, watch over her, please."

He knelt beside me. "I will, Miss Leila. I promise."

"What are you doing?" Ronan asked as I stood.

"I'm coming with you," I said adamantly. "You won't be able to leave the palace without me. If Caelan has already told my father his lies, then all exits will have been cut off. There's no way out."

"I'm not putting you in danger, Leila," Ronan declared.

"It's safer if you stay put and explain things when everyone arrives. Once I cross the Central Plains and reach the Grasslands, I'll be fine."

I shook my head. "They'll be expecting that. You'll never make it." I stepped toward him. "You need to cut through Keldara."

His eyes widened and he looked around the garden to make sure no one was listening. "Leila, you *know* I can't go through Keldara! My people are slaves there. If I'm caught …"

"I have a plan," I said quickly. "But we need to act fast."

"No. Leila, no," Ronan said unyieldingly, stepping around me to leave.

I grabbed his arm to stop him. "Ronan, wait!"

"Leila, I'm losing time," he urged.

"And you'll get caught if you don't listen to me!" I turned to the young boy kneeling with my fallen guard. "Henry, watch over Tessa until Viktor returns with the healer. Tell Viktor everything you told us; he'll know what to do."

"Lyanna!" Marcellus rushed toward us from across the garden, holding hands with Selene. "I came to warn you! Father—"

"We heard," I interrupted brusquely. "Tell me you know a way out of here, baby brother."

"Of course I do." He smirked, then eyed Ronan warily. "He didn't really try to…"

I shook my head. "Of course not. This was Caelan's grand plan to get rid of Ronan and force me to be with him. Look – we need to get out of here *now*."

Selene rushed forward, her eyes wild. "You're leaving with him?"

I nodded. "I'm not leaving him to fend for himself."

"No," Selene said. "You can't. You'll be in danger!"

"No I won't," I sighed. "I have a plan."

What the others failed to realize was that Commander Mykal had spies everywhere. I was banking on the fact that he had them posted here in Valoria. If he heard about my escape, he may just come and find us. Possibly. It might put Ronan at risk, but I had to pray to the goddess that Mykal could be reasoned with. This was our only option. Staying here was a death sentence, and cutting through the Central Plains was even worse since the governor was in Caelan's pocket.

Selene glanced around nervously. "What's your plan?"

Before I could answer, Ronan spoke up. "Can we talk and walk at the same time? My life is sort of on the line right now."

"Right!" Marcel snapped his fingers. "Follow me."

I dropped down beside Henry. "Stay safe. Whatever you do, don't get involved. Viktor will protect you."

Although he wore a forlorn look, Henry nodded. "Yes, Miss Leila."

With nervous anxiety buzzing through all four of us, we left Henry behind and Marcellus led us out of the gardens. Under the bright noon sun, we hastened across the manicured grounds of the Eastern Palace, dodging the prying eyes of courtiers and servants. Marcellus, with a brisk pace, navigated us through less frequented paths, lined with blooming flowers and towering hedges that provided a semblance of cover.

Selene's gaze darted around as she observed the lush surroundings with a mixture of awe and anxiety. "This place is like a labyrinth!" she commented, her voice hushed.

"Keep up," Ronan urged, casting a wary glance over his shoulder at her. His alertness was palpable, a stark contrast to the serene beauty around us.

Marcellus, leading with confidence, pointed towards a distant archway that marked the transition from the Eastern to the Western Palace. "We'll need to cross the open courtyard of the Central palace," he said, his tone serious. "Stay close and act natural."

As we stepped into the square, the vast expanse of the courtyard stretched before us, bustling with activity. Nobles strolled leisurely, guards patrolled the area, and servants hurried about their duties. We blended into the crowd, our group appearing as nothing more than a casual assembly of palace dwellers enjoying the day.

Moving swiftly across the courtyard, the Western Palace loomed closer, its grandeur casting a long shadow over us. I felt a tug on my sleeve and looked over to see Selene, her face etched with concern. "There are a lot of guards, Leila," she whispered, her voice barely audible over the chatter of the courtyard.

With a reassuring smile, I gently squeezed her hand. "It'll be fine. The guards searching for Ronan probably went to the Northern palace, and when they can't find him there, they'll head to the Eastern palace," I whispered back.

As we hastened across the sunlit courtyard, the sudden, sharp call of a guard cut through the air, shattering our brief illusion of anonymity. "There they are! *Stop!*" The command was directed at us, an authoritative voice slicing through the casual hustle and bustle.

We quickened our pace and tried to blend into the crowd, but it was too late. The distinctive clank of armor grew louder as more guards joined the pursuit, alerted by their comrade's call. Panic knotted in my stomach as I glanced over my shoulder to see several guards breaking through the throng, their eyes locked on our group.

"This way, quickly!" Marcellus urged, his voice tight with

urgency. He veered off the main path and raced down a less trodden garden trail. His knowledge of the palace's layout was our only advantage.

The sound of our pursuers' boots against the cobblestones grew louder, a relentless echo that spurred us forward. Ronan, ever the protector, moved to the rear of our group, casting wary glances behind us, his posture tense and ready.

"Keep moving!" I heard him say, the determination in his voice bolstering my resolve.

The once peaceful courtyard transformed into a maze of fear and desperation as we dodged statues and barreled through archways, the looming Western Palace our only beacon of hope amidst the chaos.

As we neared the secluded door Marcellus was aiming for, the guards' shouts grew ominously close, their presence an ever-looming threat at our backs.

Beside me, Selene ran with a grace born of her time at sea, her breaths measured despite the panic. "We're almost there," she panted, her encouragement mingling with the adrenaline that coursed through my veins.

Finally, Marcellus pushed open the concealed door and we slipped through one by one, the dim corridor of the Western Palace swallowing us whole. The door shut with a quiet thud behind us, momentarily silencing the clamor of the chase.

"We can't stop now," Marcellus whispered, leading us deeper into the labyrinth of the palace, the sound of our hurried footsteps the only evidence of our flight.

As we navigated the shadowed passageways, the reality of our situation weighed heavily on me. The palace, my home, had become a prison from which we had to flee, our freedom hinging on the success of our desperate escape.

Marcellus guided us through a series of winding, dimly lit passageways that felt increasingly claustrophobic as silence pressed in on us from all sides. Eventually, we arrived at a nondescript wooden door that seemed to blend seamlessly into the surrounding stone wall. Marcellus pushed it open with a firm shove.

"These are the underground tunnels—a network of forgotten passages that run like veins beneath the palace and its grounds," he explained as we tried to peer inside the darkness. "No one but me knows they exist. I use them to sneak out of the palace once in a while. It'll spit you out close to the border of Keldara."

"Good." I nodded. "That's where we need to go."

Marcel frowned. "You're going to cross the border?"

"Yes. It's the only way."

Marcellus sighed. "Be careful, Lyanna. They might not be after you, but they could definitely leverage you if they needed to."

"We'll be careful," I promised.

The air within the tunnel was cool and musty, filled with the scent of damp earth and the whisper of secrets long buried. As we stepped into the shadowy confines of the passageway, Marcellus produced a torch from a nook by the entrance and lit it, the flickering flame casting eerie shadows on the earthen walls.

"This is where we part ways," Marcellus said, his voice echoing slightly in the confined space. "These tunnels will lead you out beyond the palace grounds. Just follow the main passage until you reach the old oak tree. You'll find another exit there."

Ronan nodded, his expression grim. "Thank you, Marcellus. For everything."

Marcellus clapped him on the shoulder, a silent message

of camaraderie between them. "Just make sure you both stay safe. And Ronan, take care of my sister for me."

Ronan's gaze met mine, filled with a promise that needed no words.

Selene stepped forward and hugged me tightly. "Be careful, Leila," she whispered. "I'll see you soon."

With one last look at my brother and my best friend, Ronan and I turned to face the darkness of the tunnel before us. Hand in hand, we began our descent into the bowels of Valoria, the torchlight casting our elongated shadows ahead of us as we navigated the uneven ground.

The tunnel was narrow, the walls rough and cool to the touch, moisture glistening on the stones in the dim light. Our footsteps were muffled by the soft earth beneath us, the only sounds the distant drip of water and our own steady breathing.

As we walked, the weight of our departure settled over me—a mix of fear, sadness, and a burgeoning sense of freedom. With each step, we moved further away from the life I had known and into an uncertain future.

"Watch your step," Ronan whispered as he led the way, our hands interlocked.

"How far do you think this tunnel goes?" I whispered in return.

Ronan shrugged. "It must be fairly long, if it exits on the other side of the palace. We'd literally have to cut through the Western palace to get there."

Other than the sound of our hurried footsteps, the tunnel was quiet. "I'm sorry, Ronan," I murmured.

His steps faltered and he peered over his shoulder at me. "Sorry for what?"

I fought the tears that pricked at my eyes. "This is all my fault. Everything that happened—"

Ronan resumed walking. "It would have eventually happened, Leila. Caelan wants me out of the picture so he can make you his. Whether it was now or a year from now, he would have devised a plan to make it happen. None of this is your fault. It's *his*."

While deep down I knew he was right, I couldn't help the feeling of guilt that weighed down my shoulders. If Ronan had never met me, he'd probably still be living comfortably in the Grasslands.

"Do you ever regret it?"

"Regret what?" he asked as we continued our trek through the tunnels, guided solely by torchlight.

"Regret *us*," I said, my voice low.

"Never," he said confidently. "Do you?"

I shook my head. "No, I don't. But in times like these, I just wonder …"

"Stop wondering," Ronan interrupted. "Living life filled with what-ifs will never bring you peace. Live in the moment, Leila, and live for the future. *Our* future. The one where we're together. Safe, healthy, and happy."

A smile stretched across my face at his words. He always knew the right thing to say. He was right. I needed to stop worrying so much. I wouldn't accomplish a single thing if I continued to second-guess everything that led to this moment.

Eventually, the narrow passage gave way to a wider cavern and fresh air heralded the exit. The old oak tree Marcellus mentioned loomed ahead, its gnarled roots encircling the hidden door that would lead to freedom.

Ronan pushed the door open and we stepped out into the cool air, the sun beaming down on us and over the landscape. The palace was behind us now, both a part of us and a world away.

"We did it!" I said, my voice a whisper.

Ronan squeezed my hand. "Do you know how far away Keldara's border is from here?"

"Not far," I answered. "That's why they were able to attack us so easily. The palace is close to the border."

He nodded, then took a moment to survey the palace behind us with a thoughtful expression. "Then we must be cautious. Keldara still poses a threat – both to you *and* me."

Concern etched deeper lines on Ronan's face. The weight of responsibility and the burden of keeping us both safe visibly wore on him. Yet, his grip on my hand was firm, a silent promise that he wouldn't let anything happen to me.

"We'll stick to the shadows," he said, scanning the horizon as if already mapping our path. "Avoid main roads and use the forest for cover. We can't afford to be spotted."

21

Ronan and I began our clandestine journey away from the palace and toward Keldara. Valoria's vast, open landscape unfurled before us, a mix of verdant fields and rolling hills, the boundary between the two lands marked by a dense forest that stretched as far as the eye could see. The lands were deceptively peaceful under the bright sun, but every leaf rustle and distant birdcall seemed to carry a warning. We were exposed, vulnerable. The urgency to put distance between us and any potential pursuers pushed us to move faster.

The sun's position declared it was no later than three in the afternoon, although it seemed a world of time had passed since the stillness was severed by poison and pursuing guards. Its warmth was a stark contrast to the coolness of the hidden cavern from which we had just emerged. We walked in silence with our hands clasped firmly in the other's, each lost in our thoughts though frightfully aware of the dangers that lay ahead.

The underbrush crunched with each step as we trekked across wildflower-strewn fields. Even though fear of capture dogged our path, I couldn't help but marvel at the beauty of Valoria's wilderness. The vibrant greens of the forest and cheery wildflowers that dotted our path offered a brief distraction from the constant vigilance.

"We should reach the outskirts of a small village by nightfall," I said after a while, breaking the silence. "We can find shelter there, and maybe even some allies."

"Allies?" Ronan questioned. The concept seemed almost foreign in our current state of isolation.

I offered a small, reassuring smile. "Not everyone in Keldara needs to be our enemy. You might be surprised at who may be willing to help us." At least I hoped.

Ronan nodded and looked ahead with a thoughtful expression. "Let's hope you're right," he finally said. The idea that we could find allies in a land that had always been portrayed as hostile was a sliver of hope in an otherwise grim situation.

As we put more distance between us and the palace, the reality of our situation sank in. Ronan was a fugitive now, and my parents most likely thought he'd kidnapped me. They didn't know we were merely running for our lives from Caelan's schemes. My heart was heavy, but I pushed the world behind us aside and focused on the journey ahead.

Just as the sun began its slow descent toward the horizon, painting the sky in blinding streaks of orange and pink, we spotted the village. It was a modest community of thatched-roof cottages along with a few larger buildings that likely served as the village center. Smoke curled from chimneys and faint laughter and conversation carried on the cooling breeze.

Approaching with caution, we avoided the main paths and skirted around to the less populated areas. Ronan's hand tightened around mine, offering silent reassurance that he was there, ready to protect me at a moment's notice.

Finding shelter for the night was our priority, but we also needed to be careful about whom we trusted. The fear of being recognized and our presence being reported back to the palace was ever-present in our minds. We stopped next to a tavern hidden in the shadows.

"Wait here," I whispered.

"What are you doing?" he asked.

"I can blend in," I pointed to the crescent moon birthmark on my forehead, "but you can't," I said, tugging on his long hair. "It's obvious you're from the Crimson Clan. If word gets out that someone from the Crimson Clan is creeping around the borders of Keldara, my father and Caelan won't hesitate to send troops this way. We need to stay hidden."

Reluctantly, Ronan released my hand and I hurried inside. The place was packed with mages drinking their fill. With quiet steps, I darted to the coat rack and searched for two cloaks. Casually draping them over one arm, I scurried out of the tavern and back to Ronan. Ronan quickly covered himself up. I did the same and took his hand again.

Walking through the dimly lit streets of the village, we tried to appear casual on stone paths that had been worn by generations of villagers going about their daily lives. The village was nestled in a small valley surrounded by gentle hills that seemed to embrace it protectively. Houses with thatched roofs and walls made of stone or wood huddled together, their windows glowing softly in the twilight. Gardens bloomed with late flowers, adding splashes of color to an otherwise muted landscape.

We located an inn on the outskirts of the village, a modest two-story building with a sign swinging gently in the breeze. The sign depicted a full moon over a sleeping village, an inviting image that promised a warm bed and a safe haven for weary travelers.

As we approached the inn, the scent of cooking food wafting on the breeze made my stomach grumble in anticipation. The innkeeper, a stout woman with a kind face and calloused hands that spoke of years of hard work, greeted us with a nod as we entered.

I removed my hood to show her my birthmark and then covered myself up again. "I'm looking for a place for the night, and possibly a messenger who can cross into Keldara," I said quietly, trying not to draw too much attention from the few patrons scattered around the common room.

The innkeeper's eyes narrowed slightly, but she quickly masked her reaction with a warm smile. "I can certainly provide a room for the night," she said, leaning closer and lowering her voice. "As for a messenger, there might be someone who can help. Go to the back of the inn, near the stables. Look for a man with a scar across his left cheek. Tell him Mira sent you."

I nodded. "Could we have two meals sent up to our room as well?"

"Will do," Mira said with a curt nod.

Grateful for the information, I thanked the innkeeper and followed her directions to our room. Once we were settled in, I would seek out the mysterious messenger. The room was simple but clean with a single bed, a modest table with two rickety chairs, and a tiny window that looked out over the village.

"This bed is ... small," Ronan noted dryly as he closed and locked the door behind us.

I sighed. "It is."

Ronan removed his cloak and hung it on a wooden peg on the wall before he plopped down on the bed, wincing as the frame groaned. "I guess this means you'll have to latch onto me so you don't roll off." He winked, and I laughed.

My laughter wasn't due to his suggestion, but more because of the absurdity of our situation. It was a lot of change to deal with in the matter of a few hours, and it was catching up to me.

Sitting on the edge of the bed beside Ronan, I allowed myself a moment to just breathe and let the whirlwind of emotions and events settle. The room, with its sparse furnishings and soft light filtering through the window, was a sanctuary from the chaos outside.

"We've been through so much in such a short time," I murmured, turning to look at him, his presence a constant reassurance. "I never imagined this would be our journey."

Ronan reached out and his hand found mine, intertwining our fingers. "Life has a funny way of throwing the unexpected at us. But as long as we're together, I believe we can handle anything."

His confidence was contagious. In that moment, I believed we were unstoppable.

When a knock sounded at the door, my stomach clenched in fear. Ronan stood and walked to the door, opening it to reveal a servant holding a tray of food. Ronan took the tray and gave the young boy a coin before closing the door.

My stomach groaned when the aroma of seasoned meat and warm soup hit my nostrils. I realized I hadn't eaten since breakfast, our day spoiled by Caelan and his diabolical machinations. We settled at the small wooden table. Ronan placed the tray in the middle and I beheld our feast: two bowls of steaming soup, bread still warm from the oven, and a plate of roasted meat that was seasoned so perfectly, the aroma alone was enough to make the day's stresses fade away. It was a far cry from the food we enjoyed in the palace, but at least here I didn't have to worry about someone poisoning my food.

My sobering thoughts turned to Tessa and the ultimate sacrifice she made to ensure my safety. I pushed through my turbulent grief and picked up my spoon. "Looks like we're in for a treat," I said with a smile as I tried the soup. Its warmth spread through me, a comforting embrace against the cool evening air seeping through the window.

Ronan chuckled and took the other chair across from me, which looked comically small compared to his hulking frame. "Anything less would be a disservice to our adventurous day." He broke off a chunk of bread and dipped it into the hearty stew.

We ate in comfortable silence, filled with shared glances and knowing smiles. The food was delicious, or maybe we were simply starved. The simple meal felt like a luxury after the day we'd experienced.

Ronan finally cleared his throat and peered over at me. "Do I want to know who you want to send a message to across the border?"

I shook my head. "No. You don't."

Ronan sighed. "Leila ... I'd like to say I'm not a jealous man, but the gods would know I was lying. If you're reaching out to Mykal—"

My eyes widened. "Nothing happened—"

"Don't lie to me, Leila," he interrupted. "I overheard part of your conversation with him at the banquet. He kissed you."

I bit my lip, embarrassed to be caught in a lie. I didn't *intend* to lie, but it would complicate things less if he didn't know. And truthfully, there was nothing between me and the commander.

"It was a mistake," I admitted quickly. "I was panicking, and kissing me was his way of calming me down."

Ronan quirked a brow and nodded. "I see."

But it was obvious he *didn't* see.

"Ronan—"

"It's okay, Leila. This was before you and I were together, and it was during a time when you thought I'd betrayed you. I don't hold it against you, but I know the effect you have on a man, and it's obvious Mykal has developed feelings for you."

I frowned and shook my head vehemently. "No. Impossible. We've known each other all of two seconds."

"Yet here you are, seeking his aid," he countered.

That shut me up. He was right. I fought the urge to roll my eyes because it seemed that Ronan was always right.

"Are you done eating?" I changed the subject, not wanting to delve deeper. "We should probably seek out the messenger before he heads home for the night."

Ronan watched me intently before nodding in agreement. I knew he wanted to say more, but he wisely decided to remain quiet.

∽

WITH OUR CLOAKS drawn tight to hide our identities, we crept to the back of the inn. The stables were quiet, save for the soft sounds of horses shifting in their stalls. Under the faint glow of a lantern, I spotted a man who fit the description the innkeeper had given. The scar across his left cheek was prominent, a stark reminder of the dangers that lay in crossing borders.

Taking a deep breath, I stepped forward to speak with the man, ready to navigate the next step in our journey away from the palace and into the uncertain future that awaited us in Keldara. "Excuse me?" When the man turned to face me, I immediately noticed he wasn't Valorian. I wondered if he was Keldaran.

"Aye? What do you need?" he replied in a gruff voice.

I peered around the stables and whispered, "I need to send a message ... across the border."

He huffed. "I only deal with horses, ma'am. If you need anything else, I can't help you."

"Mira sent us," Ronan interjected.

The man paused and looked us up and down. "Who do you need to get this message to?"

I gulped and whispered, "Commander Mykal Kaiser."

The man paused and narrowed his gaze on me. "That's one odd request, little lady. Are you sure?"

I nodded. "Yes."

He sighed and stood. "Very well." The man reached for parchment, quill, and ink, handing it over to Ronan. "Keep it short and don't add too many details in case it gets intercepted. I imagine you don't want anyone reading it other than the commander."

Ronan took the materials, then glanced at me before he began to write.

I leaned into him and whispered in his ear, "Tomorrow at noon. The border. Bring aid." The weight of our message pressed heavily on my shoulders. This wasn't just any letter; it was a plea, a negotiation, a connection to Keldara that would either save us or damn us.

As Ronan wrote, the man leaned against a wooden post and watched us with an unreadable expression. I wondered about his story and the series of events that led him to this place, acting as a bridge between two nations fraught with tension.

Once Ronan finished, he signed it *Leila* instead of *Lyanna*, then folded the parchment carefully and sealed it with a piece of string. "It's ready," he said, his voice low.

The man took the letter and tucked it into his coat. "I'll see it gets there by dawn. Anything else?"

Ronan shook his head. "No, that's it. How much do we owe you?"

"Since you're Mira's friends, five Glints. But know this: this is a one-time deal. I don't make a habit of this."

"Thank you," I said, my heart lightened by a fraction as Ronan paid him. This was a step, albeit a small one, towards a resolution we desperately needed.

As we turned to leave, the man called out, "Stay safe, you two. Keldara's no place for the faint-hearted, much less Valorians."

22

We returned to our room quietly, taking care to ensure no one followed us and we hadn't raised any suspicions.

"We should get some rest," I suggested, though the last thing on my mind was sleep.

"Agreed." Ronan removed his shirt, then turned to me and extended his hand. I took it and let him lead me to the bed, where we kicked off our shoes and climbed in.

As we settled under the covers, the room's simplicity faded away, leaving just a man and a woman finding solace in each other's company. Ronan wrapped an arm around me and pulled me closer until there was no space left between us. My head found a comfortable spot on his chest where I listened to the steady rhythm of his heart. The soft glow of moonlight filtered through the curtains, casting a silver sheen over Ronan's chiseled features. His crimson eyes held a glint of something wild and untamed. I traced the lines of his tattoos, delighting in the warmth of his skin beneath my touch.

Our breaths mingled in the intimate space between us,

creating a symphony of desire that pulsed in the air. Ronan's lips grazed my forehead gently before capturing my lips in a searing kiss. The world around us faded into oblivion as we surrendered to the connection sparking between us.

Clothes became mere obstacles as we shed them in a frenzy, our bodies fitting together like two halves of a whole. Every touch and caress sent shivers down my spine, setting my senses ablaze with a fierce longing that consumed us both.

Part of me knew it was wrong to find joy amidst all the chaos and danger surrounding us. But when Ronan looked at me with those intense eyes filled with longing and tenderness, I couldn't resist.

"You know," he whispered, his voice sending shivers down my spine, "although it's been a day from hell, I've been looking forward to this moment all day."

I chuckled and traced the tattoos on his bare chest. "Me too," I admitted, feeling a rush of heat between us.

Ronan leaned in, his lips brushing against mine in a tantalizing tease before claiming them in a passionate kiss. The world around us melted away as we lost ourselves in each other, our passion igniting like wildfire. Our bodies moved together in perfect harmony, every touch and caress fueling the flames of our desire. The room was filled with soft sighs and whispered words of longing as we gave in to the undeniable pull drawing us closer.

In that fleeting moment, it was as if time stood still and there was only us, our hearts beating in perfect synchronicity. The weight of his warm body against mine brought a sense of comfort I desperately needed. But just as quickly as the moment came, it disappeared as my mind flooded with memories from earlier in the day. The sight of Tessa's lifeless body in my arms replayed on repeat in my mind and anguished guilt settled in my chest.

"Wait," I murmured, pulling away from Ronan's embrace.

His brows furrowed in concern. "Are you alright?" he asked, his voice laced with worry.

I shook my head, unable to fully articulate my jumbled thoughts and emotions. "I don't know, I just ..."

"You feel guilty," Ronan finished for me, his grip on me loosening as he laid back on the bed.

I nodded slowly as tears pricked at the corners of my eyes. "Yes. I do."

Ronan's understanding nod and quiet acceptance offered some solace in the midst of my turmoil. "But you know it's not your fault. It's Caelan's. *He* killed Tessa. Not you."

"Yes ... you're right, but you're also wrong. He might have killed her, but he used me as his tool." I blew out a shaky breath. "I never even asked about her family."

Ronan wrapped his arms around me and pulled me to his chest. "Let go of the guilt. It won't do you any good. All we can do now is pray that the gods have guided Tessa into the afterlife safely, where she'll be watching over you." He grabbed the blanket and pulled it up to our shoulders. "Come on, let's get some sleep," he whispered.

"But—"

"Shh," he quieted me. "Now's not the time. You need rest. Your mind needs to rest. I'll be right here if you need anything."

His soothing voice and touch lulled me into a state of drowsiness, and before I realized it, sleep had claimed me. The darkness enveloped me, offering respite from the weight of my swirling thoughts and emotions.

THE FOLLOWING MORNING, we were awakened by a light knock on our door. Drowsily, I sat up and nudged Ronan awake. When the knocking grew louder, Ronan and I became fully alert.

Ronan grabbed his clothes from the floor and put them on haphazardly, then went to the door. He turned the knob slowly and pulled the door slightly ajar to see who it was. There was a flurry of hushed whispers and after a few moments, Ronan shut the door.

Dressing quickly, I went over to him as he ran a hand through his long hair. "Who was it?" I asked.

"The messenger," he said. "Mykal received our message, but he didn't send one in return."

I bit my lip. It was too large of a risk to attempt to cross the border without knowing Mykal's stance, but if we didn't leave now, we would be sitting ducks until the Valorian army arrived en masse and discovered us.

Ronan eyed me. "What do you think?"

"I say we risk it," I said. "Unless you want to turn back?"

Ronan shook his head. "No, I don't. We've come this far."

"Then let's head to the border."

We gathered our few belongings and wrapped our cloaks once more before stepping out into the early morning. The village was just beginning to stir, with a few early risers in the streets. The air held a crisp chill, a reminder that we were still in dawn's early grasp.

The innkeeper, Mira, caught my eye as we stepped toward the door. She gave us a knowing nod, her expression solemn. I felt a wave of gratitude towards her for her help, however small it might have been in the grand scheme of things.

The journey to the border was tense. Each step took us closer to an uncertain confrontation, and while I shouldered the responsibility of our decision, part of me was relieved. We were taking action, no longer hiding in the shadows and waiting for the threat to find us.

The landscape gradually shifted as we walked, the village's quaint homes and bustling streets giving way to the wild, untamed beauty of Valoria's borderlands. The forest grew denser, the path less defined, and I constantly scanned our surroundings for any signs of danger.

Hand in hand, Ronan and I walked in relative silence until I couldn't keep quiet any longer. I knew what I was about to say would piss him off, but I needed to get it off my chest. "I can only go with you until we reach the Central Plains border," I said. There was a small patch of land of the Central Plains between Keldara and the Grasslands that could be crossed in just a few hours. "Although Marcellus is back at the palace to plead our case, I wouldn't put it past Caelan to suggest to my father that you kidnapped me. To avoid any further conflict and clear your name, I need to return. I just want to see you safely home."

Ronan stopped walking and turned to me. "Do you really think I would leave you in Keldara ... alone?"

"Ronan ..."

He shook his head and continued walking. "No, Leila. You can't ask that of me. I'll cross through Keldara alone; you don't need to come with me. Return to the palace. No one in Valoria will hurt you."

I tugged on his hand and forced him to turn to me. "No! I won't be at peace if I don't know what has happened to you. I'll accompany you until we reach the Central Plains. Once we get there, we'll figure things out. Maybe I can send word to my brother to come get me. But we're not parting ways yet."

He huffed and grumbled, "You're so damn stubborn."

I snorted. "As if *you* aren't." I tugged on his hand to start walking again. "Come on. Let's get a move on."

Time crawled at a slow pace as we walked to the Valorian – Keldaran border. The fear of what to expect when we arrived gnawed at my insides. I could only hope that what Mykal said to me at the banquet was true and I could come to him if I needed help.

"We're almost there," Ronan said, his hand gripping mine a little tighter.

The forest provided a sense of security with its dense foliage, but soon we would have to cross a clearing that served as the distinct border between the two nations. Just as the clearing came into view, we heard yelling.

"*There!* There they are!"

Ronan and I whirled around to see a cadre of mage warriors come out of hiding, ready to ambush us.

My eyes went wide and I tightened my hold on Ronan's hand. "I think it's time to run!" I muttered as I watched in horror.

"I think you're right!"

We spun on our heels and ran at top speed toward the border, hopeful we could secure sanctuary on the other side.

"Catch them! But don't hurt the princess!"

The mage warriors' shouts echoed through the dense forest as Ronan and I pushed our legs to their limits, dodging trees and leaping over underbrush. My heart pounded, not just from exertion, but from the fear of what being caught could mean. Their voices grew louder, closer, and our chances of escaping without confrontation dwindled with every step.

As we broke through the last line of trees and into the clearing that marked the border, a sense of desperation washed over me. The expanse before us was open and provided no cover, a stark contrast to the sheltered forest we'd just left behind.

Ronan glanced back, his expression grim. "We need a distraction," he said, his voice steady despite our dire situation.

Before he could attempt a foolish maneuver to save me, I released his hand and pulled one of my own. I stopped and turned to face our pursuers. Ronan gaped at me in disbelief, and when his steps faltered, I shouted, "Go! I'll hold them off!"

"No!" he protested, his voice cracking. "I'm not leaving you!"

I pressed a searing kiss to his lips. "Ronan, you need to *go*. I can handle them. I'll catch up, I promise. You know they won't hurt me."

The mage warriors were nearly upon us. With their hands lifted, their spells crackled in the air, ready to be unleashed. Tears blurred my vision as I worried for Ronan's safety. "Go!" I shouted and pushed him away. With a heavy heart, I turned my back on him, hoping he'd run to safety.

"Don't hurt the princess!" a mage warrior yelled, his words fueling my desperate fight to protect the man I loved.

I didn't dare look back at Ronan, afraid that if I did, I couldn't do what was needed. Instead, I focused on the mages as they neared the tree line. Tapping into my own mage powers, I reached for the roots of the trees, screaming from the exertion as I pushed myself to the limit.

Once the mages neared, I uprooted several nearby trees

and dropped them onto their path, blocking their way to us. Heaving, I placed my hands on my knees as sweat trickled down the sides of my face. I'd expended more power and energy than I had. With their path blocked, I spun on my heels ready to run when I ran right into Ronan's chest. The stubborn fool had never left.

His gaze was searing. "I can't leave you, Leila. Either we live together, or we die together. Don't ever ask me to leave you again." He took my hand and gripped it tightly.

As our feet pounded against the ground, each step taking us closer to safety, I couldn't shake the fear that clung to me like a second skin. Adrenaline coursed through our veins, propelling us forward.

The gap between us and the border narrowed, and we were almost there. Just mere steps away from safety, Caelan's voice cut through the brewing storm.

"Lyanna!"

Ronan and I whirled around and watched in horror as Caelan slowly approached. Although there was still a great distance between us, I was nervous by his chilling demeanor. Standing by the tree line, he'd obviously been lying in wait and watching from afar.

"You have nowhere to run!" Caelan said. "Do you think Keldara will welcome you with open arms? It's a death sentence, Lyanna. Come with me. We can fix this."

I reached for Ronan's hand and gripped it tightly. "I know what you did!" I shouted angrily. "You killed Tessa!" I cried. "I can't forgive you for that!"

Caelan scoffed. "You hardly knew her. And *I* didn't kill her ... *he* did!" he yelled, pointing in Ronan's direction. "If he hadn't gotten in our way, no one would have gotten hurt!"

I felt as if he'd slapped me. It wasn't only because of his words, which were unhinged, but because I finally realized something was seriously wrong with Caelan. He was delusional. Morally deficient. A menace.

"Leila!" a male voice called out from behind us. Ronan and I looked over to see Mykal standing on the other side of Keldara's border ... with an army at his back. "Cross the border, Leila," he said calmly as he narrowed his gaze on Caelan.

"Will Ronan be safe if we do?" I called out.

Mykal slowly nodded. "You have my word; I won't let anything happen to either of you. Now cross the border."

With Mykal's assurance echoing in my ears, I took a deep breath and felt the weight of the moment settle upon my shoulders.

"You can't believe him!" Caelan shouted, dumbstruck. "It's a trick! You'll be his hostage the instant your feet touch their soil! Lyanna, please, come to me," Caelan pleaded, reaching a leather-gloved hand to me from across the clearing.

This was it – the point of no return. I glanced at Ronan and saw the same resolve reflected in his eyes that had settled in my heart.

"There's no turning back after this," he said. "I'm ready to dive into the depths of the ocean with you. Are you?"

I nodded and we stepped forward together, crossing the invisible line that separated Valoria from Keldara.

The moment our feet touched Keldaran soil, the atmosphere shifted. It felt as if we had entered a different world, one where the possibilities were both terrifying and exhilarating. Behind us, Caelan stood frozen, his expression a mix of anger and disbelief.

Ronan's grip on my hand tightened as we approached Mykal and his army. Their presence was intimidating, yet there was a sense of order and discipline that reassured me.

Mykal stepped forward, his gaze softening slightly as he regarded me.

"Welcome to Keldara, Princess Lyanna," Mykal said, his voice carrying a hint of respect. "And you, Ronan of the Crimson Clan, are under my protection as well."

I nodded, unable to find the words to express my gratitude. The tension that had built within me started to ease, replaced by cautious hope. Here in Keldara, with Mykal's word as our shield, Ronan might be able to get home safely, after all.

Caelan's voice, now distant and powerless, drifted to us on the wind. "You'll regret this, Lyanna!"

But his threats seemed empty now, overshadowed by the safety Keldara promised, or so we thought. Until the moment my childhood best friend reached over a fallen tree and dragged a small body across it roughly, throwing it out into the clearing. The frail boy was gagged, his wrists and ankles bound.

"Henry!" I shouted and started to run across the border, but Ronan stopped me.

Caelan smirked. "You see? I have something you both treasure. Now, unless you want to see this young boy killed, come to me, Lyanna." He stalked over to Henry and removed the gag from his mouth. "Now tell her, Henry," he goaded. "Tell her to come save you."

My body trembled with unrestrained hatred. Never in my life had I ever wanted to kill someone until this moment.

Henry spit in Caelan's face. "Never!" he shouted hoarsely, then turned to me and Ronan. "She's safe, Miss Leila! I made sure no harm came to Miss Tessa's body!"

I couldn't stop the tears that streamed down my face. Even in the midst of his personal anguish, Henry didn't care about his wellbeing; he was only concerned with making sure I knew he'd done what I asked. I hated myself for putting that on him and not taking him with us. Now, my biggest fear had come to life. He was in danger ... *because of me.*

Caelan reared back and kicked him in his stomach, which shut him up quickly.

"Caelan!" I roared across the clearing. "I swear if you or anybody hurts that little boy, I will rain hellfire upon all of Eldwain! To every single person here, I will bleed you dry until there's nothing left but a dry carcass!" I memorized each mage's face, trembling in fury with impotent rage at the knowledge that I'd already exhausted my powers to reach the border.

Caelan's grin dimmed just a bit as he watched me stand rigidly, my hands fisted at my sides waiting, just *waiting* for one of them to move a single inch.

Ronan pulled me back against his chest. "Leila," he whispered in my ear. "He won't hurt him. Caelan is many things, but he wouldn't hurt an innocent boy."

"I don't believe that," I said raggedly. "Not anymore."

Caelan grabbed the collar of Henry's shirt and dragged him back to the tree line, tossing him to the mages who cowered in the forest.

"You think I fear you?" he called out, his voice full of derision. "Lyanna, I fear *no one*! Mark my words: If you do not return to Valoria, I will kill him."

"If you kill him," I looked straight into his evil hazel eyes, "you're dead to me. And if any of you—" I addressed the Valorian army and cadre of mages, pointing my clawed hands at them, "touch this little boy, I will kill three generations of your family ..." My voice dropped to a guttural roar. "As the lost heir, you should heed my warning."

The gasps that circulated the Valorian army reached all

the way to where we stood behind the Keldaran border, and I knew I'd gotten their attention. I never wanted to name myself the lost heir, but for Henry's sake, I would. Hopefully Marcellus could forgive me.

"No worries, Your Highness!" one of the mages called out. "We will protect the boy!"

"Leila?" Mykal spoke behind me. "It's best if we go."

Without another word, Ronan and I stepped deeper into Keldara's territory, leaving Henry's fate in the hands of the mage warriors who I hoped were more afraid of me than they were of Caelan.

23

As we ventured deeper into Keldara on horseback, the landscape transformed from the lush forests of Valoria to an austere terrain marked by its stark beauty. Keldara was a nation carved out of necessity and survival, its people as resilient as the land itself. Every village and town we passed was a testament to its military foundation—a nation perpetually prepared for the possibility of conflict.

The streets of each settlement were orderly, with soldiers patrolling in regular intervals. Despite the military presence, a sense of calm and efficiency permeated the air. The people of Keldara went about their daily lives with purpose, their respect for the soldiers evident in the way they greeted them with nods of acknowledgment.

Mykal led us through the heart of Keldara, passing training grounds where young warriors honed their skills. The sounds of clashing swords and shouting instructors coupled with the determined faces of the trainees provided a glimpse into the disciplined life of a Keldaran soldier.

"Discipline and duty are the cornerstones of life here,"

Mykal explained as we rode. "Every citizen has a role to play in the defense of our nation. From a young age, they are taught the importance of serving Keldara."

"Sounds more like brainwashing to me," Ronan muttered beside me.

The stark, utilitarian architecture of the buildings reflected the nation's pragmatic approach to life. There was beauty in their simplicity, in the way they blended into the landscape, as if acknowledging that the true splendor of Keldara lay in its people and their unyielding spirit.

We'd been riding for a full day with Mykal telling us about the places we passed and the culture of Keldara before he asked about our purpose.

"I'm assuming you're trying to reach the Grasslands." Mykal finally broached the subject as he led the way. "I heard about the so-called assassination attempt, but I knew Ronan would never be capable of doing such a thing," he smirked.

Ronan rolled his eyes.

"Do you really have spies in the palace?" I asked. It was the only way for him to learn what he did so quickly.

Mykal nodded. "I told you, Leila. I have eyes and ears everywhere."

"I don't know if I find that reassuring or not," I mumbled.

Mykal laughed. "In this case, you should. I expected you to cross the border. When I got your letter, I was already on my way."

I cleared my throat. "Thank you."

"But I *am* curious..." Mykal peered over his shoulder at us. "Are you really going to acknowledge yourself as the lost heir?"

My brows shot up to my hairline. "You know about that?"

He snorted. "I told you – nothing goes on in Asteria that I don't know about."

"Nosy bastard," Ronan grumbled.

I glared at Ronan before addressing Mykal. "Honestly, I didn't want to, but I was desperate back there."

Mykal nodded slowly. "Caelan has been waiting a long time for you to return. If you're named the Crown Princess, he won't let you go easily."

I frowned. "Why do you say that?"

"It's all part of his plan," he said slowly. "To unite all of Asteria under one nation—Eldwain's."

Shocked, I pulled on my horse's reins to stop it. "What?" I gasped. "What do you mean?"

Ronan stopped beside me, and Mykal turned his horse around to face us. "Don't you know? I figured your fae friend would have mentioned it."

"My fae friend?" I repeated with furrowed brows. Instead of answering, Mykal made a noncommittal sound. I gaped at Ronan, hoping he could fill in the blanks.

"Orion," Ronan clarified for me. "He's talking about Orion."

My eyes widened. "What does Orion have to do with any of this?"

Mykal chuckled as he leaned on the saddle's pommel. "And here I thought you were best friends with the fae. I guess not." He shrugged.

Ronan rolled his eyes. "For the love of the gods, can you get to the point, man?"

Mykal snorted. "All right, all right. Caelan acts like he's not fighting for the Eldwain throne, but he secretly is. His backers are the Elders from Ellyndor, who have gathered a secret army to assist him. Right now, Caelan's main mission is to marry into Valoria to acquire the lands. It's the whole reason he wants to marry you, which means he won't let you slip through his fingers so easily."

I frowned. "Why are you telling us this?"

Mykal shrugged. "Because once Caelan conquers Valoria, he'll come for Keldara and the Grasslands next. He's already got the Central Plains in his pocket. Like I told you once before, Leila: you and I don't need to be enemies."

Ronan scoffed. "Right, because Keldara has always had Asteria's best interest at heart," he said sarcastically. "Didn't you try to invade Valoria just ten years ago?"

Mykal nodded. "Yes, mistakes were made, but I'm hoping to correct them."

Ronan looked away, his rigid posture belying the fact that he didn't believe a single word Mykal said. "And what of the Crimson Clan? Will you continue to require tributes every year?"

Mykal's eyes widened as he glanced between me and Ronan. "She knows?"

"Yes, I *know*," I said clearly. "Which makes your story about wanting to help us hard to believe."

Mykal shrugged. "It's an equal trade. The Crimson Clan needs war horses and weapons, and we need people. If you truly wish to end our partnership, you need to speak with Chief Aryan."

"It's not that simple and you know it!" Ronan growled.

Mykal sighed. "Very well. It's obvious we won't solve things here tonight, but it's best if we don't linger here for long. We still have a day's trek to reach the capital. Come on." He pulled his horse's reins and trotted ahead, reclaiming his spot at the head of the line.

Ronan and I glanced at one another, unsure about

Mykal's claims. Even so, they held the ring of truth and things were starting to make sense. Now the only question was: How did we fix it?

~

As we neared the capital, the military presence became more pronounced. It was clear that the army was not a force of subjugation, but one of protection, deeply intertwined with the identity of Keldara itself.

"The King rules, but it is the military that safeguards our way of life," Mykal declared, his voice carrying a tone of admiration.

In the capital, the streets were filled with people; it was where I got my first glimpse of Crimson Clan members. Their tattoos were visible, but what startled me was their shaved heads.

"Ronan?" I whispered, glancing over at him to see his jaw locked with the force of gritting his teeth. "Why ...?"

"Our hair is very important to us," he ground out. "Taking it away is like stripping away our identity. It's *barbaric*."

I glanced around, absorbing the stark contrast between the disciplined, uniformed soldiers and the Crimson Clan members who mingled among them. Their shaved heads served as a silent reminder of the tension that lay simmering beneath the surface of this military-run nation. Despite the apparent peace and order, it was clear that sacrifices had been made and identities were altered in the name of unity and defense.

As we moved through the bustling capital, the presence of the Crimson Clan members increased. Some walked with their heads held high, a soundless rebellion against their imposed loss; others moved with a subdued air, the weight of their lost identity casting a shadow over their steps. It was a powerful statement of resilience and resistance.

"Move!" a Keldaran soldier yelled as he cracked a whip against the back of a Crimson Clan woman. She screamed in agony and almost dropped the barrel of water she was carrying. "Hurry up! *Move!*"

"He—!" I started, but Ronan sent me a look and shook his head.

"Don't interfere. It'll only make it worse for them," he muttered, his expression consumed with rage.

Many of the Crimson Clan members watched Ronan in awe as we trotted down the streets, silently begging him to save them. I watched Ronan avoid their gazes, his eyes glassy with unshed tears. I wanted to comfort him and tell him it would be okay, but that would be the biggest lie I'd ever told. The only way to free them from this enslavement was to resurrect the demon fox. And the only way to do that was to sacrifice *me*.

The idea gnawed at my insides as I watched his people being prodded like cattle. For the first time, I understood his desperation. Why he lied to me. This was their reality. For the first time ... I wanted to help.

I snapped the reins, urging my horse to trot and catch up to Mykal. "How far are we from the Central Plains border?"

"About a day and a half. And then roughly two hours from the Grasslands border." He peered over at me, then over his shoulder to where Ronan rode behind us. "You know you don't have to go with him," he whispered. "The Grasslands won't be safe for you."

I raised a brow. "Who said I'm going with him?"

Mykal smirked. "Well, if *that's* the case, would you do me the honor of staying in Keldara as my guest?"

I scoffed. "And you think I'd be safe here? I'm not *that* easily fooled."

His grin widened. "See? That's what I like about you. You're a realist. But truly, Leila, you have my word. I will keep you safe."

Feeling the weight of Mykal's gaze, as well as Ronan's on my back, I forced myself to keep my eyes trained straight ahead. I didn't know what my plans were, but for now, my priority was getting Ronan to safety. "Just get us to the border as quickly as you can," I muttered.

∼

THE REMAINDER of our trip to the border was tense, the sense of urgency palpable. Each of us was lost in our own worries and hopes for the future as the landscape of Keldara unfolded before us—a mixture of rugged terrain and serene beauty. The military presence gradually lessened as we moved further from the capital, giving way to the plains of the Central Plains. The occasional patrols we encountered nodded respectfully to Mykal, though their curious gazes lingered upon Ronan and me.

The knowledge of our impending farewell loomed over us like a shadow. I saw the tension in Ronan's rigid body, the muscles clenched and ready to spring; his usual ease was replaced by quiet solemnity. His homeland was calling him back, yet the idea of separation filled us with dread.

The day passed with little conversation. That night, we camped under the stars and listened to the fire crackling softly as we huddled close by for warmth. The time felt surreal, a temporary reprieve from the challenges that awaited us.

On the final stretch of land before we reached the border, the landscape grew increasingly desolate, a no-man's land that served as a buffer between Keldara and the Grasslands. The air was filled with a sense of desolation, a reminder of the rift that lay between the two vastly different lands.

As the border came into view, I was consumed by a mix of relief and apprehension. This was it—the moment of parting was upon us. I glanced at Ronan. His expression was unreadable, his jaw set in determination. Mykal rode silently beside us, his earlier offers of sanctuary in Keldara lingering unspoken between us.

"We're here," Mykal announced as we halted at the edge of the border near the invisible line that marked the beginning of the Central Plains.

Ronan dismounted, his gaze lingering on me. "Leila," he began, his voice thick with emotion. "I don't know how to—"

"You don't have to say anything," I interrupted, my voice steady despite the turmoil inside me. I dismounted and strode to him, then wrapped him in a tight embrace.

I ignored Mykal when he cleared his throat behind us. I didn't want to let Ronan go, even though I knew he would only be safe in the Grasslands.

Slowly, Ronan pulled away, his crimson eyes staring deep into mine. "Don't linger in Keldara. Have Mykal take you straight back to Valoria," he whispered as he brushed my hair back. "Once I reach the Crimson Clan, I'll send word to you—"

"No," I muttered and shook my head. "I can't do this. I can't let you go."

Ronan cradled my face. "Once I step over into the Grasslands, I'll be safe. You don't have to worry about me, Leila."

He pressed a soft kiss to my forehead. "I'm more worried about you."

Images of his people scattered and humiliated throughout Keldara filtered through my mind. Their silent pleas to be rescued were imprinted in my brain. I was the solution. I couldn't cross Keldara again and see them as I returned to the relative safety of my home. Their empty gazes would haunt me for all eternity.

"No," I repeated. "I'm coming with you."

Ronan's crimson eyes widened. "What? *No*! You can't."

My eyes flashed. "I can and I will."

"Leila," Mykal cut in to our conversation. "I've gotten word that your family believes you were kidnapped by Ronan. If you truly want to help him, getting back to Valoria to clear his name is the only way."

I glared at Mykal. "What about the Crimson Clan? What about the ones who are enslaved in Keldara? What you're doing is wrong!"

Mykal coughed into his closed fist and looked away sheepishly. "Things have been done this way for over a century, Leila. Change doesn't happen overnight. You must know that."

I stepped away from Ronan and edged closer to Mykal. "And what change are you trying to implement? I don't see you doing anything!"

Mykal sent me a glare. "You don't know anything about the politics of Keldara. Don't make assumptions."

"Leila," Ronan said, turning my attention back to him, "as much as I want to disagree with him, Mykal is right. You should return to Valoria and let your family know you're safe." He turned to Keldara's commander. "I trust you can get her back safely and quickly?"

Mykal nodded.

I took ahold of Ronan's arm and dragged him a few feet away. "Listen," I whispered, "I know you want to protect me, but I can protect myself. After seeing your people in Keldara, I can't go back to pretending I don't know how they're suffering. Either you let me speak to my father for an alliance, or you allow me to cross the border with you and help the only way I can."

Ronan's eyes widened in horror. "Leila, what are you saying?" he whispered.

"I'm saying yes. I'll awaken the fox demon."

Before I even finished my sentence, he was already shaking his head. "No, Leila. Trust me when I tell you, I want to help my people more than anyone, but ... things are different now. My father is different. I don't know what it is, but something rubbed me the wrong way when I saw him at the banquet. It had been months since I last spoke to him, and I don't think we're in agreement any longer."

I frowned. "What do you mean?"

He sighed and ran a hand through his tousled hair. "I believe he wants to sacrifice you and then use the wish on something else."

My stomach plummeted. "But he can't do that without your permission! It's *you* who holds the wish, and I trust *you*, Ronan. More than I've ever trusted anyone. So let your father scheme all he wants. He won't get his way."

"We're running out of time!" Mykal called out. "If word arrives to the King of Keldara that the son of Chief Aryan crossed the border and we let him go, much less that Princess Lyanna of Valoria crossed with him, there will be hell to pay!"

I looked deeply into Ronan's eyes and took his hands in my own. "Please, Ronan. Let me go with you," I whispered.

I saw the conflict in those crimson eyes and his burning

desire to reject my offer, but in those same eyes I saw a small part wanted to agree. He wanted to save his people no matter what it took.

He sighed. "Fine. Let's go." Gripping my hand tightly, Ronan pulled me over to where Mykal stood, holding the reins of our horses.

"So what's the plan?" the commander asked.

"She's coming with me." Ronan squeezed my hand. "Thank you for your assistance."

Mykal looked conflicted as he looked between us warily. "Leila ... this isn't a good idea. What Chief Aryan has planned –"

"I know. You told me," I said with a roll of my eyes. "But just trust that I know what I'm doing."

He turned his ire to Ronan, his expression darkening. "Are you truly willing to sacrifice her? I'm usually not opposed to sacrificing one for the sake of thousands, but—"

Mykal looked at me with something akin to caring in his eyes. Did he actually care whether I lived or died? I had to turn away.

"You can trust that I'd never let anything happen to her. She won't die," Ronan declared, his jaw locking as he stared Mykal down. "I assure you, I can take care of my woman."

"I doubt King Malik would agree with that sentiment," Mykal gritted between his teeth.

I tried to diffuse the situation. "This is *my* decision, and like you said, there's not much time. I appreciate your help, Mykal, but we need to go."

After a beat, Mykal nodded and handed us the reins of our horses. "Fine. Just don't say I didn't warn you."

Without another glance, he climbed atop his horse, digging his heels in its sides and leaving us at the border.

24

After crossing the small patch of land of the Central Plains, the journey into the Grasslands revealed a stark contrast to the regimented landscapes of Keldara. Here, the terrain sprawled wide and wild, a rugged expanse that seemed both untamed and inviting. Vast prairies stretched under an expansive sky, dotted with clusters of dense woods and interspersed with winding rivers that sparkled under the sun's bright rays.

As we ventured deeper, the occasional homestead appeared, their structures built from the very earth they stood upon, blending seamlessly into the natural environment. These homes were surrounded by patches of cultivated land where members of the Crimson Clan worked together, their movements synchronized in a dance of communal living.

"The Grasslands breathe with the life of its people," Ronan explained, his voice carrying a mix of pride and sorrow. "We live by the land, and the land lives by us. It's more than a home—it's part of who we are."

The closer we got to the heart of the Crimson Clan's

territory, the more vibrant the landscape became. Wildflowers in a myriad of colors blanketed the fields, creating a mosaic of hues that danced in the breeze. Occasionally, we'd pass a group of Crimson Clan members, their distinctive tattoos a vivid declaration of their identity, their greetings warm but measured as they recognized Ronan.

"Every clan member learns to harmonize with the environment here," Ronan continued, gesturing towards a group of children herding sheep using traditional techniques passed down through generations. "Our ways might seem primitive to some, but they're crafted from centuries of respect for the wilderness that sustains us."

As the sun began to set, casting long shadows over the grassy plains, the true beauty of the Grasslands revealed itself. The horizon lit up in fiery oranges and pinks, reflecting off the rivers like trails of molten gold. It was a land that demanded respect and offered solace in return, a land that fiercely protected its own.

"This is why I fight so hard to protect our way of life," Ronan said, his gaze fixed on the horizon. "It's not just about survival. It's about preserving a legacy that will outlive us all."

"It's beautiful, Ronan," I said as we passed another group of members who looked at me with open curiosity.

"Ronan!" someone called out from a distance. We peered over and saw Silas running towards us. When he reached us, he pulled Ronan into an embrace. "What are you doing here?" His crimson eyes slid to me, no doubt wondering why I was with him on their lands.

"Long story, brother." Ronan smiled and patted his back. "Do you know where my father is?"

Silas nodded. "He's in the ritual hall speaking with some of the elders."

"We need to see him," Ronan said, urgency edging his voice.

Silas cast a glance at me, his eyes narrowing slightly before returning to Ronan. "Is everything alright?" he asked, concern threading his tone.

Ronan hesitated, his gaze flitting to me before returning to his clan brother. "It's complicated. We've had a bit of a journey."

Silas nodded as understanding dawned on his face. "Alright, I'll take you to him, but Ronan, if you're bringing her—" he paused and nodded towards me, "—into the ritual hall, you know it's not without risk. The elders are there and they, along with your father might misunderstand your intention, if you know what I mean."

I felt a flicker of apprehension but met Silas's gaze steadily. "I can handle myself," I said, hoping my voice conveyed more confidence than I felt.

Silas studied me a moment longer, then sighed. "Alright. Follow me." He turned and led us through the village, which seemed to buzz with the energy of a community deeply connected to both their heritage and the land.

As we walked, children played in the fields, their laughter ringing clear and true, while adults nodded respectfully as we passed. The whole community pulsed with a vibrant life that was at once ancient and refreshingly alive.

The ritual hall was situated at the heart of the village, a large, round structure adorned with symbols that spoke of the Crimson Clan's deep spiritual and cultural roots. The air grew redolent with the scent of incense as we approached, and the murmur of deep voices echoed from inside.

Silas paused at the entrance and turned to us. "Prepare

yourselves. This might not go smoothly," he warned before pushing aside the thick cloth that served as a door.

Inside, the hall was dimly lit by the glow of firelight. Figures clad in traditional garb sat around a central fire, their faces marked by lines of age and wisdom. Chief Aryan sat amongst them, his presence commanding even in his stillness.

Ronan took a deep breath and stepped forward, with me lagging a half-step behind. The conversation inside the hall ceased abruptly as all eyes flicked to us. The weight of their gazes was palpable, filled with questions and, for some, suspicion.

Chief Aryan's eyes locked on mine, then he looked at Ronan. "Son," he began, his voice resonant and carrying through the hut, "what brings you back to us so early? I thought you would still be making your way through the Central Plains."

Ignoring his father's question, Ronan's voice was calm but firm. "Something happened in Valoria and ... they might possibly wage war on us if we don't act fast." He glanced back at me, his expression unreadable.

The room tensed. The air was thick with anticipation as the crackle of the fire punctuated the silence that followed.

"Explain yourself!" Chief Aryan demanded as he stood. "What have you done?"

Ronan swallowed deeply and hesitated. Before he could say anything, I stepped forward and took his hand in mine. "My family believes Ronan tried to poison me. My brother is there and is trying to explain the situation, so we hope nothing will come of it. But my brother is also dealing with Prince Caelan, who orchestrated the whole situation."

"What?" Silas gasped and looked to Ronan for confirmation. When he nodded, Silas shook his head.

Chief Aryan focused on me. His cold, crimson eyes were nothing like Ronan's warm eyes, which was slightly terrifying. "And why are *you* here? Not that we don't welcome you, but you had the power to stay behind and clear Ronan's name."

I nodded. "Yes ... but I want to help *you*."

Chief Aryan's brows shot up to his hairline. "What do you mean?"

"I know about the prophecy. I know what you need from me."

A collective gasp cut through the hall. All eyes fell on me and drifted to where our hands were clasped together. I saw the moment when understanding dawned on them.

"Leila ..." Silas whispered, attempting to stop me, but it was too late.

Chief Aryan's eyes brightened with excitement and a smirk slowly spread across his face. "Is that so? Well then, I guess my only question now is do you agree to help us?"

Everyone in the hall held their breath and waited for my answer, weighing the possibility of being saved.

I dipped my head. "Yes, I do."

The chief's smirk widened and the elders in the hall started to clap and stomp their feet with wide smiles.

Silas appeared beside me with worry etched on his face. "Leila ... Your Highness, are you *sure*? Do you know the whole truth?"

Ronan cleared his throat. "She knows," he said, finally finding his voice. "And she knows I'll use the wish from the fox demon to bring her back," he said loud enough so everyone in the hall would hear.

There was a pause in the celebration, and the smirk on Chief Aryan's face twitched. Ronan was right; his father had other plans.

"Of course, son," he agreed amiably. "We've waited a long time, so it goes without saying that we hope to conclude the ceremony swiftly. Agreed?"

Ronan's face tensed as he glared at his father. "How soon?" he gritted between his teeth.

The corners of Chief Aryan's mouth lifted. "How about tomorrow?"

Ronan growled and took a menacing step toward his father. I quickly tugged on his arm to stop him. "Tomorrow is fine," I answered quickly.

Ronan whipped his gaze to me. "Leila!"

"It's fine, Ronan," I whispered to him. "Your father is right. It's better to get this over with. Your people are in desperate need. We can't let them wait any longer."

Chief Aryan smirked and stepped toward us. "Your Highness is so sage. Tomorrow it is, then."

25

Silas waited outside the ritual hall with me while Ronan spoke privately to his father and the elders. I glanced around the village and noticed something strange. Although the threat of Keldara loomed over them, the Crimson Clan looked relatively happy as they enjoyed the freedom of their land.

"I'm sorry," Silas cut into my thoughts. I turned to him with a furrowed brow. "You know ... for kicking you out of our camp in the Central Plains. I should have known it was you. Ronan wouldn't have acted that way if you weren't who you are."

I nodded. "It's okay, Silas. I gave you reason to question me. Things back then were ... complicated, to say the least. It's all water under the bridge."

He gave me a tight smile. "I owe you thanks as well."

"For what?" I quirked a brow.

"For taking care of Ronan," he answered simply. "I know you were angry with him, which I assumed was because of the prophecy, which you had every reason to be upset about. Just know he would never put you in harm's way."

"I know," I said. "At least I know that *now*."

"Good," he murmured and then cleared his throat. "I know Ronan doesn't trust his father, but you have my word that I'll help him with whatever he needs. We won't let you die, Your Highness."

"Thanks." I smiled briefly. "But you don't have to keep addressing me as *Your Highness*. Ronan still calls me Leila, and I actually prefer it."

He bit his lip and winced. "You sure?"

"Positive."

He nodded. "Very well then ... Leila."

I grinned. "So, tell me what foods I must try while I'm here and alive in the Grasslands. What's your specialty?"

He gave his first genuine smile, which showed me he was passionate about food. "We don't have any signature wines like you're used to, but I know you have a sweet tooth, and while they're not mooncakes, we have the lotus cookie and it's very good. When Ronan returns, I'll go get you a batch to try."

For the moment, it seemed as if the tension that had loomed between us since we met started to lessen. We weren't the best of friends in the Central Plains, but since we both cared about Ronan, it was a relief to patch things up without too much of a fuss. I was about to thank him for his offer of lotus cookies when Ronan stepped out of the ritual hall.

"How'd it go?" Silas asked as we stepped toward him.

Ronan blew out a breath and ran a hand through his dark hair. "The ceremony has been scheduled for tomorrow night. It was the latest I could get them to agree to do it."

I frowned. "Under the full moon?"

"Tomorrow's a full moon?" Ronan questioned.

I nodded. "It's when I'm at my strongest. Why would they do it then? It can't be a coincidence."

Ronan shrugged. "I don't know."

Silas bit his lip. "I don't know, Ro. Something doesn't seem right. I understand why the chief wants to move fast, but this seems rushed. And Leila is right; completing the ceremony during a full moon when she's at her strongest doesn't make much sense."

The three of us glanced at one another before Ronan turned to Silas. "Can I ask you to do some digging around? That way we can at least be prepared for any surprises they might want to spring at us."

Silas nodded. "Of course. I'll gather some information and bring it to you by morning, unless it's an emergency. Oh! I was going to get Leila some lotus cookies."

Ronan's smile appeared. "Don't worry; I'll take her around the village and get her some. Thank you, Silas." He patted his friend's back.

"Sure thing. See you both later."

∽

THE AFTERNOON SUN cast a warm glow over the village as Ronan led me through the bustling market. The air was filled with a mix of scents that were both unfamiliar and enticing. Vendors shouted about their wares and competed for customers, selling everything from spiced meats to fresh, vibrant vegetables, but Ronan had a specific destination in mind.

"Here," Ronan said, pulling me toward a small, unassuming stall that was decorated with strings of dried flowers and herbs. "As Silas said, you *have* to try these," he insisted, his voice filled with excitement.

The stall owner, an elderly woman with a kind, wrinkled face and crimson eyes beamed at us. "Ah, Ronan, you're back! Brought a friend today?" Her eyes twinkled as she glanced at me.

Ronan nodded. "Yes, this is ... Leila. Leila, this is Hana. She makes the best lotus cookies in all the Grasslands."

Hana chuckled, her laughter as rich and warm as the afternoon sun. "Oh, you flatter me, young man. But *you*, dear," she said, turning to me, "try these and tell me if he's telling the truth." She handed me a small, delicate cookie, its edges perfectly crisp with a soft, almost translucent center.

I bit into the cookie and the taste was like nothing I had ever experienced. It was sweet, but not overwhelmingly so, with a hint of something floral that must have been the lotus. The texture was divine, melting almost instantly when it touched my tongue.

"They're incredible!" I admitted, unable to hide my delight.

Ronan's face lit up with a proud grin. "I told you," he said. "Hana, we'll take a dozen."

As Hana packaged the cookies, I took the moment to observe the village activity around me. Children ran past, playing with homemade toys, and the air buzzed with the chatter of daily life. It was peaceful here, a stark contrast to the ever-present political tensions of the palace.

Ronan handed me the package of cookies, his hand lingering on mine as he did. "There's more to see, and even more to taste," he promised, his voice low and inviting.

I nodded, excitement bubbling within me. My heart was full of anticipation for other secrets Ronan might share with me about his home.

The simplicity and warmth of the Grasslands were

infectious, and I found myself wishing the day would never end. Especially since my death was imminent. I think we were both hoping for a distraction for what lay ahead.

Ronan guided me to another vibrantly colored stall draped with various fruits and spices displayed like a painter's palette. "You must try the fire berries," he said, picking up a small, bright red fruit that looked innocent enough, but which promised a burst of intense flavor.

I wisely hesitated; I'd heard stories of their potency. "Are they as fiery as they say?"

Ronan laughed, a sound that made the worries of the past few days seem distant. "Only one way to find out." He popped one into his mouth, his expression teasing.

Encouraged by his boldness, I took one and gingerly bit into it. The berry was a burst of sweet heat that somehow didn't overwhelm but delighted with its complex flavors. "Wow, that's surprisingly good!" I exclaimed, reaching for another.

"See? There's magic in the Grasslands' food," Ronan boasted, his eyes gleaming with pride for his homeland.

We moved on, stopping here and there for Ronan to introduce me to more of the local delicacies—each one adding layers to my understanding of the Grasslands and its rich, vibrant culture. Ronan seemed to relish sharing this part of his life with me, and every smile and look he gave filled me with warmth.

Eventually, we reached the edge of the market where the crowd thinned and the view opened to a sprawling field dotted with wildflowers. The sun had begun its slow descent, casting a golden hue as its broad rays lazily brushed the land.

"Let's take a break," Ronan suggested. He pointed

towards a small hill that offered a panoramic view of the village and its surrounding fields.

We climbed the hill and sat on a patch of soft, lush grass. The village was nothing more than a gentle hum in the background as we soaked in the peaceful scene before us. I retrieved the package of lotus cookies and handed one to Ronan.

"As much as I love showing you the Grasslands, it's these quiet moments I treasure the most," he said, his voice soft.

I nodded as a deep sense of peace settled over me. "I can see why you love it here," I responded, taking in the view, the scents, and the sounds. "It feels a world away from everything."

Ronan leaned back on his hands and peered up at the sky painted in shades of deep orange and purple. "It is, and I'm glad I could share it with you. No matter where our paths take us, I hope you'll always remember this day."

I reached out and gently squeezed his hand. "How could I forget?" I whispered. No matter what happened next, this moment—this day—would be etched in my memory forever, a poignant reminder of life's simple beauties. "But my path will always lead me to you, Ronan. Don't *you* forget that."

"I won't," he murmured, reaching his hand around my neck and pulling me toward him until our lips crashed into each other. His tongue met mine and I reached for him hungrily, needing to touch him and feel his warmth.

"Ronan," I whispered against his mouth. "I need you."

He laid me down on the grass, and then his hand glided up my leg and under the skirt of my dress, his touch blazing a trail of fire on my skin. Normally, I would be embarrassed since we were out in the open and anyone could come up here, but with the knowledge that my life was about to end, I didn't care. I wanted him any way possible. It wasn't just a want; it was a *need*. A hunger I'd never felt before. And no matter how much I was fed, I always wanted more.

His fingers slid beneath my underwear and slid straight to the space between my folds, rubbing the wetness that pooled between my thighs. His finger slid inside me, making my breath hitch. He pumped in and out of me slowly before inserting another finger as his thumb rubbed my clit.

A moan slipped out of me and I wrapped an arm around his neck to bring him closer to me, feeling his hardness against my thigh as he laid partially on top of me. I felt an orgasm building and I was ready to explode when his hand suddenly stilled and his body fell on top of mine, unmoving.

"Ronan?" I croaked and shook him lightly, which was when I saw the dart imbedded in the side of his neck. "Ronan!" With unexpected strength, I pushed him off me, hurriedly adjusting my dress and searching the area for the threat. A threat I should have seen coming.

"Apologies for interrupting," Chief Aryan simpered as he climbed up the hill with half a dozen Crimson Clan warriors at his back.

I scrambled to my feet and stood, my muscles coiled and ready for their attack while simultaneously trying to protect Ronan's limp body on the ground. "What's going on?" I gritted between my teeth.

Chief Aryan shrugged one shoulder. "I thought it would be good for us to speak ... without Ronan. He seems very protective of you."

I fought the indignant anger that coiled within my blood. "What's in the dart? Is it poison?"

Chief Aryan scoffed as if the thought was distasteful. "You think I would poison my own son? What kind of monster do you take me for? No, he's just asleep for a little bit. He'll awaken tomorrow morning, no worse for wear."

I gulped as the chief's warriors surrounded me until I was stuck in the center with no way out. "You needed all of them just to *talk* to me? I don't know whether to be insulted or flattered."

"Definitely flattered," he said. "You're strong. We all know it. Just look at this as a precaution."

I narrowed my eyes at Ronan's unhinged father. "Fine. Then talk."

Chief Aryan edged closer, his eyes glinting. "I'm hoping you and I can come to a business agreement without any fuss. Are you willing to hear me out?"

I nodded slowly.

"Perfect." He rubbed his hands together eagerly. "So as you and my son may have realized, I agreed to do the sacrifice tomorrow night during a full moon."

I raised my brow and spat sarcastically, "Let me guess, change of plans?"

The chief smiled, though it lacked humor. "Yes. I hoped we could complete the ceremony *now*. Tonight. The witch doctor and elders are assembled and waiting to begin. It will be quick," he assured me as he edged closer. "Ronan selfishly wanted one more night with you, but we really don't have the time." He offered a sly smile. "I understand the passion held by young hearts, but this is a business transaction of the utmost importance for my people."

"Why does it have to be today? If we hadn't showed up, this wouldn't even be an option."

He nodded, the deepening shadows of dusk turning his face into a macabre mask. "Very true, but the gods must be on our side. Keldara is scheduled to send an envoy tomorrow to collect our tributes. If the fox demon is awakened before then, we'll be prepared to fight and save our people." He crossed his arms menacingly and his warriors edged closer. "What do you say, Your Highness? Are you willing to play your part and complete the ceremony voluntarily, or will it have to be by force?"

I bit my lip and evaluated my chances against the Crimson Clan warriors. I could take on one or two using my blood magic, but that would give the others time to attack, and then I would be too tired to fight back. I was outnumbered and with no weapons, and my sworn protector was unconscious on the ground at my feet. This wasn't how we wanted things to go. I wanted to spend my last hours with Ronan before the inevitable... Before my death.

While I trusted Ronan and knew he fully intended to bring me back with the demon fox's wish, there was a small voice in the back of my mind that doubted just a bit. Especially considering how tricky Chief Aryan was.

I narrowed my gaze on him. "It doesn't seem like I have much of a choice, now do I?"

He shook his head, his face grim.

I raised my head defiantly. "Can I ask a question?"

He nodded and motioned for me to continue.

I asked the question that had been gnawing at me; the one I was fairly certain I knew the answer to, and the one I didn't want to hear. "Will you bring me back afterward by using the fox demon's wish?"

Chief Aryan began to chuckle, which quickly turned into full-blown laughter. Once he calmed himself down, he wiped his eyes and shook his head. "Come, now, Lyanna. I didn't peg you as the naïve type. Of course not. I refuse to waste a wish on something so trite. We need that wish for far more important things, Your Highness. I'm sure you understand."

I wish I could say I was surprised by his response, but I wasn't. Even as Ronan and I cut through Keldara on our way to the so-called sanctuary of the Grasslands, I secretly knew that was Chief Aryan's plan all along.

I refused to cower or show that his words affected me, even as my insides roiled. "Your actions will start a war with Valoria. Do you understand that? My father will have your head!" I threatened, hoping to change his mind and alter his bloodstained path.

He gave a dark chuckle and the sinister glimmer in his eyes returned. "Valoria can try, but with the almighty fox demon on our side, we'll be unstoppable."

I didn't understand the history and lore of the fox demon, but from what I'd gathered, its incarnation would be as if a god was walking Asteria and the impossible would be made possible. It was a scary thought, especially when I didn't know what Chief Aryan planned to do with that newfound power. Would he be happy freeing his people, or did he thirst for more?

He met my heated stare unflinchingly. "What do you say, Your Highness? Will you lay down your life to help Ronan and his people by choice, or by force?"

"Fine," I gritted, staring deep into his cold, crimson eyes. "I'll go willingly."

Either way, I was ready to die. Truthfully, I should have died a long time ago. I'd lived on borrowed time for the last ten years. I dropped my gaze to where Ronan slept at my feet and tried to memorize every inch before we were torn apart forever.

He would never forgive his father for this, though in the years to come, he may come to terms with the benefit my sacrifice brought to his people.

"Goodbye, Ronan."

ABOUT THE AUTHOR

Join my Facebook group, **Karina's Kick-Ass Reads!**

Reviews are very important to authors and help readers discover our books. Please take a moment to leave a review on **Amazon**. Thank you!

ALSO BY KARINA ESPINOSA

Mackenzie Grey: Origins Series (Completed)

SHIFT

CAGED

ALPHA

OMEGA

Mackenzie Grey: Trials Series (Completed)

From the Grave

Curse Breaker

Bound by Magic

Stolen Relics

Bloodlust

Mackenzie Grey: The Crown Series (Completed)

Queen of the Lycan

Blood of the Wolf

Return of the Alpha

The Joey Santana Series (Completed)

Cursed

Sinner

Legacy

Wicked

The Last Valkyrie Trilogy (Completed)

The Last Valkyrie

The Sword of Souls

The Rise of the Valkyries

From the Ashes Trilogy (Completed)

Phoenix Burn

Phoenix Rise

Dark Phoenix

Fated Fae Elementals Trilogy (Completed)

A Hint of Delirium

A Blaze of Fire

A Touch of Iron

Sevyn Rose Trilogy (In Progress)

Killer Wolf

Captured Wolf

ABOUT THE AUTHOR

Karina Espinosa is the Fantasy Author of the Mackenzie Grey novels, The Last Valkyrie, Joey Santana, and From the Ashes series. An avid reader throughout her life, the world of Fantasy easily became an obsession that turned into a passion for writing strong leading characters with authentic story arcs. When she isn't writing badass heroines, you can find this self-proclaimed nomad in her South Florida home binge watching the latest K-drama or traveling far and wide for the latest inspiration for her books.

For more information:
www.karinaespinosa.com

Printed in France by Amazon
Brétigny-sur-Orge, FR